Edgar Wallace was born illeg. adopted by George Freeman, a porter at Billingsgate fish market. At eleven, Wallace sold newspapers at Ludgate Circus and on leaving school took a job with a printer. He enlisted in the Royal West Kent Regiment, later transferring to the Medical Staff Corps, and was sent to South Africa. In 1898 he published a collection of poems called *The Mission that Failed*, left the army and became a correspondent for Reuters.

Wallace became the South African war correspondent for *The Daily Mail*. His articles were later published as *Unofficial Dispatches* and his outspokenness infuriated Kitchener, who banned him as a war correspondent until the First World War. He edited the *Rand Daily Mail*, but gambled disastrously on the South African Stock Market, returning to England to report on crimes and hanging trials. He became editor of *The Evening News*, then in 1905 founded the Tallis Press, publishing *Smithy*, a collection of soldier stories, and *Four Just Men*. At various times he worked on *The Standard*, *The Star*, *The Week-End Racing Supplement* and *The Story Journal*.

In 1917 he became a Special Constable at Lincoln's Inn and also a special interrogator for the War Office. His first marriage to Ivy Caldecott, daughter of a missionary, had ended in divorce and he married his much younger secretary, Violet King.

The Daily Mail sent Wallace to investigate atrocities in the Belgian Congo, a trip that provided material for his *Sanders of the River* books. In 1923 he became Chairman of the Press Club and in 1931 stood as a Liberal candidate at Blackpool. On being offered a scriptwriting contract at RKO, Wallace went to Hollywood. He died in 1932, on his way to work on the screenplay for *King Kong*.

BY THE SAME AUTHOR
ALL PUBLISHED BY HOUSE OF STRATUS

The Daffodil
Mystery

This edition published in 2001 by House of Stratus, an imprint of
Stratus Books Ltd., 21 Beeching Park, Kelly Bray,
Cornwall, PL17 8QS, UK.
www.houseofstratus.com

Typeset, printed and bound by House of Stratus.

A catalogue record for this book is available from the British Library
and the Library of Congress.

ISBN07551-148-2-5

We would like to thank the Edgar Wallace Society for all the support they have given
House of Stratus. Enquiries on how to join the Edgar Wallace Society should be addressed to:
The Edgar Wallace Society, c/o Penny Wyrd, 84 Ridgefield Road, Oxford, OX4 3DA.
Email: info@edgarwallace.org Web: http://www.edgarwallace.org/

CONTENTS

Contents (Contd)

AN OFFER REJECTED

"I am afraid I don't understand you, Mr Lyne."

Odette Rider looked gravely at the young man who lolled against his open desk. Her clear skin was tinted with the faintest pink, and there was in the sober depths of those grey eyes of hers a light which would have warned a man less satisfied with his own genius and power of persuasion than Thornton Lyne.

He was not looking at her face. His eyes were running approvingly over her perfect figure, noting the straightness of the back, the fine poise of the head, the shapeliness of the slender hands.

He pushed back his long black hair from his forehead and smiled. It pleased him to believe that his face was cast in an intellectual mould, and that the somewhat unhealthy pastiness of his skin might be described as the "pallor of thought."

Presently he looked away from her through the big bay window which overlooked the crowded floor of Lyne's Stores.

He had had this office built in the entresol and the big windows had been put in so that he might at any time overlook the most important department which it was his good fortune to control.

Now and again, as he saw, a head would be turned in his direction, and he knew that the attention of all the girls was concentrated upon the little scene, plainly visible from the floor below, in which an unwilling employee was engaged.

She, too, was conscious of the fact, and her discomfort and dismay increased. She made a little movement as if to go, but he stopped her.

"You don't understand, Odette," he said. His voice was soft and melodious, and held the hint of a caress. "Did you read my little book?" he asked suddenly.

She nodded.

"Yes, I read – some of it," she said, and the colour deepened on her face.

He chuckled.

"I suppose you thought it rather curious that a man in my position should bother his head to write poetry, eh?" he asked. "Most of it was written before I came into this beastly shop, my dear – before I developed into a tradesman!"

She made no reply, and he looked at her curiously.

"What did you think of them?" he asked.

Her lips were trembling, and again he mistook the symptoms.

"I thought they were perfectly horrible," she said in a low voice. "Horrible!"

He raised his eyebrows.

"How very middle-class you are, Miss Rider!" he scoffed. "Those verses have been acclaimed by some of the best critics in the country as reproducing all the beauties of the old Hellenic poetry."

She went to speak, but stopped herself and stood with lips compressed.

Thornton Lyne shrugged his shoulders and strode to the other end of his luxuriously equipped office.

"Poetry, like cucumbers, is an acquired taste," he said after a while. "You have to be educated up to some kind of literature. I daresay there will come a time when you will be grateful that I have given you an opportunity of meeting beautiful thoughts dressed in beautiful language."

She looked up at this.

"May I go now, Mr Lyne?" she asked.

"Not yet," he replied coolly. "You said just now you didn't understand what I was talking about. I'll put it plainer this time. You're a very beautiful girl, as you probably know, and you are destined, in all probability, to be the mate of a very average suburban-minded person, who will give you a life tantamount to slavery. That is the life of the middle-class woman, as you probably know. And why would you submit to this bondage? Simply because a person in a black coat and a white collar has mumbled certain passages over you – passages which have neither meaning nor, to an intelligent person, significance. I would not take the trouble of going through such a foolish ceremony, but I would take a great deal of trouble to make you happy."

He walked towards her slowly and laid one hand upon her shoulder. Instinctively she shrank back and he laughed.

"What do you say?"

She swung round on him, her eyes blazing but her voice under control.

"I happen to be one of those foolish, suburban-minded people," she said, "who give significance to those mumbled words you were speaking about. Yet I am broad-minded enough to believe that the marriage ceremony would not make you any happier or more unhappy whether it was performed or omitted. But, whether it were marriage or any other kind of union, I should at least require a man."

He frowned at her.

"What do you mean?" he asked, and the soft quality of his voice underwent a change.

Her voice was full of angry tears when she answered him.

"I should not want an erratic creature who puts horrid sentiments into indifferent verse. I repeat, I should want a man."

His face went livid.

"Do you know whom you are talking to?" he asked, raising his voice.

"I am talking to Thornton Lyne," said she, breathing quickly, "the proprietor of Lyne's Stores, the employer of Odette Rider who draws three pounds every week from him."

He was breathless with anger.

"Be careful!" he gasped. "Be careful!"

"I am speaking to a man whose whole life is a reproach to the very name of man!" she went on speaking rapidly. "A man who is sincere in nothing, who is living on the brains and reputation of his father, and the money that has come through the hard work of better men.

"You can't scare me," she cried scornfully, as he took a step towards her. "Oh, yes, I know I'm going to leave your employment, and I'm leaving tonight!"

The man was hurt, humiliated, almost crushed by her scorn. This she suddenly realised and her quick woman's sympathy checked all further bitterness.

"I'm sorry I've been so unkind," she said in a more gentle tone. "But you rather provoked me, Mr Lyne."

He was incapable of speech and could only shake his head and point with unsteady finger to the door:

"Get out," he whispered.

Odette Rider walked out of the room, but the man did not move. Presently, however, he crossed to the window and, looking down upon the floor, saw her trim figure move slowly through the crowd of customers and assistants and mount the three steps which led to the chief cashier's office.

"You shall pay for this, my girl!" he muttered.

He was wounded beyond forgiveness. He was a rich man's son and had lived in a sense a sheltered life. He had been denied the advantage which a public school would have brought to him and had gone to college surrounded by sycophants and poseurs as blatant as himself, and never once had the cold breath of criticism been directed at him, except in what he was wont to describe as the "reptile Press."

He licked his dry lips, and, walking to his desk, pressed a bell. After a short wait – for he had purposely sent his secretary away – a girl came in.

"Has Mr Tarling come?" he asked.

"Yes, sir, he's in the boardroom. He has been waiting a quarter of an hour."

He nodded.

"Thank you," he said.

"Shall I tell him – "

"I will go to him myself," said Lyne.

He took a cigarette out of his gold case, struck a match and lit it. His nerves were shaken, his hands were trembling, but the storm in his heart was soothing down under the influence of this great thought. Tarling! What an inspiration! Tarling, with his reputation for ingenuity, his almost sublime uncanny cleverness. What could be more wonderful than this coincidence?

He passed with quick steps along the corridor which connected his private den with the boardroom, and came into that spacious apartment with outstretched hand.

The man who turned to greet him may have been twenty-seven or thirty-seven. He was tall, but lithe rather than broad. His face was the colour of mahogany, and the blue eyes turned to Lyne were unwinking and expressionless. That was the first impression which Lyne received.

He took Lyne's hand in his – it was as soft as a woman's. As they shook hands Lyne noticed a third figure in the room. He was below middle height and sat in the shadow thrown by a wall pillar. He too rose, but bowed his head.

"A Chinaman, eh?" said Lyne, looking at this unexpected apparition with curiosity. "Oh, of course, Mr Tarling, I had almost forgotten that you've almost come straight from China. Won't you sit down?"

He followed the other's example, threw himself into a chair and offered his cigarette case.

"The work I am going to ask you to do I will discuss later," he said. "But I must explain that I was partly attracted to you by the description I read in one of the newspapers of how you had recovered the Duchess of Henley's jewels and partly by the stories I heard of you when I was in China. You're not attached to Scotland Yard, I understand?"

Tarling shook his head.

"No," he said quietly. "I was regularly attached to the police in Shanghai, and I had intended joining up with Scotland Yard; in fact, I came over for that purpose. But several things happened which made me open my own detective agency, the most important of which happenings, was that Scotland Yard refused to give me the free hand I require!"

The other nodded quickly.

China rang with the achievements of Jack Oliver Tarling, or, as the Chinese criminal world had named him in parody of his name, "Lieh Jen," "The Hunter of Men."

Lyne judged all people by his own standard, and saw in this unemotional man a possible tool, and in all probability a likely accomplice.

The detective force in Shanghai did curious things by all accounts, and were not too scrupulous as to whether they kept within the strict letter of the law. There were even rumours that "The Hunter of Men" was not above torturing his prisoners, if by so doing he could elicit confessions which could implicate some greater criminal. Lyne did not and could not know all the legends which had grown around the name of "The Hunter" nor could he be expected in reason to differentiate between the truth and the false.

"I pretty well know why you've sent for me," Tarling went on. He spoke slowly and had a decided drawl. "You gave me a rough outline in your letter. You suspect a member of your staff of having consistently robbed the firm for many years. A Mr Milburgh, your chief departmental manager."

Lyne stopped him with a gesture and lowered his voice.

"I want you to forget that for a little while, Mr Tarling," he said. "In fact, I am going to introduce you to Milburgh, and maybe, Milburgh can help us in my scheme. I do not say that Milburgh is honest, or that my suspicions were unfounded. But for the moment I have a much greater business on hand, and you will oblige me if you forget all the things I have said about Milburgh. I will ring for him now."

He walked to a long table which ran half the length of the room, took up a telephone which stood at one end, and spoke to the operator.

"Tell Mr Milburgh to come to me in the boardroom, please," he said.

Then he went back to his visitor.

"That matter of Milburgh can wait," he said. "I'm not so sure that I shall proceed any farther with it. Did you make inquiries at all? If so, you had better tell me the gist of them before Milburgh comes."

Tarling took a small white card from his pocket and glanced at it.

"What salary are you paying Milburgh?"

"Nine hundred a year," replied Lyne.

"He is living at the rate of five thousand," said Tarling. "I may even discover that he's living at a much larger rate. He has a house up the river, entertains very lavishly – "

But the other brushed aside the report impatiently.

"No, let that wait," he cried. "I tell you I have much more important business. Milburgh may be a thief – "

"Did you send for me, sir?"

He turned round quickly. The door had opened without noise, and a man stood on the threshold of the room, an ingratiating smile on his face, his hands twining and intertwining ceaselessly as though he was washing them with invisible soap.

THE HUNTER DECLINES
HIS QUARRY

"This is Mr Milburgh," said Lyne awkwardly.

If Mr Milburgh had heard the last words of his employer, his face did not betray the fact. His smile was set, and not only curved the lips but filled the large, lustreless eyes. Tarling gave him a rapid survey and drew his own conclusions. The man was a born lackey, plump of face, bald of head, and bent of shoulder, as though he lived in a perpetual gesture of abasement.

"Shut the door, Milburgh, and sit down. This is Mr Tarling. Er – Mr Tarling is – er – a detective."

"Indeed, sir?"

Milburgh bent a deferential head in the direction of Tarling, and the detective, watching for some change in colour, some twist of face – any of those signs which had so often betrayed to him the convicted wrongdoer – looked in vain.

"A dangerous man," he thought.

He glanced out of the corner of his eye to see what impression the man had made upon Ling Chu. To the ordinary eye Ling Chu remained an impassive observer. But Tarling saw that faint curl of lip, an almost imperceptible twitch of the nostrils, which invariably showed on the face of his attendant when he "smelt" a criminal.

"Mr Tarling is a detective," repeated Lyne. "He is a gentleman I heard about when I was in China – you know I was in China for three months, when I made my tour round the world?" he asked Tarling.

Tarling nodded.

"Oh yes, I know," he said. "You stayed at the Bund Hotel. You spent a great deal of time in the native quarter, and you had rather an unpleasant experience as the result of making an experiment in opium smoking."

Lyne's face went red, and then he laughed.

"You know more about me than I know about you, Tarling," he said, with a note of asperity in his voice, and turned again to his subordinate.

"I have reason to believe that there has been money stolen in this business by one of my cashiers," he said.

"Impossible, sir!" said the shocked Mr Milburgh. "Wholly impossible! Who could have done it? And how clever of you to have found it out, sir! I always say that you see what we old ones overlook even though it's right under our noses!"

Mr Lyne smiled complacently.

"It will interest you to know, Mr Tarling," he said, "that I myself have some knowledge of and acquaintance with the criminal classes. In fact, there is one unfortunate protégé of mine whom I have tried very hard to reform for the past four years, who is coming out of prison in a couple of days. I took up this work," he said modestly, "because I feel it is the duty of us who are in a more fortunate position, to help those who have not had a chance in the cruel competition of the world."

Tarling was not impressed.

"Do you know the person who has been robbing you?" he asked.

"I have reason to believe it is a girl whom I have summarily dismissed tonight, and whom I wish you to watch."

The detective nodded.

"This is rather a primitive business," he said with the first faint hint of a smile he had shown. "Haven't you your own shop detective who could take that job in hand? Petty larceny is hardly in my line. I understood that this was bigger work – "

He stopped, because it was obviously impossible to explain just why he had thought as much, in the presence of the man whose conduct, originally, had been the subject of his inquiries.

"To you it may seem a small matter. To me, it is very important," said Mr Lyne profoundly. "Here is a girl, highly respected by all her companions and consequently a great influence on their morals, who, as I have reason to believe, has steadily and persistently falsified my books, taking money from the firm, and at the same time has secured the goodwill of all with whom she has been brought into contact. Obviously she is more dangerous than another individual who succumbs to a sudden temptation. It may be necessary to make an example of this girl, but I want you clearly to understand, Mr Tarling, that I have not sufficient evidence to convict her; otherwise I might not have called you in."

"You want me to get the evidence, eh?" said Tarling curiously.

"Who is the lady, may I venture to ask, sir?"

It was Milburgh who interposed the question.

"Miss Rider," replied Lyne.

"Miss Rider!"

Milburgh's face took on a look of blank surprise as he gasped the words.

"Miss Rider – oh, no, impossible!"

"Why impossible?" demanded Mr Lyne sharply

"Well, sir, I meant – " stammered the manager, "it is so unlikely – she is such a nice girl – "

Thornton Lyne shot a suspicious glance at him.

"You have no particular reason for wishing to shield Miss Rider, have you?" he asked coldly.

"No, sir, not at all. I beg of you not to think that," appealed the agitated Mr Milburgh, "only it seems so – extraordinary."

"All things are extraordinary that are out of the common," snapped Lyne. "It would be extraordinary if you were accused of stealing. Milburgh. It would be very extraordinary indeed, for example, if we discovered that you were living a five-thousand pounds life on a nine-hundred pounds salary."

Only for a second did Milburgh lose his self-possession. The hand that went to his mouth shook, and Tarling, whose eyes had never left the man's face, saw the tremendous effort which he was making to recover his equanimity.

"Yes, sir, that would be extraordinary," said Milburgh steadily.

Lyne had lashed himself again into the old fury, and if his vitriolic tongue was directed at Milburgh, his thoughts were centred upon that proud and scornful face which had looked down upon him in his office.

"It would be extraordinary if you were sent to penal servitude as the result of my discovery that you had been robbing the firm for years," he growled, "and I suppose everybody else in the firm would say the same as you – how extraordinary!"

"I daresay they would, sir," said Mr Milburgh, his old smile back, the twinkle again returning to his eyes, and his hands rubbing together in ceaseless ablutions. "It would sound extraordinary, and it would be extraordinary, and nobody here would be more surprised than the unfortunate victim – ha! ha!"

"Perhaps not," said Lyne coldly. "Only I want to say a few words in your presence, and I would like you to give them every attention. You have been complaining to me for a month past," he said speaking with deliberation, "about small sums of money being missing from the cashier's office."

It was a bold thing to say, and in many ways a rash thing. He was dependent for the success of his hastily-formed plan, not only upon Milburgh's guilt, but upon Milburgh's willingness to confess his guilt. If the manager agreed to stand sponsor to this lie, he admitted his own peculations, and Tarling, to whom the turn of the conversation had at first been unintelligible, began dimly to see the drift it was taking.

"I have complained that sums of money have been missing for the past month?" repeated Milburgh dully.

The smile had gone from his lips and eyes. His face was haggard – he was a man at bay.

"That is what I said," said Lyne watching him. "Isn't that the fact?"

There was a long pause, and presently Milburgh nodded.

"That is the fact, sir," he said in a low voice.

"And you have told me that you suspected Miss Rider of defalcations?"

Again the pause and again the man nodded.

"Do you hear?" asked Lyne triumphantly.

"I hear," said Tarling quietly. "Now what do you wish me to do? Isn't this a matter for the police? I mean the regular police."

Lyne frowned.

"The case has to be prepared first," he said. "I will give you full particulars as to the girl's address and her habits, and it will be your business to collect such information as will enable us to put the case in the hands of Scotland Yard."

"I see," said Tarling and smiled again. Then he shook his head. "I'm afraid I can't come into this case, Mr Lyne."

"Can't come in?" said Lyne in astonishment. "Why not?"

"Because it's not my kind of job," said Tarling. "The first time I met you I had a feeling that you were leading me to one of the biggest cases I had ever undertaken. It shows you how one's instincts can lead one astray," he smiled again, and picked up his hat.

"What do you mean? You're going to throw up a valuable client?"

"I don't know how valuable you're likely to be," said Tarling, "but at the present moment the signs are not particularly encouraging. I tell you I do not wish to be associated with this case, Mr Lyne, and I think there the matter can end."

"You don't think it's worthwhile, eh?" sneered Lyne. "Yet when I tell you that I am prepared to give you a fee of five hundred guineas – "

"If you gave me a fee of five thousand guineas, or fifty thousand guineas, I should still decline to be associated with this matter," said Tarling, and his words had the metallic quality which precludes argument.

"At any rate, I am entitled to know why you will not take up this case. Do you know the girl?" asked Lyne loudly.

"I have never met the lady and probably never shall," said Tarling. "I only know that I will not be concerned with what is called in the United States of America a 'frame-up.'"

"Frame-up?" repeated the other.

"A frame-up. I dare say you know what it means – I will put the matter more plainly and within your understanding. For some reason or other you have a sudden grudge against a member of your staff. I read your face, Mr Lyne, and the weakness of your chin and the appetite of your mouth suggest to me that you are not overscrupulous with the women who are in your charge. I guess rather than know that you have been turned down with a dull, sickening thud by a decent girl, and in your mortification you are attempting to invent a charge which has no substance and no foundation.

"Mr Milburgh," he turned to the other, and again Mr Milburgh ceased to smile, "has his own reasons for complying with your wishes. He is your subordinate, and moreover, the side threat of penal servitude for him if he refuses has carried some weight."

Thornton Lyne's face was distorted with fury.

"I will take care that your behaviour is widely advertised," he said. "You have brought a most monstrous charge against me, and I shall proceed against you for slander. The truth is that you are not equal to the job I intended giving you and you are finding an excuse for getting out."

"The truth is," replied Tarling, biting off the end of a cigar he had taken from his pocket, "that my reputation is too good to be risked in associating with such a dirty business as yours. I hate to be rude, and I hate just as much to throw away good money. But I can't take good money for bad work, Mr Lyne, and if you will be advised by me, you will drop this stupid scheme for vengeance which your hurt vanity has suggested – it is the clumsiest kind of frame-up that was ever invented – and also you will go and apologise to the young lady, whom, I have no doubt, you have grossly insulted."

He beckoned to his Chinese satellite and walked leisurely to the door. Incoherent with rage, shaking in every limb with a weak man's sense of his own impotence, Lyne watched him until the door was half-closed, then, springing forward with a strangled cry, he wrenched the door open and leapt at the detective.

Two hands gripped his arm and lifting him bodily back into the room, pushed him down into a chair. A not unkindly face blinked down at him, a face relieved from utter solemnity by the tiny laughter lines about the eyes.

"Mr Lyne," said the mocking voice of Tarling, "you are setting an awful example to the criminal classes. It is a good job your convict friend is in gaol."

Without another word he left the room.

THE MAN WHO LOVED LYNE

Two days later Thornton Lyne sat in his big limousine which was drawn up on the edge of Wandsworth Common, facing the gates of the gaol.

Poet and *poseur* he was, the strangest combination ever seen in man.

Thornton Lyne was a storekeeper, a Bachelor of Arts, the winner of the Mangate Science Prize and the author of a slim volume. The quality of the poetry therein was not very great – but it was undoubtedly a slim volume printed in queerly ornate type with old-fashioned esses and wide margins. He was a storekeeper because storekeeping supplied him with caviare and peaches, a handsome little two-seater, a six-cylinder limousine for state occasions, a country house and a flat in town, the decorations of which ran to a figure which would have purchased many stores of humbler pretensions than Lyne's Serve First Emporium.

To the elder Lyne, Joseph Emanuel of that family, the inception and prosperity of Lyne's Serve First Emporium was due. He had devised a sale system which ensured every customer being attended to the moment he or she entered one of the many departments which made up the splendid whole of the emporium. It was a system based upon the age-old principle of keeping efficient reserves within call.

Thornton Lyne succeeded to the business at a moment when his slim volume had placed him in the category of the gloriously misunderstood. Because such reviewers as had noticed his book wrote of his "poetry" using inverted commas to advertise their scorn, and because nobody bought the volume despite its slimness, he became the idol of men and women who also wrote that which nobody read, and in consequence developed souls with the celerity that a small boy develops stomach-ache.

For nothing in the wide world was more certain to the gloriously misunderstood than this: the test of excellence is scorn. Thornton Lyne might in different circumstances have drifted upward to sets even more misunderstood – yea, even to a set superior to marriage and soap and clean shirts and fresh air – only his father died of a surfeit, and Thornton became the Lyne of Lyne's Serve First.

His first inclination was to sell the property and retire to a villa in Florence or Capri. Then the absurdity, the rich humour of an idea, struck him. He, a scholar, a gentleman and a misunderstood poet, sitting in the office of a store, appealed to him. Somebody remarked in his hearing that the idea was "rich." He saw himself in "character" and the part appealed to him. To everybody's surprise he took up his father's work, which meant that he signed cheques, collected profits and left the management to the Soults and the Neys whom old Napoleon Lyne had relied upon in the foundation of his empire.

Thornton wrote an address to his 3,000 employees – which address was printed on decided antique paper in queerly ornate type with wide margins. He quoted Seneca, Aristotle, Marcus Aurelius and the "Iliad." The "address" secured better and longer reviews in the newspapers than had his book.

He had found life a pleasant experience – all the more piquant because of the amazement of innumerable ecstatic friends who clasped their hands and asked awefully: "How *can* you – a man of your temperament…!"

Life might have gone on being pleasant if every man and woman he had met had let him have his own way. Only there were at least two people with whom Thornton Lyne's millions carried no weight.

It was warm in his limousine, which was electrically heated. But outside, on that raw April morning, it was bitterly cold, and the shivering little group of women who stood at a respectful distance from the prison gates, drew their shawls tightly about them as errant flakes of snow whirled across the open. The common was covered with a white powder, and the early flowers looked supremely miserable in their wintry setting.

The prison clock struck eight, and a wicket-gate opened. A man slouched out, his jacket buttoned up to his neck, his cap pulled over his eyes. At sight of him, Lyne dropped the newspaper he had been reading, opened the door of the car and jumped out, walking towards the released prisoner.

"Well, Sam," he said, genially "you didn't expect me?

The man stopped as if he had been shot, and stood staring at the fur-coated figure. Then:

"Oh, Mr Lyne," he said brokenly. "Oh, guv'nor!" he choked, and tears streamed down his face, and he gripped the outstretched hand in both of his, unable to speak.

"You didn't think I'd desert you, Sam, eh?" said Mr Lyne, all aglow with consciousness of his virtue.

"I thought you'd given me up, sir," said Sam Stay huskily. "You're a gentleman, you are, sir, and I ought to be ashamed of myself!"

"Nonsense, nonsense, Sam! Jump into the car, my lad. Go along. People will think you're a millionaire."

The man gulped, grinned sheepishly, opened the door and stepped in, and sank with a sigh of comfort into the luxurious depths of the big brown cushions.

"Gawd! To think that there are men like you in the world, sir! Why, I believe in angels, I do!"

"Nonsense Sam. Now you come along to my flat, and I'm going to give you a good breakfast and start you fair again."

"I'm going to try and keep straight, sir, I am s'help me!"

It may be said in truth that Mr Lyne did not care very much whether Sam kept straight or not. He might indeed have been very much disappointed if Sam had kept to the straight and narrow path. He "kept" Sam as men keep chickens and prize cows, and he "collected" Sam as other men collect stamps and china. Sam was his luxury and his pose. In his club he boasted of his acquaintance with this representative of the criminal classes – for Sam was an expert burglar and knew no other trade – and Sam's adoration for him was one of his most exhilarating experiences.

And that adoration was genuine. Sam would have laid down his life for the pale-faced man with the loose mouth. He would have suffered himself to be torn limb from limb if in his agony he could have brought ease or advancement to the man who, to him, was one with the gods.

Originally, Thornton Lyne had found Sam whilst that artist was engaged in burgling the house of his future benefactor. It was a whim of Lyne's to give the criminal a good breakfast and to evince an interest in his future. Twice had Sam gone down for a short term, and once for a long term of imprisonment, and on each occasion Thornton Lyne had made a parade of collecting the returned wanderer, driving him home, giving him breakfast and a great deal of worldly and unnecessary advice, and launching him forth again upon the world with ten pounds – a sum just sufficient to buy Sam a new kit of burglar's tools.

Never before had Sam shown such gratitude: and never before had Thornton Lyne been less disinterested in his attentions. There was a hot bath – which Sam Stay could have dispensed with, but which, out of sheer politeness, he was compelled to accept, a warm and luxurious breakfast; a new suit of clothes, with not two, but four, five-pound notes in the pocket.

After breakfast, Lyne had his talk.

"It's no good, sir," said the burglar, shaking his head. "I've tried everything to get an honest living, but somehow I can't get on in the straight life. I drove a taxicab for three months after I came out, till a busy-fellow★ tumbled to me not having a licence, and brought me up under the Prevention of Crimes Act. It's no use my asking you to give me a job in your shop, sir, because couldn't stick it, I couldn't really! I'm used to the open air life; I like being my own master. I'm one of those fellows you've read about – the word begins with A."

★ Detective.

"Adventurers?" said Lyne with a little laugh. "Yes, I think you are, Sam, and I'm going to give you an adventure after your own heart."

And then he began to tell a tale of base ingratitude – of a girl he had helped, had indeed saved from starvation and who had betrayed him at every turn. Thornton Lyne was a poet. He was also a picturesque liar. The lie came as easily as the truth, and easier, since there was a certain crudeness about truth which revolted his artistic soul. And as the tale was unfolded of Odette Rider's perfidy, Sam's eyes narrowed. There was nothing too bad for such a creature as this. She was wholly undeserving of sympathy.

Presently Thornton Lyne stopped, his eyes fixed on the other to note the effect.

"Show me," said Sam, his voice trembling. "Show me a way of getting even with her, sir, and I'll go through hell to do it!"

"That's the kind of stuff I like to hear," said Lyne, and poured out from the long bottle which stood on the coffee-tray a stiff tot of Sam's favourite brandy. "Now, I'll give you my idea."

For the rest of the morning the two men sat almost head to head, plotting woe for the girl, whose chief offence had been against the dignity of Thornton Lyne, and whose virtue had incited the hate of that vicious man.

MURDER

Jack Tarling lay stretched upon his hard bed, a long cigarette-holder between his teeth, a book on Chinese metaphysics balanced on his chest, at peace with the world. The hour was eight o'clock, and it was the day that Sam Stay had been released from gaol.

It had been a busy day for Tarling, for he was engaged in a bank fraud case which would have occupied the whole of his time had he not had a little private business to attend to. This private matter was wholly unprofitable, but his curiosity had been piqued.

He lay the book flat on his chest as the soft click of the opening door announced the coming of his retainer. The impassive Ling Chu came noiselessly into the room, carrying a tray, which he placed upon a low table by the side of his master's bed. The Chinaman wore a blue silk pyjama suit – a fact which Tarling noticed.

"You are not going out tonight then, Ling Chu?"

"No, Lieh Jen," said the man.

They both spoke in the soft, sibilant patois of Shantung.

"You have been to the Man with the Cunning Face?"

For answer the other took an envelope from an inside pocket and laid it in the other's hand. Tarling glanced at the address.

"So this is where the young lady lives, eh? Miss Odette Rider, 27, Carrymore Buildings, Edgware Road."

"It is a clan house, where many people live," said Ling Chu. "I myself went, in your honourable service, and saw people coming in and going out interminably, and never the same people did I see twice."

"It is what they call in English a 'flat building,' Ling," said Tarling with a little smile. "What did the Man with the Cunning Face say to my letter?"

"Master, he said nothing. He just read and read, and then he made a face like this." Ling gave an imitation of Mr Milburgh's smile. "And then he wrote as you see."

Tarling nodded. He stared for a moment into vacancy, then he turned on his elbow and lifted the cup of tea which his servant had brought him.

"What of Face-White-and-Weak Man, Ling?" he asked in the vernacular. "You saw him?"

"I saw him, master," said the Chinaman gravely. "He is a man without a heaven."

Again Tarling nodded. The Chinese use the word "heaven" instead of "God," and he felt that Ling had very accurately sized up Mr Thornton Lyne's lack of spiritual qualities.

He finished the tea, and swung his legs over the edge of the bed.

"Ling," he said, "this place is very dull and sad. I do not think I shall live here."

"Will the master go back to Shanghai?" asked the other, without any display of emotion.

"I think so," nodded Tarling. "At any rate, this place is too dull. Just miserable little taking-money-easily cases, and wife-husband-lover cases and my soul is sick."

"These are small matters," said Ling philosophically. "But The Master" – this time he spoke of the great Master, Confucius – "has said that all greatness comes from small things, and perhaps some small-piece man will cut off the head of some big-piece man, and then they will call you to find the murderer."

Tarling laughed.

"You're an optimist, Ling," he said "No, I don't think they'll call me in for a murder. They don't call in private detectives in this country."

Ling shook his head.

"But the master must find murderers, or he will no longer be Lieb Jen, the Hunter of Men."

21

"You're a bloodthirsty soul, Ling," said Tarling, this time in English, which Ling imperfectly understood, despite the sustained efforts of eminent missionary schools. "Now I'll go out," he said with sudden resolution. "I am going to call upon the small-piece woman whom White-Face desires."

"May I come with you?" asked Ling.

Tarling hesitated.

"Yes, you may come," he said, "but you must trail me."

Carrymore Mansions is a great block of buildings sandwiched between two more aristocratic and more expensive blocks of flats in the Edgware Road. The ground floor is given up to lock-up shops which perhaps cheapened the building, but still it was a sufficiently exclusive habitation for the rents, as Tarling guessed, to be a little too high for a shop assistant, unless she were living with her family. The explanation, as he was to discover, lay in the fact that there were some very undesirable basement flats which were let at a lower rental.

He found himself standing outside the polished mahogany door of one of these, wondering exactly what excuse he was going to give to the girl for making a call so late at night. And that she needed some explanation was clear from the frank suspicion which showed in her face when she opened the door to him.

"Yes, I am Miss Rider," she said.

"Can I see you for a few moments?"

"I'm sorry," she said, shaking her head, "but I am alone in the flat, so I can't ask you to come in."

This was a bad beginning.

"Is it not possible for you to come out?" he asked anxiously, and in spite of herself, she smiled.

"I'm afraid it's quite impossible for me to go out with somebody I have never met before," she said, with just a trace of amusement in her eyes.

"I recognise the difficulty," laughed Tarling. "Here is one of my cards. I'm afraid I am not very famous in this country, so you will not know my name."

She took the card and read it.

"A private detective?" she said in a troubled voice. "Who has sent you? Not Mr – "

"Not Mr Lyne," he said.

She hesitated a moment, then threw open the door wider.

"You must come in. We can talk here in the hall. Do I understand Mr Lyne has not sent you?"

"Mr Lyne was very anxious that I should come," he said. "I am betraying his confidence, but I do not think that he has any claim upon my loyalty. I don't know why I've bothered you at all, except that I feel that you ought to be put on your guard."

"Against what?" she asked.

"Against the machinations of a gentleman to whom you have been – " he hesitated for a word.

"Very offensive," she finished for him.

"I don't know how offensive you've been," he laughed, "but I gather you have annoyed Mr Lyne for some reason or other, and that he is determined to annoy you. I do not ask your confidence in this respect, because I realise that you would hardly like to tell me. But what I want to tell you is this, that Mr Lyne is probably framing up a charge against you – that is to say, inventing a charge of theft."

"Of theft?" she cried in indignant amazement. "Against me? Of theft? It's impossible that he could be so wicked!"

"It's not impossible that anybody could be wicked," said Tarling of the impassive face and the laughing eyes. "All that I know is that he even induced Mr Milburgh to say that complaints have been made by Milburgh concerning thefts of money from your department."

"That's absolutely impossible!" she cried emphatically. "Mr Milburgh would never say such a thing. Absolutely impossible!"

"Mr Milburgh didn't want to say such a thing, I give him credit for that," said Tarling slowly, and then gave the gist of the argument, omitting any reference, direct or indirect, to the suspicion which surrounded Milburgh.

"So you see," he said in conclusion, "that you ought to be on your guard. I suggest to you that you see a solicitor and put the matter in his hands. You need not move against Mr Lyne, but it would strengthen your position tremendously if you had already detailed the scheme to some person in authority."

"Thank you very, very much, Mr Tarling," she said warmly, and looked up into his face with a smile so sweet, so pathetic, so helpless, that Tarling's heart melted towards her.

"And if you don't want a solicitor," he said, "you can depend upon me. I will help you if any trouble arises."

"You don't know how grateful I am to you, Mr Tarling. I didn't receive you very graciously!"

"If you will forgive my saying so, you would have been a fool to have received me in any other way," he said.

She held out both hands to him: he took them, and there were tears in her eyes. Presently she composed herself, and led him into her little drawing-room.

"Of course, I've lost my job," she laughed, "but I've had several offers, one of which I shall accept. I am going to have the rest of the week to myself and to take a holiday."

Tarling stopped her with a gesture. His ears were superhumanly sensitive.

"Are you expecting a visitor?" he asked softly.

"No," said the girl in surprise.

"Do you share this flat with somebody?'

"I have a woman who sleeps here," she said, "She is out for the evening."

"Has she a key?"

The girl shook her head.

The man rose, and Odette marvelled bow one so tall could move so swiftly, and without so much as a sound, across the uncarpeted hallway. He reached the door, turned the knob of the patent lock and jerked it open. A man was standing on the mat and he jumped back at the unexpectedness of Tarling's appearance. The stranger was a cadaverous-looking man, in a brand-new suit of clothes, evidently ready-made, but he still wore on his face the curious yellow tinge which is the special mark of the recently liberated gaol-bird.

"Beg pardon," he stammered, "but is this No 87?"

Tarling shot out a hand, and gripping him by the coat, drew the helpless man towards him.

"Hullo, what are you trying to do? What's this you have?"

He wrenched something from the man's hand. It was not a key but a flat-toothed instrument of strange construction.

"Come in," said Tarling, and jerked his prisoner into the hall.

A swift turning back of his prisoner's coat pinioned him, and then with dexterousness and in silence he proceeded to search. From two pockets he took a dozen jewelled rings, each bearing the tiny tag of Lyne's Store.

"Hullo!" said Tarling sarcastically, "are these intended as a loving gift from Mr Lyne to Miss Rider?"

The man was speechless with rage. If looks could kill, Tarling would have died.

"A clumsy trick," said Tarling, shaking his head mournfully. "Now go back to your boss, Mr Thornton Lyne, and tell him that I am ashamed of an intelligent man adopting so crude a method," and with a kick he dismissed Sam Stay to the outer darkness.

The girl, who had been a frightened spectator of the scene, turned her eyes imploringly upon the detective.

"What does it mean?" she pleaded. "I feel so frightened. What did that man want?"

"You need not be afraid of that man, or any other man," said Tarling briskly. "I'm sorry you were scared."

He succeeded in calming her by the time her servant had returned and then took his leave.

"Remember, I have given you my telephone number and you will call me up if there is any trouble. Particularly," he said emphatically, "if there is any trouble tomorrow."

But there was no trouble on the following day, though at three o'clock in the afternoon she called him up.

"I am going away to stay in the country," she said. "I got scared last night."

"Come and see me when you get back," said Tarling, who had found it difficult to dismiss the girl from his mind. "I am going to see

25

Lyne tomorrow. By the way, the person who called last night is a protégé of Mr Thornton Lyne's, a man who is devoted to him body and soul, and he's the fellow we've got to look after. By Jove! It almost gives me an interest in life!"

He heard the faint laugh of the girl.

"Must I be butchered to make a detective's holiday?" she mocked, and he grinned sympathetically.

"Anyway, I'll see Lyne tomorrow," he said. The interview which Jack Tarling projected was destined never to take place.

On the following morning, an early worker taking a short cut through Hyde Park, found the body of a man lying by the side of a carriage drive. He was fully dressed save that his coat and waistcoat had been removed. Wound about his body was a woman's silk night-dress stained with blood. The hands of the figure were crossed on the breast and upon them lay a handful of daffodils.

At eleven o'clock that morning the evening newspapers burst forth with the intelligence that the body had been identified as that of Thornton Lyne, and that he had been shot through the heart.

FOUND IN LYNE'S POCKET

"The London police are confronted with a new mystery, which has features so remarkable, that it would not be an exaggeration to describe this crime as the Murder Mystery of the Century. A well-known figure in London Society, Mr Thornton Lyne, head of an important commercial organisation, a poet of no mean quality, and a millionaire renowned for his philanthropic activities, was found dead in Hyde Park in the early hours of this morning, in circumstances which admit of no doubt that he was most brutally murdered.

"At half-past five, Thomas Savage, a bricklayer's labourer employed by the Cubitt Town Construction Company, was making his way across Hyde Park *en route* to his work. He had crossed the main drive which runs parallel with the Bayswater Road, when his attention was attracted to a figure lying on the grass near to the sidewalk. He made his way to the spot and discovered a man, who had obviously been dead for some hours. The body had neither coat nor waistcoat, but about the breast, on which his two hands were laid, was a silk garment tightly wound about the body, and obviously designed to stanch a wound on the left side above the heart.

"The extraordinary feature is that the murderer must not only have composed the body, but had laid upon its breast a handful of daffodils. The police were immediately summoned and the body was removed. The police theory is that the murder was not committed in Hyde Park, but the unfortunate gentleman was killed elsewhere and his body conveyed to the Park in his own motor car, which was found abandoned a hundred yards from the scene of the discovery. We

27

understand that the police are working upon a very important clue, and an arrest is imminent."

Mr J O Tarling, late of the Shanghai Detective Service, read the short account in the evening newspaper, and was unusually thoughtful.

Lyne murdered! It was an extraordinary coincidence that he had been brought into touch with this young man only a few days before.

Tarling knew nothing of Lyne's private life, though from his own knowledge of the man during his short stay in Shanghai, he guessed that that life was not wholly blameless. He had been too busy in China to bother his head about the vagaries of a tourist, but he remembered dimly some sort of scandal which had attached to the visitor's name, and puzzled his head to recall all the circumstances.

He put down the newspaper with a little grimace indicative of regret. If he had only been attached to Scotland Yard, what a case this would have been for him! Here was a mystery which promised unusual interest.

His mind wandered to the girl, Odette Rider. What would she think of it? She would be shocked, he thought – horrified. It hurt him to feel that she might be indirectly, even remotely associated with such a public scandal, and he realised with a sudden sense of dismay that nothing was less unlikely than that her name would be mentioned as one who had quarrelled with the dead man.

"Pshaw!" he muttered, shrugging off the possibility as absurd, and, walking to the door, called his Chinese servant.

Ling Chu came silently at his bidding.

"Ling Chu," he said, "the white-faced man is dead."

Ling Chu raised his imperturbable eyes to his master's face.

"All men die some time," he said calmly. "This man quick die. That is better than long die."

Tarling looked at him sharply.

"How do you know that he quick die?" he demanded.

"These things are talked about," said Ling Chu without hesitation.

"But not in the Chinese language," replied Tarling, "and, Ling Chu, you speak no English."

"I speak a little, master," said Ling Chu, "and I have heard these things in the streets,"

Tarling did not answer immediately, and the Chinaman waited.

"Ling Chu," he said after a while, "this man came to Shanghai whilst we were there, and there was trouble-trouble. Once he was thrown out from Wing Fu's tea-house, where he had been smoking opium. Also there was another trouble – do you remember?"

The Chinaman looked him straight in the eyes.

"I am forgetting," he said. "This white-face was a bad man. I am glad he is dead."

"Humph!" said Tarling, and dismissed his retainer.

Ling Chu was the cleverest of all his sleuths, a man who never lifted his nose from the trail once it was struck, and he had been the most loyal and faithful of Tarling's native trailers. But the detective never pretended that he understood Ling Chu's mind, or that he could pierce the veil which the native dropped between his own private thoughts and the curious foreigner. Even native criminals were baffled in their interpretation of Ling Chu's views, and many a man had gone to the scaffold puzzling the head, which was soon to be snicked from his body, over the method by which Ling Chu had detected his crime.

Tarling went back to the table and picked up the newspaper, but had hardly begun to read when the telephone bell rang. He picked up the receiver and listened. To his amazement it was the voice of Cresswell, the Assistant Commissioner of Police, who had been instrumental in persuading Tarling to come to England.

"Can you come round to the Yard immediately, Tarling?" said the voice. "I want to talk to you about this murder."

"Surely," said Tarling. "I'll be with you in a few minutes."

In five minutes he was at Scotland Yard and was ushered into the office of Assistant Commissioner Cresswell. The white-haired man who came across to meet him with a smile of pleasure in his eyes disclosed the object of the summons.

"I'm going to bring you into this case, Tarling," he said. "It has certain aspects which seem outside the humdrum experience of our own people. It is not unusual, as you know," he said as he motioned the other to a chair, "for Scotland Yard to engage outside help, particularly when we have a crime of this character to deal with. The facts you know," he went on, as he opened a thin folder. "These are the reports, which you can read at your leisure. Thornton Lyne was, to say the least, eccentric. His life was not a particularly wholesome one, and he had many undesirable acquaintances, amongst whom was a criminal and ex-convict who was only released from gaol a few days ago."

"That's rather extraordinary," said Tarling, lifting his eyebrows. "What had he in common with the criminal?"

Commissioner Cresswell shrugged his shoulders.

"My own view is that this acquaintance was rather a pose of Lyne's. He liked to be talked about. It gave him a certain reputation for character amongst his friends."

"Who is the criminal?" asked Tarling.

"He is a man named Stay, a petty larcenist, and in my opinion a much more dangerous character than the police have realised."

"Is he – " began Tarling. But the Commissioner shook his head.

"I think we can rule him out from the list of people who may be suspected of this murder," he said. "Sam Stay has very few qualities that would commend themselves to the average man, but there can be no doubt at all that he was devoted to Lyne, body and soul. When the detective temporarily in charge of the case went down to Lambeth to interview Stay, he found him lying on his bed prostrate with grief, with a newspaper containing the particulars of the murder by his side. The man is beside himself with sorrow, and threatens to 'do in' the person who is responsible for this crime. You can interview him later. I doubt whether you will get much out of him, because he is absolutely incoherent. Lyne was something more than human in his eyes, and I should imagine that the only decent emotion he has had in his life is this affection for a man who was certainly good to him, whether he was sincere in his philanthropy or otherwise. Now here are a few of the facts which have not been made public." Cresswell settled himself back in his chair and ticked off on his fingers the points as he made them.

"You know that around Lyne's chest a silk night-dress was discovered?"

Tarling nodded.

"Under the nightdress, made into a pad, evidently with the object of arresting the bleeding, were two handkerchiefs, neatly folded, as though they had been taken from a drawer. They were ladies' handkerchiefs, so we may start on the supposition that there is a woman in the case."

Tarling nodded.

"Now another peculiar feature of the case, which happily has escaped the attention of those who saw the body first and gave particulars to the newspapers, was that Lyne, though fully dressed, wore a pair of thick felt slippers. They were taken out of his own store yesterday evening, as we have ascertained, by Lyne himself, who sent for one of his assistants to his office and told him to get a pair of very soft-soled slippers.

"The third item is that Lyne's boots were discovered in the deserted motor car which was drawn up by the side of the road a hundred yards from where the body was lying.

"And the fourth feature – and this explains why I have brought you into the case – is that in the car was discovered his bloodstained coat and waistcoat. In the right-hand pocket of the latter garment," said Cresswell, speaking slowly, "was found this." He took from his drawer a small piece of crimson paper two inches square, and handed it without comment to the detective.

Tarling took the paper and stared. Written in thick black ink were four Chinese characters, "*tzu chao fan nao*" – "He brought this trouble upon himself."

THE MOTHER OF ODETTE RIDER

The two men looked at one another in silence.

"Well?" said the Commissioner at last. Tarling shook his head.

"That's amazing," he said, and looked at the little slip of paper between his finger and thumb.

"You see why I am bringing you in," said the Commissioner. "If there is a Chinese end to this crime, nobody knows better than you how to deal with it. I have had this slip translated. It means 'He brought this trouble upon himself.' "

"Literally, 'self look for trouble,' " said Tarling. "But there is one fact which you may not have noticed. If you will look at the slip, you will see that it is not written but printed."

He passed the little red square across the table, and the Commissioner examined it.

"That's true," he said in surprise. "I did not notice that. Have you seen these slips before?"

Tarling nodded.

"A few years ago," he said. "There was a very bad outbreak of crime in Shanghai, mostly under the leadership of a notorious criminal whom I was instrumental in getting beheaded. He ran a gang called 'The Cheerful Hearts' – you know the fantastic titles which these Chinese gangs adopt. It was their custom to leave on the scene of their depredations the *Hong*, or sign-manual of the gang. It was worded exactly as this slip, only it was written. These visiting cards of 'The Cheerful Hearts' were bought up as curios, and commanded high prices until some enterprising Chinaman started printing them,

32

so that you could buy them at almost any stationer's shop in Shanghai – just as you buy picture postcards."

The Commissioner nodded.

"And this is one of those?"

"This is such a one. How it came here, heaven knows," he said. "It is certainly the most remarkable discovery."

The Commissioner went to a cupboard, unlocked it and took out a suitcase, which he placed upon the table and opened.

"Now," said the Commissioner, "look at this, Tarling."

"This" was a stained garment, which Tarling had no difficulty in recognising as a nightdress. He took it out and examined it. Save for two sprays of forget-me-nots upon the sleeves it was perfectly plain and was innocent of lace or embroidery.

"It was found round his body, and here are the handkerchiefs." He pointed to two tiny squares of linen, so discoloured as to be hardly recognisable.

Tarling lifted the flimsy garment, with its evidence of the terrible purpose for which it had been employed, and carried it to the light.

"Are there laundry marks?"

"None whatever," said the Commissioner.

"Or on the handkerchiefs?"

"None," replied Mr Cresswell.

"The property of a girl who lived alone," said Tarling. "She is not very well off, but extremely neat, fond of good things, but not extravagant, eh?"

"How do you know that?" asked the Commissioner, surprised.

Tarling laughed.

"The absence of laundry marks shows that she washes her silk garments at home, and probably her handkerchiefs also, which places her amongst the girls who aren't blessed with too many of this world's goods. The fact that it is silk, and good silk, and that the handkerchiefs are good linen, suggests a woman who takes a great deal of trouble, yet whom one would not expect to find over dressed. Have you any other clue?"

"None," said the Commissioner. "We have discovered that Mr Lyne had rather a serious quarrel with one of his employees, a Miss Odette Rider – "

Tarling caught his breath. It was, he told himself, absurd to take so keen an interest in a person whom he had not seen for more than ten minutes, and who a week before was a perfect stranger. But somehow the girl had made a deeper impression upon him than he had realised. This man, who had spent his life in the investigation of crime and in the study of criminals, had found little time to interest himself in womanhood, and Odette Rider had been a revelation to him.

"I happen to know there was a quarrel. I also know the cause," he said, and related briefly the circumstances under which he himself had met Thornton Lyne. "What have you against her?" he said, with an assumption of carelessness which he did not feel.

"Nothing definite," said the Commissioner. "Her principal accuser is the man Stay. Even he did not accuse her directly, but he hinted that she was responsible, in some way which he did not particularise, for Thornton Lyne's death. I thought it curious that he should know anything about this girl, but I am inclined to think that Thornton Lyne made this man his confidant."

"What about the man?" asked Tarling. "Can he account for his movements last night and early this morning?"

"His statement," replied the Commissioner, "is that he saw Mr Lyne at his flat at nine o'clock, and that Mr Lyne gave him five pounds in the presence of Lyne's butler. He said he left the flat and went to his lodgings in Lambeth, where he went to bed very early. All the evidence we have been able to collect supports his statement. We have interviewed Lyne's butler, and his account agrees with Stay's. Stay left at five minutes past nine, and at twenty-five minutes to ten – exactly half an hour later – Lyne himself left the house, driving his two-seater. He was alone, and told the butler he was going to his club."

"How was he dressed?" asked Tarling.

"That is rather important," nodded the Commissioner. "For he was in evening dress until nine o'clock – in fact, until after Stay had gone – when he changed into the kit in which he was found dead."

Tarling pursed his lips.

"He'd hardly change from evening into day dress to go to his club," he said.

He left Scotland Yard a little while after this, a much puzzled man. His first call was at the flat in Edgware Road which Odette Rider occupied. She was not at home, and the hall porter told him that she had been away since the afternoon of the previous day. Her letters were to be sent on to Hertford. He had the address, because it was his business to intercept the postman and send forward the letters.

"Hillington Grove, Hertford."

Tarling was worried. There was really no reason why he should be, he told himself, but he was undoubtedly worried. And he was disappointed too. He felt that, if he could have seen the girl and spoken with her for a few minutes, he could have completely disassociated her from any suspicion which might attach. In fact, that she was away from home, that she had "disappeared" from her flat on the eve of the murder, would be quite enough, as he knew, to set the official policeman nosing on her trail.

"Do you know whether Miss Rider has friends at Hertford?" he asked the porter.

"Oh, yes, sir," said the man nodding. "Miss Rider's mother lives there."

Tarling was going, when the man detained him with a remark which switched his mind back to the murder and filled him with a momentary sense of hopeless dismay.

"I'm rather glad Miss Rider didn't happen to be in last night, sir," he said. "Some of the tenants upstairs were making complaints."

"Complaints about what?" asked Tarling, and the man hesitated.

"I suppose you're a friend of the young lady's aren't you?" and Tarling nodded,

"Well, it only shows you," said the porter confidentially, "how people are very often blamed for something they did not do. The tenant in the next flat is a bit crotchety; he's a musician, and rather deaf. If he hadn't been deaf, he wouldn't have said that Miss Rider was the cause of his being wakened up. I suppose it was something that happened outside."

"What did he hear?" asked Tarling quickly, and the porter laughed.

"Well, sir, he thought he heard a shot, and a scream like a woman's. It woke him up. I should have thought he had dreamt it, but another tenant, who also lives in the basement, heard the same sound, and the rum thing was they both thought it was in Miss Rider's flat."

"What time was this?"

"They say about midnight, sir," said the porter; "but, of course, it couldn't have happened, because Miss Rider had not been in, and the flat was empty."

Here was a disconcerting piece of news for Tarling to carry with him on his railway journey to Hertford. He was determined to see the girl and put her on her guard, and though he realised that it was not exactly his duty to put a suspected criminal upon her guard, and that his conduct was, to say the least of it, irregular, such did not trouble him very much.

He had taken his ticket and was making his way to the platform when he espied a familiar figure hurrying as from a train which had just come in, and apparently the man saw Tarling even before Tarling had recognised him, for he turned abruptly aside and would have disappeared into the press of people had not the detective overtaken him.

"Hullo, Mr Milburgh!" he said. "Your name is Milburgh, if I remember aright?"

The manager of Lyne's Store turned, rubbing his hands, his habitual smile upon his face.

"Why, to be sure," he said genially, "it's Mr Tarling, the detective gentleman. What sad news this is, Mr Tarling! How dreadful for everybody concerned!"

"I suppose it has meant an upset at the Stores, this terrible happening?"

"Oh, yes, sir," said Milburgh in a shocked voice. "Of course we closed the Store for the day. It is dreadful – the most dreadful thing within my experience. Is anybody suspected, sir?" he asked.

Tarling shook his head.

"It is a most mysterious circumstance, Mr Milburgh," he said. And then: "May I ask if any provision had been made to carry on the business in the event of Mr Lyne's sudden death?"

Again Milburgh hesitated, and seemed reluctant to reply.

"I am, of course, in control," he said, "as I was when Mr Lyne took his trip around the world. I have received authority also from Mr Lyne's solicitors to continue the direction of the business until the Court appoints a trustee."

Tarling eyed him narrowly.

"What effect has this murder had upon you personally?" he asked bluntly. "Does it enhance or depreciate your position?"

Milburgh smiled.

"Unhappily," he said, "it enhances my position, because it gives me a greater authority and a greater responsibility. I would that the occasion had never arisen, Mr Tarling."

"I'm sure you do," said Tarling dryly, remembering Lyne's accusations against the other's probity.

After a few commonplaces the men parted.

Milburgh! On the journey to Hertford Tarling analysed that urbane man, and found him deficient in certain essential qualities; weighed him and found him wanting in elements which should certainly form part of the equipment of a trustworthy man.

At Hertford he jumped into a cab and gave the address.

"Hillington Grove, sir? That's about two miles out," said the cabman. "It's Mrs Rider you want?"

Tarling nodded.

"You ain't come with the young lady she was expecting?" said the driver.

"No," replied Tarling in surprise.

"I was told to keep my eyes open for a young lady," explained the cabman vaguely.

A further surprise awaited the detective. He expected to discover that Hillington Grove was a small suburban house bearing a grandiose title. He was amazed when the cabman turned through a pair of impressive gates, and drove up a wide drive of some considerable length, turning eventually on to a gravelled space before a large mansion. It was hardly the kind of home he would have expected for the parent of a cashier at Lyne's Store, and his surprise was increased when the door was opened by a footman.

He was ushered into a drawing-room, beautifully and artistically furnished. He began to think that some mistake had been made, and was framing an apology to the mistress of the house, when the door opened and a lady entered.

Her age was nearer forty than thirty, but she was still a beautiful woman and carried herself with the air of a grand dame. She was graciousness itself to the visitor, but Tarling thought he detected a note of anxiety both in her mien and in her voice.

"I'm afraid there's some mistake," he began "I have probably found the wrong Mrs Rider – I wanted to see Miss Odette Rider."

The lady nodded.

"That is my daughter," she said. "Have you any news of her? I am quite worried about her."

"Worried about her?" said Tarling quickly. "Why, what has happened? Isn't she here?"

"Here?" said Mrs Rider, wide-eyed. "Of course she is not."

"But hasn't she been here?" asked Tarling. "Didn't she arrive here two nights ago?"

Mrs Rider shook her head.

"My daughter has not been," she replied. "But she promised to come and spend a few days with me, and last night I received a telegram – wait a moment, I will get it for you."

She was gone a few moments and came back with a little buff form, which she handed to the detective. He looked and read:

"My visit cancelled. Do not write to me at flat. I will communicate with you when I reach my destination."

The telegram had been handed in at the General Post Office, London, and was dated nine o'clock – three hours, according to expert opinion, before the murder was committed!

THE WOMAN IN THE CASE

"May I keep this telegram?" asked Tarling. The woman nodded, He saw that she was nervous, ill at ease and worried.

"I can't quite understand why Odette should not come," she said. "Is there any particular reason?"

"That I can't say," said Tarling. "But please don't let it worry you, Mrs Rider. She probably changed her mind at the last moment and is staying with friends in town."

"Then you haven't seen her?" asked Mrs Rider anxiously.

"I haven't seen her for several days."

"Is anything wrong?" Her voice shook for a second, but she recovered herself. "You see," she made an attempt to smile. "I have been in the house for two or three days, and I have seen neither Odette nor – nor anybody else," she added quickly.

Who was she expecting to see, wondered Tarling, and why did she check herself? Was it possible that she had not heard of the murder? He determined to test her.

"Your daughter is probably detained in town owing to Mr Lyne's death," he said, watching her closely.

She started and went white.

"Mr Lyne's death?" she stammered. "Has he died? That young man?"

"He was murdered in Hyde Park yesterday morning," said Tarling, and she staggered back and collapsed into a chair.

"Murdered! Murdered!" she whispered. "Oh, God! Not that, not that!"

Her face was ashen white, and she was shaking in every limb, this stately woman who had walked so serenely into the drawing-room a few minutes before.

Presently she covered her face with her hands and began to weep softly and Tarling waited.

"Did you know Mr Lyne?" he asked after a while.

She shook her head.

"Have you heard any stories about Mr Lyne?"

She looked up.

"None," she said listlessly, "except that he was – not a very nice man."

"Forgive me asking you, but are you very much interested – " He hesitated, and she lifted her head.

He did not know how to put this question into words. It puzzled him that the daughter of this woman, who was evidently well off, should be engaged in a more or less humble capacity in Lyne's Store. He wanted to know whether she knew that the girl had been dismissed, and whether that made much difference to her. Then again, his conversation with Odette Rider had not led him to the conclusion that she could afford to throw up her work. She spoke of finding another job, and that did not sound as though her mother was in a good position.

"Is there any necessity for your daughter working for a living?" he asked bluntly, and she dropped her eyes.

"It is her wish," she said in a low voice, "She does not get on with people about here," she added hastily.

There was a brief silence, then he rose and offered his hand.

"I do hope I haven't worried you with my questions," he said, "and I daresay you wonder why I have come. I will tell you candidly that I am engaged in investigating this murder, and I was hoping to hear that your daughter, in common with the other people who were brought into contact with Mr Lyne, might give me some thread of a clue which would lead to more important things."

"A detective?" she asked, and he could have sworn there was horror in her eyes.

"A sort of detective," he laughed, "but not a formidable one, I hope, Mrs Rider."

She saw him to the door, and watched him as he disappeared down the drive; then walked slowly back to the room and stood against the marble mantelpiece, her head upon her arms, weeping softly.

Jack Tarling left Hertford more confused than ever. He had instructed the fly driver to wait for him at the gates, and this worthy he proceeded to pump.

Mrs Rider had been living in Hertford for four years, and was greatly respected. Did the cabman know the daughter? Oh yes, he had seen the young lady once or twice, but "She don't come very often," he explained. "By all accounts she doesn't get on with her father."

"Her father? I did not know she had a father," said Tarling in surprise.

Yes, there was a father. He was an infrequent visitor, and usually came up from London by the late train and was driven in his own brougham to the house. He had not seen him – indeed, very few people had, but by all accounts he was a very nice man, and well-connected in the City.

Tarling had telegraphed to the assistant who had been placed at his disposal by Scotland Yard, and Detective-Inspector Whiteside was waiting for him at the station.

"Any fresh news?" asked Tarling.

"Yes, sir, there's rather an important clue come to light," said Whiteside. "I've got the car here, sir, and we might discuss it on the way back to the Yard."

"What is it?" asked Tarling.

"We got it from Mr Lyne's manservant," said the inspector. "It appears that the butler had been going through Mr Lyne's things, acting on instructions from headquarters, and in a corner of his writing-desk a telegram was discovered. I'll show it you when I get to the Yard. It has a very important bearing upon the case, and I think may lead us to the murderer."

"On the word "telegram" Tarling felt mechanically in his pockets for the wire which Mrs Rider had given him from her daughter. Now he took it out and read it again. It had been handed in at the General Post Office at nine o'clock exactly.

"That's extraordinary, sir," Detective-Inspector Whiteside, sitting by his side, had overlooked the wire.

"What is extraordinary?" asked Tarling with an air of surprise.

"I happened to see the signature to that wire – 'Odette,' isn't it?" said the Scotland Yard man.

"Yes," nodded Tarling. "Why? What is there extraordinary in that?"

"Well, sir," said Whiteside, "it's something of a coincidence that the telegram which was found in Mr Lyne's desk, and making an appointment with him at a certain flat in the Edgware Road, was also signed 'Odette,' and," he bent forward, looking at the wire still in the astonished Tarling's hand, "and," he said in triumph, "it was handed in exactly at the same time as that!"

An examination of the telegram at Scotland Yard left no doubt in the detective's mind that Whiteside had spoken nothing but the truth. An urgent message was despatched to the General Post Office, and in two hours the original telegrams were before him. They were both written in the same hand. The first to her mother, saying that she could not come; the second to Lyne, running:

"Will you see me at my flat tonight at eleven o'clock?
                                        ODETTE RIDER."

Tarling's heart sank within him. This amazing news was stunning. It was impossible, impossible, he told himself again and again, that this girl could have killed Lyne. Suppose she had? Where had they met? Had they gone driving together, and had she shot him in making the circuit of the Park? But why should he be wearing list slippers? Why should his coat be off, and why should the nightdress be bound round and round his body?

He thought the matter out, but the more he thought the more puzzled he became. It was a very depressed man who interviewed an authority that night and secured from him a search warrant.

Armed with this and accompanied by Whiteside he made his way to the flat in Edgware Road, and, showing his authority, secured a pass-key from the hall porter, who was also the caretaker of the building. Tarling remembered the last time he had gone to the flat, and it was with a feeling of intense pity for the girl that he turned the key in the lock and stepped into the little hall, reaching out his hand and switching on the light as he did so.

There was nothing in the hall to suggest anything unusual. There was just that close and musty smell which is peculiar to all buildings which have been shut up, even for a few days.

But there was something else.

Tarling sniffed and Whiteside sniffed. A dull, "burnt" smell, some pungent, "scorched" odour, which he recognised as the stale stench of exploded cordite. He went into the tiny dining-room; everything was neat, nothing displaced.

"That's curious," said Whiteside, pointing to the sideboard, and Tarling saw a deep glass vase half filled with daffodils. Two or three blossoms had either fallen or had been pulled out, and were lying, shrivelled and dead, on the polished surface of the sideboard.

"Humph!" said Tarling. "I don't like this very much."

He turned and walked back into the hall and opened another door, which stood ajar. Again he turned on the light. He was in the girl's bedroom. He stopped dead, and slowly examined the room. But for the disordered appearance of the chest of drawers, there was nothing unusual in the appearance of the room. At the open doors of the bureau a little heap of female attire had been thrown pell-mell upon the floor. All these were eloquent of hasty action. Still more was a small suitcase, half packed, on the bed, also left in a great hurry.

Tarling stepped into the room, and if he had been half blind he could not have missed the last and most damning evidence of all. The carpet was of a biscuit colour and covered the room flush to the wainscot. Opposite the fireplace was a big, dark red, irregular stain.

Tarling's face grew tense.

"This is where Lyne was shot," he said.

"And look there!" said Whiteside excitedly. pointing to the chest of drawers.

Tarling stepped quickly across the room and pulled out a garment which hung over the edge of the drawer. It was a nightdress – a silk nightdress with two little sprays of forget-me-nots embroidered on the sleeves. It was the companion to that which had been found about Lyne's body. And there was something more. The removal of the garment from the drawer disclosed a mark on the white enamel of the bureau. It was a bloody thumb print!

The detective looked round at his assistant, and the expression of his face was set in its hardest mask.

"Whiteside," he said quietly, "swear out a warrant for the arrest of Odette Rider on a charge of wilful murder. Telegraph all stations to detain this girl, and let me know the result."

Without another word he turned from the room and walked back to his lodgings.

THE SILENCING OF SAM STAY

There was a criminal in London who was watched day and night. It was no new experience to Sam Stay to find an unconcerned-looking detective strolling along behind him; but for the first time in his life the burglar was neither disconcerted nor embarrassed by these attentions.

The death of Thornton Lyne had been the most tragic blow which had ever overtaken him. And if they had arrested him he would have been indifferent. For this hang-dog criminal, with the long, melancholy face, lined and seamed and puckered so that he appeared to be an old man, had loved Thornton Lyne as he had loved nothing in his wild and barren life. Lyne to him had been some divine creature, possessed gifts and qualities which no other would have recognised in him. In Sam's eyes Lyne could have done no wrong. By Sam Stay's standard he stood for all that was beautiful in human nature.

Thornton Lyne was dead! Dead, dead, dead.

Every footfall echoed the horrible, unbelievable word. The man was incapable of feeling – every other pain was deadened in this great suffering which was his.

And who had been the cause of it all? Whose treachery had cut short this wonderful life? He ground his teeth at the thought. Odette Rider! He remembered the name. He remembered all the injuries she had done to this man, his benefactor. He remembered that long conversation which Lyne and he had had on the morning of Sam's release from prison and the plannings which had followed.

He could not know that his hero was lying, and that in his piqué and hurt vanity he was inventing grievances which had no foundation, and offences which had never been committed. He only knew that, because of the hate which lay in Thornton Lyne's heart, justifiable hate from Sam's view, the death of this great man had been encompassed.

He walked aimlessly westward, unconscious of and uncaring for his shadower, and had reached the end of Piccadilly when somebody took him gently by the arm. He turned, and as he recognised an acquaintance, his thick lips went back in an ugly snarl.

"It's all right, Sam," said the plain-clothes policeman with a grin. "There's no trouble coming to you. I just want to ask you a few questions."

"You fellows have been asking questions day and night since – since that happened," growled Sam.

Nevertheless, he permitted himself to be mollified and led to a seat in the Park.

"Now, I'm putting it to you straight, Sam," said the policeman. "We've got nothing against you at the Yard, but we think you might be able to help us. You knew Mr Lyne; he was very decent to you."

"Here, shut up," said Sam savagely. "I don't want to talk about it. I don't want to think about it! D'ye hear? He was the grandest fellow that ever was, was Mr Lyne, God bless him! Oh, my God! My God!" he wailed, and to the detective's surprise this hardened criminal buried his face in his hands.

"That's all right, Sam. I know he was a nice fellow. Had he any enemies – he might have talked to a chap like you where he wouldn't have talked to his friends."

Sam, red-eyed, looked up suspiciously.

"Am I going to get into any trouble for talking?" he said.

"None at all, Sam," said the policeman quickly. "Now, you be a good lad and do all you can to help us, and maybe, if you ever get into trouble, we'll put one in for you. Do you see? Did anybody hate him?"

Sam nodded.

"Was it a woman?" asked the detective with studied indifference.

"It was," replied the other with an oath. "Damn her, it was! He treated her well, did Mr Lyne. She was broke, half-starving; he took her out of the gutter and put her into a good place, and she went about making accusations against him!"

He poured forth a stream of the foulest abuse which the policeman had ever heard.

"That's the kind of girl she was, Slade," he went on, addressing the detective, as criminals will, familiarly by their surnames. "She ain't fit to walk the earth – "

His voice broke.

"Might I ask her name?" demanded Slade.

Again Sam looked suspiciously around.

"Look here," he said, "leave me to deal with her. I'll settle with her, and don't you worry!"

"That would only get you into trouble, Sam," mused Slade. "Just give us her name. Did it begin with an 'R'?"

"How do I know?" growled the criminal. "I can't spell. Her name was Odette."

"Rider?" said the other eagerly.

"That's her. She used to be cashier in Lyne's Store."

"Now, just quieten yourself down and tell me all Lyne told you about her, will you, my lad?"

Sam Stay stared at him, and then a slow look of cunning passed over his face.

"If it was her!" he breathed. "If I could only put her away for it!"

Nothing better illustrated the mentality of this man than the fact that the thought of "shopping" the girl had not occurred to him before. That was the idea, a splendid idea! Again his lips curled back, and he eyed the detective with a queer little smile.

"All right, sir," he said. "I'll tell the head-split. I'm not going to tell you."

"That's as it ought to be, Sam," said the detective genially. "You can tell Mr Tarling or Mr Whiteside and they'll make it worth your while."

The detective called a cab and together they drove, not to Scotland Yard, but to Tarling's little office in Bond Street. It was here that the man from Shanghai had established his detective agency, and here he waited with the phlegmatic Whiteside for the return of the detective he had sent to withdraw Sam Stay from his shadower.

The man shuffled into the room, looked resentfully from one to the other, nodded to both, and declined the chair which was pushed forward for him. His head was throbbing in an unaccountable way, as it had never throbbed before. There were curious buzzes and noises in his ears. It was strange that he had not noticed this until he came into the quiet room, to meet the grave eyes of a hard-faced man, whom he did not remember having seen before.

"Now, Stay," said Whiteside, whom at least the criminal recognised, "we want to hear what you know about this murder."

Stay pressed his lips together and made no reply.

"Sit down," said Tarling, and this time the man obeyed. "Now, my lad," Tarling went on – and when he was in a persuasive mood his voice was silky – "they tell me that you were a friend of Mr Lyne's."

Sam nodded.

"He was good to you, was he not?"

"Good?" The man drew a deep breath. "I'd have given my heart and soul to save him from a minute's pain, I would, sir! I'm telling you straight, and may I be struck dead if I'm lying! He was an angel on earth – my God, if ever I lay me hands on that woman, I'll strangle her. I'll put her out! I'll not leave her till she's torn to rags!"

His voice rose, specks of foam stood on his lips, his whole face seemed transfigured in an ecstasy of hate.

"She's been robbing him and robbing him for years," he shouted. "He looked after her and protected her, and she went and told lies about him, she did. She trapped him!"

His voice rose to a scream, and he made a move forward towards the desk, both fists clenched till the knuckles showed white. Tarling sprang up, for he recognised the signs. Before another word could be spoken, the man collapsed in a heap on the floor, and lay like one dead.

Tarling was round the table in an instant, turned the unconscious man on his back, and, lifting one eyelid, examined the pupil.

"Epilepsy or something worse," he said. "This thing has been preying on the poor devil's mind – 'phone an ambulance, Whiteside, will you?"

"Shall I give him some water?"

Tarling shook his head.

"He won't recover for hours, if he recovers at all," he said. "If Sam Stay knows anything to the detriment of Odette Rider, he is likely to carry his knowledge to the grave."

And in his heart of hearts J O Tarling felt a little sense of satisfaction that the mouth of this man was closed.

WHERE THE FLOWERS CAME FROM

Where was Odette Rider? That was a problem which had to be solved. She had disappeared as though the earth had opened and swallowed her up. Every police station in the country had been warned; all outgoing ships were being watched; tactful inquiries had been made in every direction where it was likely she might be found; and the house at Hertford was under observation day and night.

Tarling had procured an adjournment of the inquest; for, whatever might be his sentiments towards Odette Rider, he was, it seemed, more anxious to perform his duty to the State, and it was very necessary that no prurient-minded coroner should investigate too deeply into the cause and the circumstances leading up to Thornton Lyne's death, lest the suspected criminal be warned.

Accompanied by Inspector Whiteside, he re-examined the flat to which the bloodstained carpet pointed unmistakably as being the scene of the murder. The red thumbprints on the bureau had been photographed and were awaiting comparison with the girl's the moment she was apprehended.

Carrymore Mansions, where Odette Rider lived, were, as has been described, a block of good-class flats, the ground floor being given over to shops. The entrance to the flats was between two of these, and a flight of stairs led down to the basement. Here were six sets of apartments, with windows giving out to the narrow areas which ran parallel to the side streets on either side of the block.

The centre of the basement consisted of a large concrete store-room, about which were set little cubicles or cellars in which the tenants stored such of their baggage, furniture, etc., as they did not need. It was possible, he discovered, to pass from the corridor of the basement flat, into the storeroom, and out through a door at the back of the building into a small courtyard. Access to the street was secured through a fairly large door, placed there for the convenience of tenants who wished to get their coal and heavy stores delivered. In the street behind the block of flats was a mews, consisting of about a dozen shut-up stables, all of which were rented by a taxicab company, and now used as a garage.

If the murder was committed in the flat, it was by this way the body would have been carried to the mews, and here, too, a car would attract little attention. Inquiries made amongst employees of the cab company, some of whom occupied little rooms above their garages, elicited the important information that the car had been seen in the mews on the night of the murder – a fact, it seemed, which had been overlooked in the preliminary police investigations.

The car was a two-seater Daimler with a yellow body and a hood. This was an exact description of Thornton Lyne's machine which had been found near the place where his body was discovered. The hood of the car was up when it was seen in the mews and the time apparently was between ten and eleven on the night of the murder. But though he pursued the most diligent inquiries, Tarling failed to discover any human being who had either recognised Lyne or observed the car arrive or depart.

The hall porter of the flats, on being interviewed, was very emphatic that nobody had come into the building by the main entrance between the hours of ten and half-past. It was possible, he admitted, that they could have come between half-past ten and a quarter to eleven because he had gone to his "office," which proved to be a stuffy little place under the stairs, to change from his uniform into his private clothes before going home. He was in the habit of locking the front door at eleven o'clock. Tenants of the mansions had pass-keys to the main door, and of all that happened after eleven he would be ignorant. He admitted that he may have gone a little before eleven that night, but even as to this he was not prepared to swear.

"In fact," said Whiteside afterwards, "his evidence would lead nowhere. At the very hour when somebody might have come into the flat – that is to say, between half-past ten and a quarter to eleven – he admits he was not on duty."

Tarling nodded. He had made a diligent search of the floor of the basement corridor through the storeroom into the courtyard, but had found no trace of blood. Nor did he expect to find any such trace, since it was clear that, if the murder had been committed in the flat and the nightdress which was wound about the dead man's body was Odette Rider's, there would be no bleeding.

"Of one thing I am satisfied," he said; "if Odette Rider committed this murder she had an accomplice. It was impossible that she could have carried or dragged this man into the open and put him into the car, carried him again from the car and laid him on the grass."

"The daffodils puzzle me," said Whiteside. "Why should he be found with daffodils on his chest? And why, if he was murdered here, should she trouble to pay that tribute of her respect?"

Tarling shook his head. He was nearer a solution to the latter mystery than either of them knew.

His search of the flat completed, he drove to Hyde Park and, guided by Whiteside, made his way to the spot where the body was found. It was on a gravelled sidewalk, nearer to the grass than to the road, and Whiteside described the position of the body. Tarling looked round, and suddenly uttered an exclamation.

"I wonder," he said, pointing to a flower-bed.

Whiteside stared, then laughed.

"That's curious," he said. "We seem to see nothing but daffodils in this murder!"

The big bed to which Tarling walked was smothered with great feathery bells that danced and swayed in the light spring breezes.

"Humph!" said Tarling. "Do you know anything about daffodils, Whiteside?"

Whiteside shook his head with a laugh.

"All daffodils are daffodils to me. Is there any difference in them? I suppose there must be."

Tarling nodded.

"These are known as Golden Spurs," he said, "a kind which is very common in England. The daffodils in Miss Rider's flat are the variety known as the Emperor."

"Well?" said Whiteside.

"Well," said the other slowly, "the daffodils I saw this morning which were found on Lyne's chest were Golden Spurs."

He knelt down by the side of the bed and began pushing aside the stems, examining the ground carefully.

"Here you are," he said.

He pointed to a dozen jagged stems.

"That is where the daffodils were plucked, I'd like to swear to that. Look, they were all pulled together by one hand. Somebody leaned over and pulled a handful."

Whiteside looked dubious.

"Mischievous boys sometimes do these things."

Only in single stalks," said Tarling, "and the regular flower thieves are careful to steal from various parts of the bed so that the loss should not be reported by the Park gardeners."

"Then you suggest – "

"I suggest that whoever killed Thornton Lyne found it convenient, for some reason best known to himself or herself, to ornament the body as it was found, and the flowers were got from here."

"Not from the girl's flat at all?"

"I'm sure of that," replied Tarling emphatically "In fact, I knew that this morning when I'd seen the daffodils which you had taken to Scotland Yard."

Whiteside scratched his nose in perplexity.

"The further this case goes, the more puzzled I am," he said. "Here is a man, a wealthy man, who has apparently no bitter enemies, discovered dead in Hyde Park, with a woman's silk nightdress wound round his chest, with list slippers on his feet, and a Chinese inscription in his pocket – and further, to puzzle the police, a bunch of daffodils on the chest. That was a woman's act, Mr Tarling," he said suddenly.

Tarling started. "How do you mean?" he asked.

"It was a woman's act to put flowers on the man," said Whiteside quietly. "Those daffodils tell me of pity and compassion, and perhaps repentance."

A slow smile dawned on Tarling's face.

"My dear Whiteside," he said, "you are getting sentimental! And here," he added, looking up, "attracted to the spot, is a gentleman I seem to be always meeting – Mr Milburgh, I think."

Milburgh had stopped at the sight of the detective, and looked as if he would have been glad to have faded away unobserved. But Tarling had seen him, and Milburgh came forward with his curious little shuffling walk, a set smile on his face, the same worried look in his eyes, which Tarling had seen once before.

"Good morning, gentlemen," he said, with a flourish of his top hat. "I suppose, Mr Tarling, nothing has been discovered?"

"At any rate, I didn't expect to discover *you* here this morning!" smiled Tarling. "I thought you were busy at the Stores."

Milburgh shifted uneasily.

"The place has a fascination for me," he said huskily, I – I can't keep away from it."

He dropped his eyes before Tarling's keen gaze and repeated the question.

"Is there any fresh news?"

"I ought to ask you that," said Tarling quietly.

The other looked up.

"You mean Miss Rider?" he asked. "No, sir, nothing has been found to her detriment and I cannot trace her present address, although I have pursued the most diligent inquiries. It is very upsetting"

There was a new emphasis in his voice. Tarling remembered that when Lyne had spoken to Milburgh before, and had suggested that the girl had been guilty of some act of predation, Milburgh had been quick to deny the possibility. Now his manner was hostile to the girl – indefinitely so, but sufficiently marked for Tarling to notice it.

"Do you think that Miss Rider had any reason for running away?" asked the detective.

Milburgh shrugged his shoulders.

"In this world," he said unctuously, "one is constantly being deceived by people in whom one has put one's trust."

"In other words, you suspect Miss Rider of robbing the firm?"

Up went Mr Milburgh's plump hands.

"I would not say that," he said. "I would not accuse a young woman of such an act of treachery to her employers, and I distinctly refuse to make any charges until the auditors have completed their work. There is no doubt," he added carefully, "that Miss Rider had the handling of large sums of money, and she of all people in the business, and particularly in the cashier's department would have been able to rob the firm without the knowledge of either myself or poor Mr Lyne. This, of course, is confidential." He laid one hand appealingly on Tarling's arm, and that worthy nodded.

"Have you any idea where she would be?"

Again Milburgh shook his head.

"The only thing – " he hesitated and looked into Tarling's eyes.

"Well?" asked the detective impatiently.

"There is a suggestion, of course, that she may have gone abroad. I do not offer that suggestion, only I know that she spoke French very well and that she had been to the Continent before."

Tarling stroked his chin thoughtfully.

"To the Continent, eh?" he said softly. "Well, in that case I shall search the Continent; for on one thing I am determined, and that is to find Odette Rider," and, beckoning to his companion, he turned on his heel and left the obsequious Mr Milburgh staring after him.

THE WOMAN AT ASHFORD

Tarling went back to his lodgings that afternoon, a puzzled and baffled man. Ling Chu, his impassive Chinese servant, had observed those symptoms of perplexity before, but now there was something new in his master's demeanour – a kind of curt irritation, an anxiety which in the Hunter of Men had not been observed before.

The Chinaman went silently about the business of preparing his chief's tea and made no reference to the tragedy or to any of its details. He had set the table by the side of the bed, and was gliding from the room in that cat-like way of his when Tarling stopped him.

"Ling Chu," he said, speaking in the vernacular, "you remember in Shanghai when the 'Cheerful Hearts' committed a crime, how they used to leave behind their *hong*?"

"Yes, master, I remember it very well," said Ling Chu calmly. "They were certain words on red paper, and afterwards you could buy them from the shops, because people desired to have these signs to show to their friends."

"Many people carried these things," said Tarling slowly, "and the sign of the 'Cheerful Hearts' was found in the pocket of the murdered man."

Ling Chu met the other's eyes with imperturbable calmness.

Master," he said, " may not the white-faced man who is now dead have brought such a thing from Shanghai? He was a tourist, and tourists buy these foolish souvenirs."

Tarling nodded again.

"That is possible," he said. "I have already thought that such might have been the case. Yet, why should he have this sign of the 'Cheerful Hearts' in his pocket on the night he was murdered?"

"Master," said the Chinaman, "why should he have been murdered?"

Tarling's lips curled in a half smile.

"By which I suppose you mean that one question is as difficult to answer as the other," he said. "All right, Ling Chu, that will do."

His principal anxiety for the moment was not this, or any other clue which had been offered, but the discovery of Odette Rider's present hiding-place. Again and again he turned the problem over in his mind. At every point he was baffled by the wild improbability of the facts that he had discovered. Why should Odette Rider be content to accept a servile position in Lyne's Stores when her mother was living in luxury at Hertford? Who was her father – that mysterious father who appeared and disappeared at Hertford, and what part did he play in the crime? And if she was innocent, why had she disappeared so completely and in circumstances so suspicious? And what did Sam Stay know? The man's hatred of the girl was uncanny. At the mention of her name a veritable fountain of venom had bubbled up, and Tarling had sensed the abysmal depths of this man's hate and something of his boundless love for the dead man.

He turned impatiently on the couch and reached out his hand for his tea, when there came a soft tap at the door and Ling Chu slipped into the room.

"The Bright Man is here," he said, and in these words announced Whiteside, who brought into the room something of his alert, fresh personality which had earned him the pseudonym which Ling Chu had affixed.

"Well, Mr Tarling," said the Inspector, taking out a little notebook, "I'm afraid I haven't done very much in the way of discovering the movements of Miss Rider, but so far as I can find out by inquiries made at Charing Cross booking office, several young ladies unattended have left for the Continent in the past few days."

"You cannot identify any of these with Miss Rider?" asked Tarling in a tone of disappointment.

The detective shook his head. Despite his apparent unsuccess, he had evidently made some discovery which pleased him, for there was nothing gloomy in his admission of failure.

"You have found out something, though?" suggested Tarling quickly, and Whiteside nodded.

"Yes," he said, "by the greatest of luck I've got hold of a very curious story. I was chatting with some of the ticket collectors and trying to discover a man who might have seen the girl – I have a photograph of her taken in a group of Stores employees, and this I have had enlarged, as it may be very useful."

Tarling nodded.

"Whilst I was talking with the man on the gate," Whiteside proceeded, "a travelling ticket inspector came up and he brought rather an extraordinary story from Ashford. On the night of the murder there was an accident to the Continental Express."

"I remember seeing something about it," said Tarling, "but my mind has been occupied by this other matter. What happened?"

"A luggage truck which was standing on the platform fell between two of the carriages and derailed one of them," explained Whiteside. "The only passenger who was hurt was a Miss Stevens. Apparently it was a case of simple concussion, and when the train was brought to a standstill she was removed to the Cottage Hospital, where she is today. Apparently the daughter of the travelling ticket inspector is a nurse at the hospital, and she told her father that this Miss Stevens, before she recovered consciousness, made several references to a 'Mr Lyne' and a 'Mr Milburgh'!"

Tarling was sitting erect now, watching the other through narrowed lids.

"Go on," he said quietly.

"I could get very little from the travelling inspector, except that his daughter was under the impression that the lady had a grudge against Mr Lyne, and that she spoke even more disparagingly of Mr Milburgh."

Tarling had risen and slipped off his silk dressing-gown before the other could put away his notebook. He struck a gong with his knuckles, and when Ling Chu appeared, gave him an order in Chinese, which Whiteside could not follow.

"You're going to Ashford? I thought you would," said Whiteside. "Would you like me to come along?"

"No, thank you," said the other. "I'll go myself. I have an idea that Miss Stevens may be the missing witness in the case and may throw greater light upon the happenings of the night before last than any other witness we have yet interviewed."

He found he had to wait an hour before he could get a train for Ashford, and he passed that hour impatiently walking up and down the broad platform. Here was a new complication in the case. Who was Miss Stevens, and why should she be journeying to Dover on the night of the murder?

He reached Ashford, and with difficulty found a cab, for it was raining heavily, and he had come provided with neither mackintosh nor umbrella.

The matron of the Cottage Hospital reassured him on one point.

"Oh, yes, Miss Stevens is still in the hospital," she said, and he breathed a sigh of relief. There was just a chance that she might have been discharged, and again the possibility that she would be difficult to trace.

The matron showed him the way through a long corridor, terminating in a big ward. Before reaching the door of the ward there was a smaller door on the right.

"We put her in this private ward, because we thought it might be necessary to operate," said the matron and opened the door.

Tarling walked in. Facing him was the foot of the bed, and in that bed lay a girl whose eyes met his. He stopped dead as though he were shot. For "Miss Stevens" was Odette Rider!

"THORNTON LYNE IS DEAD"

For a time neither spoke. Tarling walked slowly forward, pulled a chair to the side of the bed and sat down, never once taking his eyes off the girl.

Odette Rider! The woman for whom the police of England were searching, against whom a warrant had been issued on a charge of wilful murder – and here, in a little country hospital. For a moment, and a moment only, Tarling was in doubt. Had he been standing outside the case and watching it as a disinterested spectator, or had this girl never come so closely into his life, bringing a new and a disturbing influence so that the very balance of his judgment was upset, he would have said that she was in hiding and had chosen this hospital for a safe retreat. The very name under which she was passing was fictitious – a suspicious circumstance in itself.

The girl's eyes did not leave his. He read in their clear depths a hint of terror and his heart fell. He had not realised before that the chief incentive he found in this case was not to discover the murderer of Thornton Lyne, but to prove that the girl was innocent.

"Mr Tarling," she said with a queer little break in her voice, "I – I did not expect to see you."

It was a lame opening, and it seemed all the more feeble to her since she had so carefully rehearsed the statement she had intended making. For her waking moments, since the accident, had been filled with thoughts of this hard-faced man, what he would think, what he would say, and what, in certain eventualities, he would do.

"I suppose not," said Tarling gently. "I am sorry to hear you have had rather a shaking, Miss Rider."

She nodded, and a faint smile played about the corners of her mouth.

"It was nothing very much," she said. "Of course, it was very horrid at first and – what do you want?"

The last words were blurted out. She could not keep up the farce of a polite conversation.

There was a moment's silence, and then Tarling spoke.

"I wanted to find you," he said, speaking slowly, and again he read her fear.

"Well," she hesitated, and then said desperately and just a little defiantly, "you have found me!"

Tarling nodded.

"And now that you have found me," she went on, speaking rapidly, "what do you want?"

She was resting on her elbow, her strained face turned towards him, her eyes slightly narrowed, watching him with an intensity of gaze which betrayed her agitation.

"I want to ask you a few questions," said Tarling, and slipped a little notebook from his pocket, balancing it upon his knee.

To his dismay the girl shook her head.

"I don't know that I am prepared to answer your questions," she said more calmly, "but there is no reason why you should not ask them."

Here was an attitude wholly unexpected. And Odette Rider panic-stricken he could understand.

If she had burst into a fit of weeping, if she had grown incoherent in her terror, if she had been indignant or shame-faced – any of these displays would have fitted in with his conception of her innocence or apprehension of her guilt.

"In the first place," he asked bluntly, "why are you here under the name of Miss Stevens?"

She thought a moment, then shook her head.

"That is a question I am not prepared to answer," she said quietly.

"I won't press it for a moment," said Tarling, "because I realise that it is bound up in certain other extraordinary actions of yours, Miss Rider."

The girl flushed and dropped her eyes, and Tarling went on:

"Why did you leave London secretly, without giving your friends or your mother any inkling of your plans?"

She looked up sharply.

"Have you seen mother?" she asked quietly, and again her eyes were troubled.

"I've seen your mother," said Tarling. "I have also seen the telegram you sent to her. Come, Miss Rider, won't you let me help you? Believe me, a great deal more depends upon your answers than the satisfaction of my curiosity. You must realise how very serious your position is."

He saw her lips close tightly and she shook her head.

"I have nothing to say," she said with a catch of her breath. "If – if you think I have – "

She stopped dead.

"Finish your sentence," said Tarling sternly. "If I think you have committed this crime?"

She nodded.

He put away his notebook before he spoke again, and, leaning over the bed, took her hand.

"Miss Rider, I want to help you," he said earnestly, "and I can help you best if you're frank with me. I tell you I do not believe that you committed this act. I tell you now that though all the circumstances point to your guilt, I have absolute confidence that you can produce an answer to the charge."

For a moment her eyes filled with tears, but she bit her lip and smiled bravely into his face.

"That is good and sweet of you, Mr Tarling, and I do appreciate your kindness. But I can't tell you anything – I can't, I can't!" She gripped his wrist in her vehemence, and he thought she was going to break down, but again, with an extraordinary effort of will which excited his secret admiration, she controlled herself.

"You're going to think very badly of me," she said, "and I hate the thought, Mr Tarling – you don't know how I hate it. I want you to think that I am innocent, but I am going to make no effort to prove that I was not guilty."

"You're mad!" he interrupted her roughly. "Stark, raving mad! You must do something, do you hear? You've got to do something."

She shook her head, and the little hand which rested on his closed gently about two of his fingers.

"I can't," she said simply. "I just can't,"

Tarling pushed back the chair from the bed. He could have groaned at the hopelessness of the girl's case. If she had only given him one thread that would lead him to another clue, if she only protested her innocence! His heart sank within him, and he could only shake his head helplessly.

"Suppose," he said huskily, "that you are charged with this – crime. Do you mean to tell me that you will not produce evidence that could prove your innocence, that you will make no attempt to defend yourself?"

She nodded.

"I mean that," she said.

"My God! You don't know what you're saying," he cried, starting up. "You're mad, Odette, stark mad!"

She only smiled for the fraction of a second, and that at the unconscious employment of her Christian name.

"I'm not at all mad," she said. "I am very sane."

She looked at him thoughtfully, and then of a sudden seemed to shrink back, and her face went whiter. "You – you have a warrant for me!" she whispered.

He nodded.

"And you're going to arrest me?"

He shook his head.

"No," he said briefly. "I am leaving that to somebody else. I have sickened of the case, and I'm going out of it."

"He sent you here," she said slowly.

"He?"

"Yes – I remember. You were working with him, or he wanted you to work with him."

"Of whom are you speaking?" asked Tarling quickly.

"Thornton Lyne," said the girl.

Tarling leaped to his feet and stared down at her.

"Thornton Lyne?" he repeated. "Don't you know?"

"Know what?" asked the girl with a frown.

"That Thornton Lyne is dead," said Tarling, "and that it is for his murder that a warrant has been issued for your arrest?"

She looked at him for a moment with wide, staring eyes.

"Dead!" she gasped. "Dead! Thornton Lyne dead! You don't mean that, you don't mean that?" She clutched at Tarling's arm. "Tell me that isn't true! He did not do it, he dare not do it!"

She swayed forward, and Tarling, dropping on his knees beside the bed, caught her in his arms as she fainted.

THE HOSPITAL BOOK

While the nurse was attending to the girl Tarling sought an interview with the medical officer in charge of the hospital.

"I don't think there's a great deal the matter with her," said the doctor. "In fact, she was fit for discharge from hospital two or three days ago, and it was only at her request that we let her stay. Do I understand that she is wanted in connection with the Daffodil Murder?"

"As a witness," said Tarling glibly. He realised that he was saying a ridiculous thing, because the fact that a warrant was out for Odette Rider must have been generally known to the local authorities. Her description had been carefully circulated, and that description must have come to the heads of hospitals and public institutions. The next words of the doctor confirmed his knowledge.

"As a witness, eh?" he said dryly. "Well, I don't want to pry into your secrets, or rather into the secrets of Scotland Yard, but she is fit to travel just as soon as you like."

There was a knock on the door, and the matron came into the doctor's office.

"Miss Rider wishes to see you, sir," she said, addressing Tarling, and the detective, taking up his hat, went back to the little ward.

He found the girl more composed but still deathly white. She was out of bed, sitting in a big armchair, wrapped in a dressing-gown, and she motioned Tarling to pull up a chair to her side. She waited until after the door had closed behind the nurse, then she spoke.

"It was very silly of me to faint, Mr Tarling but the news was so horrible and so unexpected. Won't you tell me all about it? You see, I have not read a newspaper since I have been in the hospital. I heard one of the nurses talk about the Daffodil Murder – that is not the – "

She hesitated, and Tarling nodded. He was lighter of heart now, almost cheerful. He had no doubt in his mind that the girl was innocent, and life had taken on a rosier aspect.

"Thornton Lyne," he began, "was murdered on the night of the 14th. He was last seen alive by his valet about half-past nine in the evening. Early next morning his body was found in Hyde Park. He had been shot dead, and an effort had been made to stanch the wound in his breast by binding a woman's silk nightdress round and round his body. On his breast somebody had laid a bunch of daffodils."

"Daffodils?" repeated the girl wonderingly. "But how – "

"His car was discovered a hundred yards from the place," Tarling continued, "and it was clear that he had been murdered elsewhere, brought to the Park in his car, and left on the sidewalk. At the time he was discovered he had on neither coat nor vest, and on his feet were a pair of list slippers."

"But I don't understand," said the bewildered girl. "What does it mean? Who had – " She stopped suddenly, and the detective saw her lips tighten together, as though to restrain her speech. Then suddenly she covered her face with her hands.

"Oh, it's terrible, terrible!" she whispered. "I never thought, I never dreamed – oh, it is terrible!"

Tarling laid his hand gently on her shoulder.

"Miss Rider," he said, "you suspect somebody of this crime. Won't you tell me?"

She shook her head without looking up.

"I can say nothing," she said.

"But don't you see that suspicion will attach to you?" urged Tarling. "A telegram was discovered amongst his belongings, asking him to call at your flat that evening."

She looked up quickly.

"A telegram from me?" she said. "I sent no telegram."

"Thank God for that!" cried Tarling fervently. "Thank God for that!"

"But I don't understand, Mr Tarling. A telegram was sent to Mr Lyne asking him to come to my flat? Did he go to my flat?"

Tarling nodded.

"I have reason to believe he did," he said gravely. "The murder was committed in your flat."

"My God!" she whispered. "You don't mean that? Oh, no, no, it is impossible!"

Briefly he recited all his discoveries. He knew that he was acting in a manner which, from the point of view of police ethics, was wholly wrong and disloyal. He was placing her in possession of all the clues and giving her an opportunity to meet and refute the evidence which had been collected against her. He told her of the bloodstains on the floor, and described the nightdress which had been found around Thornton Lyne's body.

"That was my nightdress," she said simply and without hesitation. "Go on, please, Mr Tarling."

He told her of the bloody thumb-prints upon the door of the bureau.

"On your bed," he went on, "I found your dressing-case, half-packed."

She swayed forward, and threw out her hands, groping blindly.

"Oh, how wicked, how wicked!" she wailed "He did it, he did it!"

"Who?" demanded Tarling.

He took the girl by the shoulder and shook her.

"Who was the man? You must tell me. Your own life depends upon it. Don't you see, Odette, I want to help you? I want to clear your name of this terrible charge. You suspect somebody. I must have his name."

She shook her head and turned her pathetic face to his.

"I can't tell you," she said in a low voice. "I can say no more. I knew nothing of the murder until you told me. I had no idea, no thought…

I hated Thornton Lyne, I hated him, but I would not have hurt him…
it is dreadful, dreadful!"

Presently she grew calmer.

"I must go to London at once," she said. "Will you please take me
back?"

She saw his embarrassment and was quick to understand its cause.

"You – you have a warrant, haven't you?"

He nodded.

"On the charge of – murder?"

He nodded again. She looked at him in silence for some
moments.

"I shall be ready in half an hour," she said, and without a word the
detective left the room.

He made his way back to the doctor's sanctum, and found that
gentleman awaiting him impatiently.

"I say," said the doctor, "that's all bunkum about this girl being
wanted as a witness. I had my doubts and I looked up the Scotland
Yard warning which I received a couple of days ago. She's Odette
Rider, and she's wanted on a charge of murder."

"Got it first time," said Tarling, dropping wearily into a chair. "Do
you mind if I smoke?"

"Not a bit," said the doctor cheerfully. "I suppose you're taking her
with you?"

Tarling nodded.

"I can't imagine a girl like that committing a murder," said Dr
Saunders. "She doesn't seem to possess the physique necessary to have
carried out all the etceteras of the crime. I read the particulars in the
Morning Globe. The person who murdered Thornton Lyne must have
carried him from his car and laid him on the grass, or wherever he
was found – and that girl couldn't lift a large-sized baby."

Tarling jerked his head in agreement.

"Besides," Dr Saunders went on, "she hasn't the face of a murderer.
I don't mean to say that because she's pretty she couldn't commit a
crime, but there are certain types of prettiness which have their origin

in spiritual beauty, and Miss Stevens, or Rider, as I suppose I should call her, is one of that type."

"I'm one with you there," said Tarling. "I am satisfied in my own mind that she did not commit the crime, but the circumstances are all against her."

The telephone bell jingled, and the doctor took up the receiver and spoke a few words.

"A trunk call," he said, explaining the delay in receiving acknowledgment from the other end of the wire.

He spoke again into the receiver and then handed the instrument across the table to Tarling.

"It's for you," he said. "I think it is Scotland Yard."

Tarling put the receiver to his ear.

"It is Whiteside," said a voice. "Is that you, Mr Tarling? We've found the revolver."

"Where?" asked Tarling quickly.

"In the girl's flat," came the reply.

Tarling's face fell. But after all, that was nothing unexpected. He had no doubt in his mind at all that the murder had been committed in Odette Rider's flat, and, if that theory were accepted, the details were unimportant, as there was no reason in the world why the pistol should not be also found near the scene of the crime. In fact, it would have been remarkable if the weapon had not been discovered on those premises.

"Where was it?" he asked.

"In the lady's work-basket," said Whiteside. "Pushed to the bottom and covered with a lot of wool and odds and ends of tape."

"What sort of a revolver is it?" asked Tarling after a pause.

"A Colt automatic," was the reply. "There were six live cartridges in the magazine and one in the breach. The pistol had evidently been fired, for the barrel was foul. We've also found the spent bullet in the fireplace. Have you found your Miss Stevens?"

"Yes," said Tarling quietly. "Miss Stevens is Odette Rider."

He heard the other's whistle of surprise.

"Have you arrested her?"

"Not yet," said Tarling. "Will you meet the next train in from Ashford? I shall be leaving here in half an hour."

He hung up the receiver and turned to the doctor. "I gather they've found the weapon," said the interested medico.

"Yes," replied Tailing, "they have found the weapon."

"Humph!" said the doctor, rubbing his chin thoughtfully. "A pretty bad business." He looked at the other curiously. "What sort of a man was Thornton Lyne?" he asked.

Tarling shrugged his shoulders.

"Not the best of men, I'm afraid," he said; "but even the worst of men are protected by the law, and the punishment which will fall to the murderer – "

"Or murderess," smiled the doctor.

"Murderer," said Tarling shortly. "The punishment will not be affected by the character of the dead man."

Dr Saunders puffed steadily at his pipe.

"It's rum a girl like that being mixed up in a case of this description," he said. "Most extraordinary."

There was a little tap at the door and the matron appeared.

"Miss Stevens is ready," she said, and Tarling rose. Dr Saunders rose with him, and, going to a shelf took down a large ledger, and placing it on his table, opened it and took up a pen.

"I shall have to mark her discharge," he said, turning over the leaves, and running his finger down the page. "Here she is – Miss Stevens, concussion and shock."

He looked at the writing under his hand and then lifted his eyes to the detective.

"When was this murder committed?" he asked.

"On the night of the fourteenth."

"On the night of the fourteenth?" repeated the doctor thoughtfully. "At what time?"

"The hour is uncertain," said Tarling, impatient and anxious to finish his conversation with this gossiping surgeon; "some time after eleven."

"Some time after eleven," repeated the doctor. "It couldn't have been committed before. When was the man last seen alive?"

"At half-past nine," said Tarling with a little smile. "You're not going in for criminal investigation, are you, doctor?"

"Not exactly," smiled Saunders. "Though I am naturally pleased to be in a position to prove the girl's innocence."

"Prove her innocence? What do you mean?" demanded Tarling quickly.

"The murder could not have been committed before eleven o'clock. The dead man was last seen alive at half-past nine."

"Well?" said Tarling.

"Well," repeated Dr Saunders, "at nine o'clock the boat train left Charing Cross, and at half-past ten Miss Rider was admitted to this hospital suffering from shock and concussion."

For a moment Tarling said nothing and did nothing. He stood as though turned to stone, staring at the doctor with open mouth. Then he lurched forward, gripped the astonished medical man by the hand, and wrung it.

"That's the best bit of news I have had in my life," he said huskily.

TWO SHOTS IN THE NIGHT

The journey back to London was one the details of which were registered with photographic realism in Tarling's mind for the rest of his life. The girl spoke little, and he himself was content to meditate and turn over in his mind the puzzling circumstances which had surrounded Odette Rider's flight.

In the very silences which occurred between the interchanges of conversation was a comradeship and a sympathetic understanding which both the man and the girl would have found it difficult to define. Was he in love with her? He was shocked at the possibility of such a catastrophe overtaking him. Love had never come into his life. It was a hypothetical condition which he had never even considered. He had known men to fall in love, just as he had known men to suffer from malaria or yellow fever, without considering that the same experience might overtake him. A shy, reticent man, behind that hard mask was a diffidence unsuspected by his closest friends.

So that the possibility of being in love with Odette Rider disturbed his mind, because he lacked sufficient conceit to believe that such a passion could be anything but hopeless. That any woman could love him he could not conceive. And now her very presence, the fragrant nearness of her, at once soothed and alarmed him. Here was a detective virtually in charge of a woman suspected of murder – and he was frightened of her! He knew the warrant in his pocket would never be executed, and that Scotland Yard would not proceed with the prosecution, because, though Scotland Yard makes some big errors, it does not like to have its errors made public.

The journey was all too short, and it was not until the train was running slowly through a thin fog which had descended on London that he returned to the subject of the murder, and only then with an effort.

"I am going to take you to an hotel for the night," he said, "and in the morning I will ask you to come with me to Scotland Yard to talk to the Chief."

"Then I am not arrested?" she smiled.

"No, I don't think you're arrested." He smiled responsively. "But I'm afraid that you are going to be asked a number of questions which may be distressing to you. You see, Miss Rider, your actions have been very suspicious. You leave for the Continent under an assumed name, and undoubtedly the murder was committed in your flat."

She shivered.

"Please, please don't talk about that," she said in a low voice.

He felt a brute, but he knew that she must undergo an examination at the hands of men who had less regard for her feelings.

"I do wish you would be frank with me," he pleaded. "I am sure I could get you out of all your troubles without any difficulty."

"Mr Lyne hated me," she said. "I think I touched him on his tenderest spot – poor man – his vanity. You yourself know how he sent that criminal to my flat in order to create evidence against me."

He nodded.

"Did you ever meet Stay before?" he asked.

She shook her head.

"I think I have heard of him," she said. "I know that Mr Lyne was interested in a criminal, and that this criminal worshipped him. Once Mr Lyne brought him to the Stores and wanted to give him a job but the man would not accept it. Mr Lyne once told me that Sam Stay would do anything in the world for him."

"Stay thinks you committed the murder," said Tailing bluntly. "Lyne has evidently told stories about you and your hatred for him, and I really think that Stay would have been more dangerous to you than the police, only fortunately the little crook has gone off his head."

She looked at him in astonishment.

"Mad?" she asked. "Poor fellow! Has this awful thing driven him…"

Tarling nodded.

"He was taken to the County Asylum this morning. He had a fit in my office, and when he recovered he seemed to have lost his mind completely. Now, Miss Rider, you're going to be frank with me, aren't you?"

She looked at him again and smiled sadly.

"I'm afraid I shan't be any more frank than I have been, Mr Tarling," she said. "If you want me to tell you why I assumed the name of Stevens, or why I ran away from London, I cannot tell you. I had a good reason – " she paused, "and I may yet have a better reason for running away…"

She nearly said "again" but checked the word.

He laid his hand on hers.

"When I told you of this murder," he said earnestly, "I knew by your surprise and agitation that you were innocent. Later the doctor was able to prove an alibi which cannot be shaken. But, Miss Rider, when I surprised you, you spoke as though you knew who committed the crime. You spoke of a man and it is that man's name I want."

She shook her head.

"That I shall never tell you," she said simply.

"But don't you realise that you may be charged with being an accessory before or after the act?" he urged. "Don't you see what it means to you and to your mother?"

. Her eyes closed at the mention of her mother's name, as though to shut out the vision of some unpleasant possibility.

"Don't talk about it, don't talk about it!" she murmured, "please, Mr Tarling! Do as you wish. Let the police arrest me or try me or hang me – but do not ask me to say any more, because I will not, I will not!"

Tarling sank back amongst the cushions, baffled and bewildered, and no more was said.

Whiteside was waiting for the train, and with him were two men who were unmistakably branded "Scotland Yard." Tarling drew him aside and explained the situation in a few words.

"Under the circumstances," he said, "I shall not execute the warrant."

Whiteside agreed.

"It is quite impossible that she could have committed the murder," he said. "I suppose the doctor's evidence is unshakable?"

"Absolutely," said Tarling, "and it is confirmed by the station master at Ashford, who has the time of the accident logged in his diary, and himself assisted to lift the girl from the train."

"Why did she call herself Miss Stevens?" asked Whiteside. "And what induced her to leave London so hurriedly?"

Tarling gave a despairing gesture.

"That is one of the things I should like to know," he said, "and the very matter upon which Miss Rider refuses to enlighten me. I am taking her to an hotel," he went on. "Tomorrow I will bring her down to the Yard. But I doubt if the Chief can say anything that will induce her to talk."

"Was she surprised when you told her of the murder? Did she mention anybody's name?" asked Whiteside.

Tarling hesitated, and then, for one of the few times in his life, he lied.

"No," he said, "she was just upset…she mentioned nobody."

He took the girl by taxi to the quiet little hotel he had chosen – a journey not without its thrills, for the fog was now thick – and saw her comfortably fixed.

"I can't be sufficiently grateful to you, Mr Tarling, for your kindness," she said at parting "and if I could make your task any easier… I would."

He saw a spasm of pain pass across her face.

"I don't understand it yet; it seems like a bad dream," she said half to herself. "I don't want to understand it somehow… I want to forget, I want to forget!"

"What do you want to forget?" asked Tarling.

She shook her head.

"Don't ask me," she said. "Please, please, don't ask me!"

He walked down the big stairway, a greatly worried man. He had left the taxi at the door. To his surprise he found the cab had gone, and turned to the porter.

"What happened to my taxi?" he said. "I didn't pay him off."

"Your taxi, sir?" said the head porter. "I didn't see it go. I'll ask one of the boys."

As assistant porter who had been in the street told a surprising tale. A gentleman had come up out of the murk, had paid off the taxi, which had disappeared. The witness to this proceeding had not seen the gentleman's face. All he knew was that this mysterious benefactor had walked away in an opposite direction to that in which the cab had gone, and had vanished into the night.

Tarling frowned.

"That's curious," he said. "Get me another taxi."

"I'm afraid you'll find that difficult, sir." The hotel porter shook his head. "You see how the fog is – we always get them thick about here – it's rather late in the year for fogs.…"

Tarling cut short his lecture on meteorology, buttoned up his coat, and turned out of the hotel in the direction of the nearest underground station.

The hotel to which he had taken the girl was situated in a quiet residential street, and at this hour of the night the street was deserted, and the fog added something to its normal loneliness.

Tarling was not particularly well acquainted with London, but he had a rough idea of direction. The fog was thick, but he could see the blurred nimbus of a street lamp, and was midway between two of these when he beard a soft step behind him.

77

It was the faintest shuffle of sound, and he turned quickly. Instinctively he threw up his hands and stepped aside.

Something whizzed past his head and struck the pavement with a thud.

"Sandbag," he noted mentally, and leapt at his assailant.

As quickly his unknown attacker jumped back. There was a deafening report. His feet were scorched with burning cordite, and momentarily he released his grip of his enemy's throat, which he had seized.

He sensed rather than saw the pistol raised again, and made one of those lightning falls which he had learnt in far-off days from Japanese instructors of ju-jitsu. Head over heels he went as the pistol exploded for the second time. It was a clever trick, designed to bring the full force of his foot against his opponent's knee. But the mysterious stranger was too quick for him, and when Tarling leapt to his feet he was alone.

But he had seen the face – big and white and vengeful. It was glimpse and guesswork, but he was satisfied that he knew his man.

He ran in the direction he thought the would-be assassin must have taken, but the fog was patchy and he misjudged. He heard the sound of hurrying footsteps and ran towards them, only to find that it was a policeman attracted by the sound of shots.

The officer had met nobody.

"He must have gone the other way," said Tarling, and raced off in pursuit, without, however, coming up with his attacker.

Slowly he retraced his footsteps to where he had left the policeman searching the pavement or some clue which would identify the assailant of the night.

The constable was using a small electric lamp which he had taken from his pocket.

"Nothing here, sir," he said. "Only this bit of red paper."

Tarling took the small square of paper from the man's hand and examined it under the light of the lamp – a red square on which were written four words in Chinese: "He brought this trouble upon himself."

It was the same inscription as had been found neatly folded in the waistcoat pocket of Thornton Lyne that morning he was discovered lying starkly dead.

THE SEARCH OF MILBURGH'S COTTAGE

Mr Milburgh had a little house in one of the industrial streets of Camden Town. It was a street made up for the most part of blank walls, pierced at intervals with great gates, through which one could procure at times a view of gaunt factories and smoky-looking chimney stacks.

Mr Milburgh's house was the only residence in the road, if one excepted the quarters of caretakers and managers, and it was agreed by all who saw his tiny demesne, that Mr Milburgh had a good landlord.

The "house" was a detached cottage in about half an acre of ground, a one-storey building, monopolising the space which might have been occupied by factory extension. Both the factory to the right and the left had made generous offers to acquire the ground, but Mr Milburgh's landlord had been adamant. There were people who suggested that Mr Milburgh's landlord was Mr Milburgh himself. But how could that be? Mr Milburgh's salary was something under £400 a year, and the cottage site was worth at least £4,000.

Canvey Cottage, as it was called, stood back from the road, behind a lawn, innocent of flowers, and the lawn itself was protected from intrusion by high iron railings which Mr Milburgh's landlord had had erected at considerable cost. To reach the house it was necessary to pass through an iron gate and traverse a stone-flagged path to the door of the cottage.

On the night when Tarling of Scotland Yard was the victim of a murderous assault, Mr Milburgh unlocked the gate and passed through, locking and double-locking the gate behind him. He was alone, and, as was his wont, he was whistling a sad little refrain which had neither beginning nor end. He walked slowly up the stone pathway, unlocked the door of his cottage, and stood only a moment on the doorstep to survey the growing thickness of the night, before he closed and bolted the door and switched on the electric light.

He was in a tiny hallway, plainly hut nicely furnished. The note of luxury was struck by the Zohn etchings which hung on the wall, and which Mr Milburgh stopped to regard approvingly. He hung up his coat and hat, slipped off the galoshes he was wearing (for it was wet underfoot), and, passing through a door which opened from the passage, came to his living room. The same simple note of furniture and decoration was observable here. The furniture was good, the carpet under his feet thick and luxurious. He snicked down another switch and an electric radiator glowed in the fireplace. Then he sat down at the big table, which was the most conspicuous article of furniture in the room. It was practically covered with orderly little piles of paper, most of them encircled with rubber bands. He did not attempt to touch or read them, but sat looking moodily at his blotting-pad, preoccupied and absent.

Presently he rose with a little grunt, and, crossing the room, unlocked a very commonplace and old-fashioned cupboard, the top of which served as a sideboard. From the cupboard he took a dozen little books and carried them to the table. They were of uniform size and each bore the figures of a year. They appeared to be, and indeed were, diaries, but they were not Mr Milburgh's diaries. One day he chanced to go into Thornton Lyne's room at the Stores and had seen these books arrayed on a steel shelf of Lyne's private safe. The proprietor's room overlooked the ground floor of the Stores, and Thornton Lyne at the time was visible to his manager, and could not under any circumstances surprise him, so Mr Milburgh had taken out one volume and read, with more than ordinary interest, the somewhat frank and expansive diary which Thornton Lyne had kept.

He had only read a few pages on that occasion, but later he had an opportunity of perusing the whole year's record, and had absorbed a great deal of information which might have been useful to him in the future, had not Thornton Lyne met his untimely end at the hands of an unknown murderer.

On the day when Thornton Lyne's body was discovered in Hyde Park with a woman's nightdress wrapped around the wound in his breast, Mr Milburgh had, for reasons of expediency and assisted by a duplicate key of Lyne's safe, removed those diaries to a safer place. They contained a great deal that was unpleasant for Mr Milburgh, particularly the current diary, for Thornton Lyne had set down not only his experiences, but his daily happenings, his thoughts, poetical and otherwise, and had stated very exactly and in libellous terms his suspicions of his manager.

The diary provided Mr Milburgh with a great deal of very interesting reading matter, and now he turned to the page where he had left off the night before and continued his study. It was a page easy to find, because he had thrust between the leaves a thin envelope of foreign make containing certain slips of paper, and as he took out his improvised book mark a thought seemed to strike him, and he felt carefully in his pocket. He did not discover the thing for which he was searching, and with a smile he laid the envelope carefully on the table, and went on at the point where his studies had been interrupted.

"Lunched at the London Hotel and dozed away the afternoon. Weather fearfully hot. Had arranged to make a call upon a distant cousin – a man named Tarling – who is in the police force at Shanghai, but too much of a fag. Spent evening at Chu Han's dancing hall. Got very friendly with a pretty little Chinese girl who spoke pigeon English. Am seeing her tomorrow at Ling Foo's. She is called 'The Little Narcissus.' I called her 'My Little Daffodil ' – "

Mr Milburgh stopped in his reading.

"Little Daffodil!" he repeated, then looked at the ceiling and pinched his thick lips. "Little Daffodil!" he said again, and a big smile dawned on his face.

He was still engaged in reading when a bell shrilled in the hall. He rose to his feet and stood listening and the bell rang again. He switched off the light, pulled aside the thick curtain which hid the window, and peered out through the fog. He could just distinguish in the light of the street lamp two or three men standing at the gate. He replaced the curtain, turned up the light again, took the books in his arms and disappeared with them into the corridor. The room at the back was his bedroom, and into this he went, making no response to the repeated jingle of the bell for fully five minutes.

At the end of that time he reappeared, but now he was in his pyjamas, over which he wore a heavy dressing-gown. He unlocked the door, and shuffled in his slippers down the stone pathway to the gate.

"Who's that?" he asked.

"Tarling. You know me," said a voice.

"Mr Tarling?" said Milburgh in surprise. "Really this is an unexpected pleasure. Come in, come in, gentlemen."

"Open the gate," said Tarling briefly.

"Excuse me while I go and get the key," said Milburgh. "I didn't expect visitors at this hour of the night."

He went into the house, took a good look round his room, and then reappeared, taking the key from the pocket of his dressing-gown. It had been there all the time, if the truth be told, but Mr Milburgh was a cautious man and took few risks.

Tarling was accompanied by Inspector Whiteside and another man, whom Milburgh rightly supposed was a detective. Only Tarling and the Inspector accepted his invitation to step inside, the third man remaining on guard at the gate.

Milburgh led the way to his cosy sitting-room.

"I have been in bed some hours, and I'm sorry to have kept you so long."

"Your radiator is still warm," said Tarling quietly, stooping to feel the little stove.

Mr Milburgh chuckled.

"Isn't that clever of you to discover that?" he said admiringly. "The fact is, I was so sleepy when I went to bed, several hours ago, that I forgot to turn the radiator off, and it was only when I came down to answer the bell that I discovered I had left it switched on."

Tarling stooped and picked the butt end of a cigar out of the hearth. It was still alight.

"You've been smoking in your sleep, Mr Milburgh," he said dryly.

"No, no," said the airy Mr Milburgh. "I was smoking that when I came downstairs to let you in. I instinctively put a cigar in my mouth the moment I wake up in the morning, it is a disgraceful habit, and really is one of my few vices." he admitted. "I threw it down when I turned out the radiator."

Tarling smiled.

"Won't you sit down?" said Milburgh, seating himself in the least comfortable of the chairs. "You see," his smile was apologetic as he waved his hand to the table, "the work is frightfully heavy now that poor Mr Lyne is dead. I am obliged to bring it home, and I can assure you, Mr Tarling, that there are some nights when I work till daylight, getting things ready for the auditor."

"Do you ever take exercise?" asked Tarling innocently. "Little night walks in the fog for the benefit of your health?"

A puzzled frown gathered on Milburgh's face.

"Exercise, Mr Tarling?" he said with an air of mystification. "I don't quite understand you. Naturally I shouldn't walk out on a night like this. What an extraordinary fog for this time of the year!"

"Do you know Paddington at all?"

"No," said Mr Milburgh, "except that there is a station there which I sometimes use. But perhaps you will explain to me the meaning of this visit?"

"The meaning is," said Tarling shortly, "that I have been attacked tonight by a man of your build and height, who fired twice at me at close quarters. I have a warrant – " Mr Milburgh's eyes narrowed – "I have a warrant to search this house."

"For what?" demanded Milburgh boldly.

"For a revolver or an automatic pistol and anything else I can find."

Milburgh rose.

"You're at liberty to search the house from end to end," he said. "Happily, it is a small one, as my salary does not allow of an expensive establishment."

"Do you live here alone?" asked Tarling.

"Quite," replied Milburgh. "A woman comes in at eight o'clock tomorrow morning to cook my breakfast and make the place tidy, but I sleep here by myself. I am very much hurt," he was going on.

"You will be hurt much worse," said Tarling dryly and proceeded to the search.

It proved to be a disappointing one, for there was no trace of any weapon, and certainly no trace of the little red slips which he had expected to find in Milburgh's possession. For he was not searching for the man who had assailed him, but for the man who had killed Thornton Lyne.

He came back to the little sitting-room where Milburgh had been left with the Inspector and apparently he was unruffled by his failure.

"Now, Mr Milburgh," he said brusquely, "I want to ask you: Have you ever seen a piece of paper like this before?"

He took a slip from his pocket and spread it on the table, Milburgh looked hard at the Chinese characters on the crimson square, and then nodded.

"You have?" said Tarling in surprise.

"Yes, sir," said Mr Milburgh complacently. "I should be telling an untruth if I said I had not. Nothing is more repugnant to me than to deceive anybody."

"That I can imagine," said Tarling.

"I am sorry you are sarcastic, Mr Tarling," said the reproachful Milburgh, "but I assure you that I hate and loathe an untruth."

"Where have you seen these papers?"

"On Mr Lyne's desk," was the surprising answer.

"On Lyne's desk?"

Milburgh nodded.

"The late Mr Thornton Lyne," he said, "came back from the East with a great number of curios, and amongst them were a number of slips of paper covered with Chinese characters similar to this. I do not understand Chinese," he said, "because I have never had occasion to go to China. The characters may have been different one from the other, but to my unsophisticated eye they all look alike."

"You've seen these slips on Lyne's desk?" said Tarling. "Then why did you not tell the police before? You know that the police attach a great deal of importance to the discovery of one of these things in the dead man's pocket?"

Mr Milburgh nodded.

"It is perfectly true that I did not mention the fact to the police," he said, "but you understand Mr Tarling that I was very much upset by the sad occurrence, which drove everything else out of my mind. It would have been quite possible that you would have found one or two of these strange inscriptions in this very house." He smiled in the detective's face. "Mr Lyne was very fond of distributing the curios he brought from the East to his friends," he went on. "He gave me that dagger you see hanging on the wall, which he bought at some outlandish place in his travels. He may have given me a sample of these slips. I remember his telling me a story about them, which I cannot for the moment recall."

He would have continued retailing reminiscences of his late employer, but Tarling cut him short, and with a curt good night withdrew. Milburgh accompanied him to the front gate and locked the door upon the three men before he went back to his sitting-room smiling quietly to himself.

"I am certain that the man was Milburgh," said Taming. "I am as certain as that I am standing here."

"Have you any idea why he should want to out you?" asked Whiteside.

"None in the world," replied Tarling. "Evidently my assailant was a man who had watched my movements and had probably followed the girl and myself to the hotel in a cab. When I disappeared inside he dismissed his own and then took the course of dismissing my cab, which he could easily do by paying the man his fare and sending him off. A cabman would accept that dismissal without suspicion. He then waited for me in the fog and followed me until he got me into a quiet part of the road, where he first attempted to sandbag and then to shoot me."

"But why?" asked Whiteside again. "Suppose Milburgh knew something about this murder – which is very doubtful – what benefit would it be to him to have you put out of the way?"

"If I could answer that question," replied Tarling grimly, "I could tell you who killed Thornton Lyne."

THE OWNER OF THE PISTOL

All trace of the fog of the night before had disappeared when Tarling looked out from his bedroom window later that morning. The streets were flooded with yellow sunshine, and there was a tang in the air which brought the colour to the cheek and light to the eye of the patient Londoner.

Tarling stretched his arms and yawned in the sheer luxury of living, before he took down his silk dressing-gown and went in to the breakfast which Ling Chu had laid for him.

The blue-bloused Chinaman who stood behind his master's chair, poured out the tea and laid a newspaper on one side of the plate and letters on the other. Tarling ate his breakfast in silence and pushed away the plate.

"Ling Chu," he said in the vernacular of Lower China, "I shall lose my name as the Man Hunter, for this case puzzles me beyond any other."

"Master," said the Chinaman in the same language, "there is a time in all cases, when the hunter feels that he must stop and weep. I myself had this feeling when I hunted down Wu Fung, the strangler of Hankow. Yet," he added philosophically, "one day I found him and he is sleeping on the Terrace of Night."

He employed the beautiful Chinese simile for death.

"Yesterday I found the little-young-woman," said Tarling after a pause. In this quaint way did he refer to Odette Rider.

"You may find the little-young-woman and yet not find the killer," said Ling Chu, standing by the side of the table, his hands respectfully hidden under his sleeves. "For the little-young-woman did not kill the white-faced man."

"How do you know?" asked Tarling; and the Chinaman shook his head.

"The little-young-woman has no strength, master," he said. "Also it is not known that she has skill in the driving of the quick cart."

"You mean the motor?" asked Tarling quickly, and Ling Chu nodded.

"By Jove! I never thought of that," said Tarling. "Of course, whoever killed Thornton Lyne must have put his body in the car and driven him to the Park. But how do you know that she does not drive?"

"Because I have asked," said the Chinaman simply. "Many people know the little-young-woman at the great Stores where the white-faced man lived, and they all say that she does not drive the quick cart."

Tarling considered for a while.

"Yes, it is true talk," he said. "The little-young-woman did not kill the white-faced man, because she was many miles away when the murder was committed. That we know. The question is, who did?"

"The Hunter of Men will discover," said Ling Chu

"I wonder," said Tarling.

He dressed and went to Scotland Yard. He had an appointment with Whiteside, and later intended accompanying Odette Rider to an interview before the Assistant Commissioner. Whiteside was at Scotland Yard before him, and when Tarling walked into his room was curiously examining an object which lay before him on a sheet of paper. It was a short-barrelled automatic pistol.

"Hullo!" he said, interested. "Is that the gun that killed Thornton Lyne?"

"That's the weapon," said the cheerful Whiteside. "An ugly-looking brute, isn't it?"

"Where did you say it was discovered?"

"At the bottom of the girl's work-basket."

"This has a familiar look to me," said Tarling, lifting the instrument from the table. "By the way, is the cartridge still in the chamber?"

Whiteside shook his head.

"No, I removed it," he said. "I've taken the magazine out too."

"I suppose you've sent out the description and the number to all the gunsmiths?"

Whiteside nodded.

"Not that it's likely to be of much use," he said. "This is an American-made pistol, and unless it happens to have been sold in England there is precious little chance of our discovering its owner."

Tarling was looking at the weapon, turning it over and over in his hand. Presently he looked at the butt and uttered an exclamation. Following the direction of his eyes, Whiteside saw two deep furrows running diagonally across the grip.

"What are they?" he asked.

"They look like two bullets fired at the holder of the revolver some years ago, which missed him but caught the butt."

Whiteside laughed.

"Is that a piece of your deduction, Mr Tarling?" he asked.

"No," said Tarling, "that is a bit of fact. That pistol is my own!"

THE HEIR

"*Your* pistol?" said Whiteside incredulously, "my dear good chap, you are mad! How could it be your pistol?"

"It is nevertheless my pistol," said Tarling quietly. "I recognised it the moment I saw it on your desk, and thought there must be some mistake. These furrows prove that there is no mistake at all. It has been one of my most faithful friends; and I carried it with me in China for six years."

Whiteside gasped.

"And you mean to tell me," he demanded, "that Thornton Lyne was killed with your pistol?

Tarling nodded.

"It is an amazing but bewildering fact," he said. "That is undoubtedly my pistol, and it is the same that was found in Miss Rider's room at Carrymore Mansions, and I have not the slightest doubt in my mind that it was by a shot fired from this weapon that Thornton Lyne lost his life."

There was a long silence.

"Well, that beats me," said Whiteside, laying the weapon on the table. "At every turn some new mystery arises. This is the second jar I've had today."

"The second?" said Tarling. He put the question idly, for his mind was absorbed in this new and to him tremendous aspect of the crime. Thornton Lyne had been killed by his pistol! That to him was the most staggering circumstance which had been revealed since he had come into the case.

"Yes," Whiteside was saying, "it's the second setback."

With an effort Tarling brought his mind back from speculating upon the new mystery.

"Do you remember this?" said Whiteside. He opened his safe and took out a big envelope, from which he extracted a telegram.

"Yes, this is the telegram supposed to have been sent by Odette Rider, asking Mr Lyne to call at her flat. It was found amongst the dead man's effects when the house was searched.

"To be exact," corrected Whiteside, "it was discovered by Lyne's valet – a man named Cole, who seems to be a very honest person, against whom no suspicion could be attached. I had him here this morning early to make further inquiries into Lyne's movements on the night of the murder. He's in the next room, by the way. I'll bring him in."

He pushed a bell and gave his instructions to the uniformed policeman who came. Presently the door opened again and the officer ushered in a respectable-looking, middle-aged man, who had "domestic service" written all over him.

"Just tell Mr Tarling what you told me," said Whiteside.

"About that telegram, sir? " asked Cole. "Yes, I'm afraid I made a bit of a mistake there, but I got flurried with this awful business and I suppose I lost my head a bit."

"What happened?" asked Tarling.

"Well, sir, this telegram I brought up the next day to Mr Whiteside – that is to say, the day after the murder – " Tarling nodded. "And when I brought it up I made a false statement. It's a thing I've never done before in my life, but I tell you I was scared by all these police inquiries."

"What was the false statement?" asked Tarling quickly.

"Well, sir," said the servant, twisting his hat nervously, "I said that it had been opened by Mr Lyne. As a matter of fact, the telegram wasn't delivered until a quarter of an hour after Mr Lyne left the place. It was I who opened it when I heard of the murder. Then, thinking that I should get into trouble for sticking my nose into police business, I told Mr Whiteside that Mr Lyne had opened it."

"He didn't receive the telegram?" asked Tarling.

"No, sir."

The two detectives looked at one another.

"Well, what do you make of that, Whiteside?"

"I'm blest if I know what to think of it," said Whiteside, scratching his head. "We depended upon that telegram to implicate the girl. It breaks a big link in the chain against her."

"Supposing it was not already broken," said Tarling almost aggressively.

"And it certainly removes the only possible explanation for Lyne going to the flat on the night of the murder. You're perfectly sure, Cole, that that telegram did not reach Mr Lyne?"

"Perfectly, sir," said Cole emphatically. "I took it in myself. After Mr Lyne drove off I went to the door of the house to get a little fresh air, and I was standing on the top step when it came up. If you notice, sir, it's marked 'received at 9.20' – that means the time it was received at the District Post Office, and that's about two miles from our place. It couldn't possibly have got to the house before Mr Lyne left, and I was scared to death that you clever gentlemen would have seen that."

"I was so clever that I didn't see it," admitted Tarling with a smile. "Thank you, Mr Cole, that will do."

When the man had gone, he sat down on a chair opposite Whiteside and thrust his hands into his pockets with a gesture of helplessness.

"Well, I'm baffled," he said. "Let me recite the case, Whiteside, because it's getting so complicated that I'm almost forgetting its plainest features. On the night of the fourteenth Thornton Lyne is murdered by some person or persons unknown, presumably in the flat of Odette Rider, his former cashier, residing at Carrymore Mansions. Bloodstains are found upon the floor, and there is other evidence, such as the discovery of the pistol and the spent bullet, which emphasises the accuracy of that conclusion. Nobody sees Mr Lyne come into the flat or go out. He is found in Hyde Park the next morning without his coat or vest, a lady's silk nightdress, identified as Odette Rider's, wrapped tightly round his breast, and two of Odette Rider's handkerchiefs are found over the wound. Upon his body are a number of daffodils, and his car, containing his coat, vest and boots, is found by the side of the road a hundred yards away. Have I got it right?"

Whiteside nodded.

"Whatever else is at fault," he smiled, "your memory is unchallengeable."

"A search of the bedroom in which the crime was committed reveals a bloodstained thumbprint on the white bureau, and a suit-case, identified as Odette Rider's, half-packed upon the bed. Later, a pistol, which is mine, is found in the lady's work-basket, hidden under repairing material The first suggestion is that Miss Rider is the murderess. That suggestion is refuted, first by the fact that she was at Ashford when the murder was committed, unconscious as a result of a railway accident; and the second point in her favour is that the telegram discovered by Lyne's valet, purporting to be signed by the girl, inviting Lyne to her flat at a certain hour, was not delivered to the murdered man."

He rose to his feet.

"Come along and see Cresswell," he said. "This case is going to drive me mad!"

Assistant Commissioner Cresswell heard the story the two men had to tell, and if he was astounded he did not betray any signs of his surprise.

"This looks like being the murder case of the century," he said. "Of course, you cannot proceed any further against Miss Rider, and you were wise not to make the arrest. However, she must be kept under observation, because apparently she knows, or think she knows, the person who did commit the murder. She must be watched day and night, and sooner or later, she will lead you to the man upon whom her suspicions rest.

"Whiteside had better see her," he said, turning to Tarling. "He may get a new angle of her view. I don't think there's much use in bringing her down here. And, by the way, Tarling, all the accounts of Lyne's Stores have been placed in the hands of a clever firm of chartered accountants – Dashwood and Solomon, of St Mary Axe. If you suspect there has been any peculation on the part of Lyne's employees, and if that peculation is behind the murder, we shall probably learn something which will give you a clue."

Tarling nodded.

"How long will the examination take?" he asked.

"They think a week. The books have been taken away this morning – which reminds me that your friend, Mr Milburgh – I think that is his name – is giving every assistance to the police to procure a faithful record of the firm's financial position."

He looked up at Tarling and scratched his nose.

"So it was committed with your pistol, Tarling?" he said with a little smile. "That sounds bad."

"It sounds mad," laughed Tarling. "I'm going straight back to discover what happened to my pistol and how it got into that room. I know that it was safe a fortnight ago because I took it to a gunsmith to be oiled."

"Where do you keep it as a rule?"

"In the cupboard with my colonial kit," said Tarling. "Nobody has access to my room except Ling Chu, who is always there when I'm out."

"Ling Chu is your Chinese servant?"

"Not exactly a servant," smiled Tarling. "He is one of the best native thief catchers I have ever met. He is a man of the greatest integrity and I would trust him with my life."

"Murdered with your pistol, eh?" asked the Commissioner.

There was a little pause and then:

"I suppose Lyne's estate will go to the Crown? He has no relations and no heir."

"You're wrong there," said Tarling quietly.

The Commissioner looked up in surprise.

"Has he an heir?" he asked.

"He has a cousin," said Tarling with a little smile, "a relationship close enough to qualify him for Lyne's millions, unfortunately."

"Why unfortunately?" asked Mr Cresswell.

"Because I happen to be the heir," said Tarling.

THE MISSING REVOLVER

Tarling walked out of Scotland Yard on to the sunlit Embankment, trouble in his face. He told himself that the case was getting beyond him and that it was only the case and its development which worried him. The queer little look which had dawned on the Commissioner's face when he learnt that the heir to the murdered Thornton Lyne's fortune was the detective who was investigating his murder, and that Tarling's revolver had been found in the room where the murder had been committed, aroused nothing but an inward chuckle.

That suspicion should attach to him was, he told himself, poetic justice, for in his day he himself had suspected many men, innocent or partly innocent.

He walked up the stairs to his room and found Ling Chu polishing the meagre stock of silver which Tarling possessed. Ling Chu was a thief-catcher and a great detective, but he had also taken upon himself the business of attending to Tarling's personal comfort. The detective spoke no word, but went straight to the cupboard where he kept his foreign kit. On a shelf in neat array and carefully folded, were the thin white drill suits he wore in the tropics. His sun helmet hung on a peg, and on the opposite wall was a revolver holster hanging by a strap. He lifted the holster. It was empty. He had had no doubts in his mind that the holster would be empty and closed the door with a troubled frown.

"Ling Chu," he said quietly.

"You speak me, Lieh Jen?" said the man, putting down the spoons and rubber he was handling.

"Where is my revolver?"

"It is gone, Lieh Jen," said the man calmly.

"How long has it been gone?"

"I miss him four days," said Ling Chu calmly.

"Who took it?" demanded Tarling.

"I miss him four days," said the man.

There was an interval of silence, and Tarling nodded his head slowly.

"Very good, Ling Chu," he said, "there is no more to be said."

For all his outward calm, he was distressed in mind.

Was it possible that anybody could have got into the room in Ling Chu's absence – he could only remember one occasion when they had been out together, and that was the night he had gone to the girl's flat and Ling Chu had shadowed him.

What if Ling Chu – ?

He dismissed the thought as palpably absurd. What interest could Ling Chu have in the death of Lyne, whom he had only seen once, the day that Thornton Lyne had called Tarling into consultation at the Stores?

That thought was too fantastic to entertain, but nevertheless it recurred again and again to him and in the end he sent his servant away with a message to Scotland Yard, determined to give even his most fantastic theory as thorough and impartial an examination as was possible.

The flat consisted of four rooms and a kitchen. There was Tarling's bedroom communicating with his dining and sitting-room. There was a spare-room in which he kept his boxes and trunks – it was in this room that the revolver had been put aside – and there was the small room occupied by Ling Chu. He gave his attendant time to get out of the house and well on his journey before he rose from the deep chair where he had been sitting in puzzled thought and began his inspection.

Ling Chu's room was small and scrupulously clean. Save for the bed and a plain black-painted box beneath the bed, there was no furniture. The well-scrubbed boards were covered with a strip of

Chinese matting and the only ornamentation in the room was supplied by a tiny red lacquer vase which stood on the mantelpiece.

Tarling went back to the outer door of the flat and locked it before continuing his search. If there was any clue to the mystery of the stolen revolver it would be found here, in this black box. A Chinaman keeps all his possessions "within six sides," as the saying goes, and certainly the box was very well secured. It was ten minutes before he managed to find a key to shift the two locks with which it was fastened.

The contents of the box were few. Ling Chu's wardrobe was not an extensive one and did little more than half fill the receptacle. Very carefully he lifted out the one suit of clothes, the silk shirts, the slippers and the odds and ends of the Chinaman's toilet and came quickly to the lower layer. Here he discovered two lacquer boxes, neither of which were locked or fastened.

The first of these contained sewing material, the second a small package wrapped in native paper and carefully tied about with ribbon. Tarling undid the ribbon, opened the package and found to his surprise a small pad of newspaper cuttings. In the main they were cuttings from colloquial journals printed in Chinese characters, but there were one or two paragraphs evidently cut from one of the English papers published in Shanghai.

He thought at first that these were records of cases in which Ling Chu had been engaged, and though he was surprised that the Chinaman should have taken the trouble to collect these souvenirs – especially the English cuttings – he did not think at first that there was any significance in the act. He was looking for some clue – what he knew not – which would enable him to explain to his own satisfaction the mystery of the filched pistol.

He read the first of the European cuttings idly, but presently his eyes opened wide.

"There was a fracas at Ho Hans' tea-room last night, due apparently to the too-persistent attentions paid by an English visitor to the dancing girl, the little Narcissus, who is known to the English, or such as frequent Ho Hans' rooms, as The Little Daffodil – "

He gasped. The Little Daffodil! He let the cutting drop on his knee and frowned in an effort of memory. He knew Shanghai well. He knew its mysterious underworld and had more than a passing acquaintance with Ho Hans' tea-rooms. Ho Hans' tea-room was, in fact, the mask which hid an opium den that he had been instrumental in cleaning up just before he departed from China. And he distinctly remembered the Little Daffodil. He had had no dealings with her in the way of business, for when he had had occasion to go into Ho Hans' tearooms, he was usually after bigger game than the graceful little dancer.

It all came back to him in a flash. He had heard men at the club speaking of the grace of the Little Daffodil and her dancing had enjoyed something of a vogue amongst the young Britishers who were exiled in Shanghai.

The next cutting was also in English and ran:

"A sad fatality occurred this morning, a young Chinese girl, Ling, the sister of Inspector Ling Chu, of the Native Police, being found in a dying condition in the yard at the back of Ho Hans' tea-rooms. The girl had been employed at the shop as a dancer, much against her brother's wishes, and figured in a very unpleasant affair reported in these columns last week. It is believed that the tragic act was one of those 'save-face' suicides which are all too common amongst native women."

Tarling whistled, a soft, long, understanding whistle.

The Little Daffodil! And the sister of Ling Chu! He knew something of the Chinese, something of their uncanny patience, something of their unforgiving nature. This dead man had put an insult not only upon the little dancing girl, but upon the whole of her family. In China disgrace to one is a disgrace to all and she, realising

99

the shame that the notoriety had brought upon her brother, had taken what to her, as a Chinese girl, had been the only way out.

But what was the shame? Tarling searched through the native papers and found several flowery accounts, not any two agreed save on one point, that an Englishman, and a tourist, had made public love to the girl, no very great injury from the standpoint of the Westerner, a Chinaman had interfered and there had been a "rough house."

Tarling read the cuttings through from beginning to end, then carefully replaced them in the paper package and put them away in the little lacquer box at the bottom of the trunk. As carefully he returned all the clothes he had removed, relocked the lid and pushed it under the iron bedstead. Swiftly he reviewed all the circumstances. Ling Chu had seen Thornton Lyne and had planned his vengeance. To extract Tarling's revolver was an easy matter – but why, if he had murdered Lyne, would he have left the incriminating weapon behind? That was not like Ling Chu – that was the act of a novice.

But how had he lured Thornton Lyne to the flat? And how did he know – a thought struck him.

Three nights before the murder, Ling Chu, discussing the interview which had taken place at Lyne's Stores, had very correctly diagnosed the situation. Ling Chu knew that Thornton Lyne was in love with the girl and desired her, and it would not be remarkable if he had utilised his knowledge to his own ends.

But the telegram which was designed to bring Lyne to the flat was in English and Ling Chu did not admit to a knowledge of that language. Here again Tarling came to a dead end. Though he might trust the Chinaman with his life, he was perfectly satisfied that this man would not reveal all that he knew, and it was quite possible that Ling Chu spoke English as well as he spoke his own native tongue and the four dialects of China.

"I give it up," said Tarling, half to himself and half aloud.

He was undecided as to whether be should wait for his subordinate's return from Scotland Yard and tax him with the crime, or whether he should let matters slide for a day or two and carry out his intention to visit Odette Rider. He took that decision, leaving a note for the

Chinaman, and a quarter of an hour later got out of his taxi at the door of the West Somerset Hotel.

Odette Rider was in (that he knew) and waiting for him. She looked pale and her eyes were tired, as though she had slept little on the previous night, but she greeted him with that half smile of hers.

"I've come to tell you that you are to be spared the ordeal of meeting the third degree men of Scotland Yard," he said laughingly, and her eyes spoke her relief.

"Haven't you been out this beautiful morning?" he asked innocently, and this time she laughed aloud.

"What a hypocrite you are, Mr Tarling!" she replied. "You know very well I haven't been out, and you know too that there are three Scotland Yard men watching this hotel who would accompany me in any constitutional I took."

"How did you know that?" he asked without denying the charge.

"Because I've been out," she said naïvely and laughed again. "You aren't so clever as I thought you were," she rallied him. "I quite expected when I said I'd not been out, to hear you tell me just where I'd been, how far I walked and just what I bought."

"Some green sewing silk, six handkerchiefs, and a toothbrush," said Tarling promptly and the girl stared at him in comic dismay.

"Why, of course, I ought to have known you better than that," she said. "Then you do have watchers?"

"Watchers and talkers," said Tarling gaily. "I had a little interview with the gentleman in the vestibule of the hotel and he supplied me with quite a lot of information. Did he shadow you?"

She shook her head.

"I saw nobody," she confessed, "though I looked most carefully. Now what are you going to do with me, Mr Tarling?"

For answer, Tarling took from his pocket a flat oblong box. The girl looked wonderingly as he opened the lid and drew forth a slip of porcelain covered with a thin film of black ink and two white cards. His hand shook as he placed them on the table and suddenly the girl understood.

"You want my finger prints?" she asked and he nodded.

"I just hate asking you," he said, "but – "

"Show me how to do it," she interrupted and he guided her.

He felt disloyal – a very traitor, and perhaps she realised what he was thinking, for she laughed as she wiped her stained fingertips.

"Duty's duty," she mocked him, "and now tell me this – are you going to keep me under observation all the time?"

"For a little while," said Tarling gravely. "In fact, until we get the kind of information we want."

He put away the box into his pocket as she shook her head.

"That means you're not going to tell us anything," said Tarling. "I think you are making a very great mistake, but really I am not depending upon your saying a word. I depend entirely upon – "

"Upon what?" she asked curiously as he hesitated.

"Upon what others will tell me," said Tarling.

"Others? What others?"

Her steady eyes met his.

"There was once a famous politician who said 'Wait and see,' " said Tarling, "advice which I am going to ask you to follow. Now, I will tell you something, Miss Rider," he went on. "Tomorrow I am going to take away your watchers, though I should advise you to remain at this hotel for a while. It is obviously impossible for you to go back to your flat."

The girl shivered.

"Don't talk about that," she said in a low voice. "But is it necessary that I should stay here?"

"There is an alternative," he said, speaking slowly, "an alternative," he said looking at her steadily, "and it is that you should go to your mother's place at Hertford."

She looked up quickly.

"That is impossible," she said.

He was silent for a moment.

"Why don't you make a confidant of me, Miss Rider?" he said. "I should not abuse your trust. Why don't you tell me something about your father?"

"My father?" she looked at him in amazement. "My father, did you say?"

He nodded.

"But I have no father," said the girl.

"Have you – " he found a difficulty in framing his words and it seemed to him that she must have guessed what was coming. "Have you a lover?" he asked at length.

"What do you mean?" she countered, and there was a note of hauteur in her voice.

"I mean this," said Tarling steadily. "What is Mr Milburgh to you?"

Her hand went up to her mouth and she looked at him in wide-eyed distress, then:

"Nothing!" she said huskily. "Nothing, nothing!"

THE FINGERPRINTS

Tarling, his hands thrust into his pockets, his chin dropped, his shoulders bent, slowly walked the broad pavement of the Edgware Road on his way from the girl's hotel to his flat. He dismissed with good reason the not unimportant fact that he himself was suspect. He, a comparatively unknown detective from Shanghai was by reason of his relationship to Thornton Lyne, and even more so because his own revolver had been found on the scene of the tragedy, the object of some suspicion on the part of the higher authorities who certainly would not pooh-pooh the suggestion that he was innocent of any association with the crime because be happened to be engaged in the case.

He knew that the whole complex machinery of Scotland Yard was working, and working at top speed, to implicate him in the tragedy. Silent and invisible though that work may be, it would nevertheless be sure. He smiled a little, and shrugged himself from the category of the suspected.

First and most important of the suspects was Odette Rider. That Thornton Lyne had loved her, he did not for one moment imagine. Thornton Lyne was not the kind of man who loved. Rather had he desired, and very few women had thwarted him. Odette Rider was an exception. Tarling only knew of the scene which had occurred between Lyne and the girl on the day he had been called in, but there must have beep many other painful interviews, painful for the girl, humiliating for the dead millionaire.

Anyway, he thought thankfully, it would not be Odette. He had got into the habit of thinking of her as "Odette," a discovery which had amused him. He could rule her out, because obviously she could not be in two places at once. When Thornton Lyne was discovered in Hyde Park, with Odette Rider's nightdress round about his wound, the girl herself was lying in a cottage hospital at Ashford fifty miles away.

But what of Milburgh, that suave and oily man? Tarling recalled the fact that he had been sent for by his dead relative to inquire into Milburgh's mode of living and that Milburgh was under suspicion of having robbed the firm. Suppose Milburgh had committed the crime? Suppose, to hide his defalcations, he had shot his employer dead? There was a flaw in this reasoning because the death of Thornton Lyne would be more likely to precipitate the discovery of the manager's embezzlements – there would be an examination of accounts and everything would come out. Milburgh himself was not unmindful of this argument in his favour, as was to be revealed.

As against this, Tarling thought, it was notorious that criminals did foolish things. They took little or no account of the immediate consequences of their act, and a man like Milburgh, in his desperation, might in his very frenzy overlook the possibility of his crime coming to light through the very deed he had committed to cover himself up.

He had reached the bottom of Edgware Road and was turning the corner of the street, looking across to the Marble Arch, when he heard a voice hail him and turning, saw a cab breaking violently to the edge of the pavement.

It was Inspector Whiteside who jumped out.

"I was just coming to see you," he said. "I thought your interview with the young lady would be longer. Just wait a moment, till I've paid the cabman – by the way, I saw your Chink servant and gather you sent him to the Yard on a spoof errand."

When he returned, he met Tarling's eye and grinned sympathetically.

"I know what's in your mind," he said frankly, "but really the Chief thinks it no more than an extraordinary coincidence. I suppose you made inquiries about your revolver?"

Tarling nodded.

"And can you discover how it came to be in the possession of – " he paused, "the murderer of Thornton Lyne?"

"I have a theory, half-formed, it is true, but still a theory," said Tarling. "In fact, it's hardly so much a theory as an hypothesis."

Whiteside grinned again.

"This hair-splitting in the matter of logical terms never did mean much in my young life," he said, "but I take it you have a hunch."

Without any more to-do, Tarling told the other of the discovery he had made in Ling Chu's box, the press cuttings, descriptive of the late Mr Lyne's conduct in Shanghai and its tragic sequel.

Whiteside listened in silence.

"There may be something on that side," he said at last when Tarling had finished. "I've heard about your Ling Chu. He's a pretty good policeman, isn't he?"

"The best in China," said Tarling promptly, "but I'm not going to pretend that I understand his mind. These are the facts. The revolver, or rather the pistol, was in my cupboard and the only person who could get at it was Ling Chu. There is the second and more important fact imputing motive, that Ling Chu had every reason to hate Thornton Lyne, the man who had indirectly been responsible for his sister's death. I have been thinking the matter over and I now recall that Ling Chu was unusually silent after he had seen Lyne. He has admitted to me that he has been to Lyne's Store and in fact has been pursuing inquiries there. We happened to be discussing the possibility of Miss Rider committing the murder and Ling Chu told me that Miss Rider could not drive a motor car and when I questioned him as to how he knew this, he told me that he had made several inquiries at the Store. This I knew nothing about.

"Here is another curious fact," Tarling went on. "I have always been under the impression that Ling Chu did not speak English, except a few words of 'pigeon' that Chinamen pick up through mixing with foreign devils. Yet he pushed his inquiries at Lyne's Store amongst the employees, and it is a million to one against his finding any shop-girl who spoke Cantonese!"

"I'll put a couple of men on to watch him," said Whiteside, but Tailing shook his head.

"It would be a waste of good men," he said, "because Ling Chu could lead them just where he wanted to. I tell you he is a better sleuth than any you have got at Scotland Yard, and he has an absolute gift for fading out of the picture under your very nose. Leave Ling Chu to me, I know the way to deal with him," he added grimly.

"The Little Daffodil!" said Whiteside thoughtfully, repeating the phrase which Tarling had quoted. "That was the Chinese girl's name, eh? By Jove! It's something more than a coincidence, don't you think, Tarling?"

"It may be or may not he," said Tarling; "there is no such word as daffodil in Chinese. In fact, I am not so certain that the daffodil is a native of China at all, though China's a mighty big place. Strictly speaking the girl was called 'The Little Narcissus,' but as you say, it may be something more than a coincidence that the man who insulted her, is murdered whilst her brother is in London."

They had crossed the broad roadway as they were speaking and had passed into Hyde Park. Tarling thought whimsically that this open space exercised the same attraction on him as it did upon Mr Milburgh.

"What were you going to see me about?" he asked suddenly, remembering that Whiteside had been on his way to the hotel when they had met.

"I wanted to give you the last report about Milburgh."

Milburgh again! All conversation, all thought, all clues led to that mystery man. But what Whiteside had to tell was not especially thrilling. Milburgh had been shadowed day and night, and the record of his doings was a very prosaic one.

But it is out of prosaic happenings that big clues are born.

"I don't know how Milburgh expects the inquiry into Lyne's accounts will go," said Whiteside, "but he is evidently connected, or expects to be connected, with some other business."

"What makes you say that?" asked Tarling.

"Well," replied Whiteside, "he has been buying ledgers," and Tarling laughed.

"That doesn't seem to be a very offensive proceeding," he said good-humouredly. "What sort of ledgers?"

"Those heavy things which are used in big offices. You know, the sort of thing that it takes one man all his time to lift. He bought three at Roebuck's, in City Road, and took them to his house by taxi. Now my theory," said Whiteside earnestly, "is that this fellow is no ordinary criminal, if he is a criminal at all. It may be that he has been keeping a duplicate set of books."

"That is unlikely," interrupted Tarling, "and I say this with due respect for your judgment, Whiteside. It would want to be something more than an ordinary criminal to carry all the details of Lyne's mammoth business in his head, and it is more than possible that your first theory was right, namely, that he contemplates either going with another firm, or starting a new business of his own. The second supposition is more likely. Anyway, it is no crime to own a ledger, or even three. By the way, when did he buy these books?"

"Yesterday," said Whiteside, "early in the morning, before Lyne's opened. How did your interview with Miss Rider go off?"

Tailing shrugged his shoulders. He felt a strange reluctance to discuss the girl with the police officer, and realised just how big a fool he was in allowing her sweetness to drug him.

"I am convinced that, whoever she may suspect, she knows nothing of the murder," he said shortly.

"Then she *does* suspect somebody?"

Tarling nodded.

"Who?"

Again Tarling hesitated.

"I think she suspects Milburgh," he said.

He put his hand in the inside of his jacket and took out a pocket case, opened it, and drew forth the two cards bearing the finger impressions he had taken of Odette Rider. It required more than an ordinary effort of will to do this, though he would have found it difficult to explain just what tricks his emotions were playing.

"Here are the impressions you wanted," he said. "Will you take them?"

Whiteside took the cards with a nod and examined the inky smudges, and all the time Tarling's heart stood still, for Inspector Whiteside was the recognised authority of the Police Intelligence Department on fingerprints and their characteristics.

The survey was a long one.

Tarling remembered the scene for years afterwards; the sunlit path, the straggling idlers, the carriages pursuing their leisurely way along the walks, and the stiff military figure of Whiteside standing almost to attention, his keen eyes peering down at the little cards which he held in the fingertips of both hands. Then:

"Interesting," he said. "You notice that the two figures are almost the same – which is rather extraordinary. Very interesting."

"Well?" asked Tarling impatiently, almost savagely.

"Interesting," said Whiteside again, "but none of these correspond to the thumbprints on the bureau."

"Thank God for that!" said Tarling fervently "Thank God for that!"

LING CHU TELLS THE TRUTH

The firm of Dashwood and Solomon occupied a narrow-fronted building in the heart of the City of London. Its reputation stood as high as any, and it numbered amongst its clients the best houses in Britain. Both partners had been knighted, and it was Sir Felix Solomon who received Tarling in his private office.

Sir Felix was a tall, good-looking man, well past middle age, rather brusque of manner but kindly withal, and he looked up over his glasses as the detective entered.

"Scotland Yard, eh?" he said, glancing at Tarling's card. "Well, I can give you exactly five minutes, Mr Tarling. I presume you've come to see me about the Lyne accounts?"

Tarling nodded.

"We have not been able to start on these yet," said Sir Felix, "though we are hoping to go into them tomorrow. We're terribly rushed just now, and we've had to get in an extra staff to deal with this new work the Government has put on us – by the way, you know that we are not Lyne's accountants; they are Messrs Purbrake & Store, but we have taken on the work at the request of Mr Purbrake, who very naturally wishes to have an independent investigation, as there seems to be some question of defalcation on the part of one of the employees. This, coupled with the tragic death of Mr Lyne, has made it all the more necessary that an outside firm should be called in to look into the books."

"That I understand," said Tarling, "and of course, the Commissioner quite appreciates the difficulty of your task. I've come along rather to procure information for my own purpose as I am doubly interested – "

Sir Felix looked up sharply.

"Mr Tarling?" he repeated, looking at the card again. "Why, of course! I understand that letters of administration are to be applied for on your behalf?"

"I believe that is so," said Tarling quietly.

"But my interest in the property is more or less impersonal at the moment. The manager of the business is a Mr Milburgh."

Sir Felix nodded.

"He has been most useful and helpful," he said. "And certainly, if the vague rumours I have heard have any substantial foundation – namely, that Milburgh is suspected of robbing the firm – then he is assuredly giving us every assistance to convict himself."

"You have all the books in your keeping?"

"Absolutely," replied Sir Felix emphatically. "The last three books, unearthed by Mr Milburgh himself, came to us only this morning. In fact, those are they," he pointed to a brown paper parcel standing on a smaller table near the window. The parcel was heavily corded and was secured again by red tape, which was sealed.

Sir Felix leaned over and pressed a bell on the table, and a clerk came in.

"Put those books with the others in the strongroom," he said, and when the man had disappeared, staggering under the weight of the heavy volumes he turned to Tarling.

"We're keeping all the books and accounts of Lyne's Stores in a special strongroom," he said. "They are all under seal, and those seals will be broken in the presence of Mr Milburgh, as an interested party, and a representative of the Public Prosecutor."

"When will this be?" asked Tarling.

"Tomorrow afternoon, or possibly tomorrow morning. We will notify Scotland Yard as to the exact hour, because I suppose you will wish to be represented."

He rose briskly, thereby ending the interview.

It was another dead end, thought Tarling, as he went out into St Mary Axe and boarded a westward-bound omnibus. The case abounded in these culs-de-sac which seemed to lead nowhere. Cul-de-sac No. 1 had been supplied by Odette Rider; cul-de-sac No. 2 might very easily lead to the dead end of Milburgh's innocence.

He felt a sense of relief, however, that the authorities had acted so promptly in impounding Lyne's books. An examination into these might lead to the discovery of the murderer, and at any rate would dispel the cloud of suspicion which still surrounded Odette Rider.

He had gone to Dashwood and Solomon to make himself personally acquainted with that string in the tangled skein which he was determined to unravel; and now, with his mind at rest upon that subject, he was returning to settle matters with Ling Chu, that Chinese assistant of his who was now as deeply under suspicion as any suspect in the case.

He had spoken no more than the truth when he had told Inspector Whiteside that he knew the way to deal with Ling Chu. A Chinese criminal – and he was loath to believe that Ling Chu, that faithful servant, came under that description – is not to be handled in the Occidental manner; and he, who had been known throughout Southern China as the "Hunter of Men" had a reputation for extracting truth by methods which no code of laws would sanction.

He walked into his Bond Street flat, shut the door behind him and locked it, putting the key in his pocket. He knew Ling Chu would be in, because he had given him instructions that morning to await his return.

The Chinaman came into the hall to take his coat and hat, and followed Tarling into the sitting-room.

"Close the door, Ling Chu," said Tarling in Chinese. "I have something to say to you."

The last words were spoken in English, and the Chinaman looked at him quickly. Tarling had never addressed him in that language before, and the Chinaman knew just what this departure portended.

"Ling Chu," said Tarling, sitting at the table, his chin in his hand, watching the other with steady eyes, "you did not tell me that you spoke English."

"The master has never asked me," said the Chinaman quietly, and to Tarling's surprise his English was without accent and his pronunciation perfect.

"That is not true," said Tarling sternly. "When you told me that you had heard of the murder, I said that you did not understand English, and you did not deny it."

"It is not for me to deny the master," said Ling Chu as coolly as ever. "I speak very good English. I was trained at the Jesuit School in Hangkow, but it is not good for a Chinaman to speak English in China, or for any to know that he understands. Yet the master must have known I spoke English and read the language, for why should I keep the little cuttings from the newspapers in the box which the master searched this morning?"

Tarling's eyes narrowed.

"So you knew that, did you?" he said.

The Chinaman smiled. It was a most unusual circumstance, for Ling Chu had never smiled within Tarling's recollection.

"The papers were in certain order – some turned one way and some turned the other. When I saw them after I came back from Scotland Yard they had been disturbed. They could not disturb themselves, master, and none but you would go to my box."

There was a pause, awkward enough for Tarling, who felt for the moment a little foolish that his carelessness had led to Ling Chu discovering the search which had been made of his private property.

"I thought I had put them back as I had found them," he said, knowing that nothing could be gained by denying the fact that he had gone through Ling Chu's trunk. "Now, you will tell me, Ling Chu, did those printed words speak the truth?"

Ling Chu nodded.

"It is true, master," he said. "The Little Narcissus, or as the foreigners called her, the Little Daffodil, was my sister. She became a dancer in a tea-house against my wish, our parents being dead. She was a very good girl, master, and as pretty as a sprig of almond blossom. Chinese women are not pretty to the foreigner's eyes, but little Daffodil was like something cast in porcelain, and she had the virtues of a thousand years."

Tarling nodded.

"She was a good girl?" he repeated, this time speaking in Chinese and using a phrase which had a more delicate shade of meaning.

"She lived good and she died good," said the Chinaman calmly. "The speech of the Englishman offended her, and he called her many bad names because she would not come and sit on his knee; and if he put shame upon her by embracing her before the eyes of men, she was yet good, and she died very honourably."

Another interval of silence.

"I see," said Tarling quietly. "And when you said you would come with me to England, did you expect to meet – the bad Englishman?"

Ling Chu shook his head.

"I had put it from my mind," he said, "until I saw him that day in the big shop. Then the evil spirit which I had thought was all burnt out inside me, blazed up again." He stopped.

"And you desired his death? "said Tarling, and a nod was his answer.

"You shall tell me all, Ling Chu," said Tarling. The man was now pacing the room with restless strides, his emotion betrayed only by the convulsive clutching and unclutching of his hands.

"The Little Daffodil was very dear to me," he said. "Soon I think she would have married and have had children, and her name would have been blessed after the fashion of our people; for did not the Great Master say: 'What is more worshipful than the mother of children?' And when she died, master, my heart was empty, for there was no other love in my life. And then the Ho Sing murder was committed, and I went into the interior to search for Lu Fang, and that helped me to forget. I had forgotten till I saw him again. Then the old sorrow grew large in my soul, and I went out – "

"To kill him," said Tarling quietly.

"To kill him," repeated the man.

"Tell me all," said Tarling, drawing a long breath.

"It was the night you went to the little girl," said Ling Chu (Tarling knew that he spoke of Odette Rider). "I had made up my mind to go out, but I could not find an excuse because, master, you have given me orders that I must not leave this place whilst you are out. So I asked if I might go with you to the house of many houses."

"To the flat?" nodded Tarling. "Yes, go on."

"I had taken your quick-quick pistol and had loaded it and put it in my overcoat pocket. You told me to trail you, but when I had seen you on your way I left you and went to the big shop."

"To the big shop?" said Tarling in surprise. "But Lyne did not live in his stores!"

"So I discovered," said Ling Chu simply. "I thought in such a large house he would have built himself a beautiful room. In China many masters live in their shops. So I went to the big store to search it."

"Did you get in?" asked Tarling in surprise, and again Ling Chu smiled.

"That was very easy," he said. "The master knows how well I climb, and there were long iron pipes leading to the roof. Up one of these I climbed. Two sides of the shop are on big streets. One side is on a smaller street, and the fourth side is in a very small-piece street with few lights. It was up this side that I went. On the roof were many doors, and to such a man as me there was no difficulty."

"Go on," said Tarling again.

"I came down from floor to floor, always in darkness, but each floor I searched carefully, but found nothing but great bundles and packing-cases and long bars – "

"Counters," corrected Tarling.

"Yes," nodded Ling Chu, "they are called counters. And then at last I came to the floor where I had seen The Man." He paused. "First I went to the great room where we had met him, and that was locked. I opened it with a key, but it was in darkness, and I knew nobody was there. Then I went along a passage very carefully, because there was a light at the other end, and I came to an office."

"Empty, of course?"

"It was empty," said the Chinaman, "but a light was burning, and the desk cover was open. I thought he must be there, and I slipped behind the bureau, taking the pistol from my pocket. Presently I heard a footstep. I peeped out and saw the big white-faced man."

"Milburgh!" said Tarling.

"So he is called," replied the Chinaman. "He sat at the young man's desk. I knew it was the young man's desk, because there were many pictures upon it and flowers, such as he would have. The big man had his back to me."

"What was he doing?" asked Tarling.

"He was searching the desk, looking for something. Presently I saw him take from one of the drawers, which he opened, an envelope. From where I stood I could see into the drawer, and there were many little things such as tourists buy in China. From the envelope he took the *Hong*."

Tarling started. He knew of the *Hong* to which the man referred. It was the little red slip of paper bearing the Chinese characters which was found upon Thornton Lyne's body that memorable morning in Hyde Park.

"Yes, yes," he said eagerly. "What happened then?"

"He put the envelope in his pocket and went out. I heard him walking along the passage, and then I crept out from my hiding place and I also looked at the desk. I put the revolver down by my side, because I wanted both hands for the search, but I found nothing – only one little-piece book that the master uses to write down from day to day all that happens to him."

"A diary?" thought Tarling. "Well, and what next?" he asked.

"I got up to search the room and tripped over a wire. It must have been the wire attached to the electric light above the desk, for the room suddenly became dark, and at that moment I heard the big man's footsteps returning and slipped out of the door. And that is all, master," said Ling Chu simply. "I went back to the roof quickly for fear I should be discovered and it should bring dishonour to you."

Tarling whistled.

"And left the pistol behind?" he said.

"That is nothing but the truth," said Ling Chu. "I have dishonoured myself in your eyes, and in my heart I am a murderer, for I went to that place to kill the man who had brought shame to me and to my honourable relation."

"And left the pistol behind?" said Tarling again. "And Milburgh found it!"

MR MILBURGH SEES IT THROUGH

Ling Chu's story was not difficult to believe It was less difficult to believe that he was lying. There is no inventor in the world so clever, so circumstantial, so exact as to detail, as the Chinaman. He is a born teller of stories and piecer together of circumstances that fit so closely that it is difficult to see the joints. Yet the man had been frank, straightforward, patently honest. He had even placed himself in Tarling's power by his confession of his murderous intention.

Tarling could reconstruct the scene after the Chinaman had left. Milburgh stumbling in in the dark, striking a match and discovering a wall plug had been pulled away, reconnecting the lamp, and seeing to his amazement a murderous-looking pistol on the desk. It was possible that Milburgh, finding the pistol, had been deceived into believing that he had overlooked it on his previous search.

But what had happened to the weapon between the moment that Ling Chu left it on Thornton Lyne's private desk and when it was discovered in the work-basket of Odette Rider in the flat at Carrymore Mansions? And what had Milburgh been doing in the store by himself so late at night? And more particularly, what had he been doing in Thornton Lyne's private room? It was unlikely that Lyne would leave his desk unlocked, and the only inference to be drawn was that Milburgh had unlocked it himself with the object of searching its contents.

And the *Hong*? Those sinister little squares of red paper with the Chinese characters, one of which had been found in Thornton Lyne's pocket? The explanation of their presence in Thornton Lyne's desk was simple. He had been a globetrotter and had collected curios, and it was only natural that he should collect these slips of paper, which were on sale in most of the big Chinese towns as a souvenir of the predatory methods of the "Cheerful Hearts."

His conversation with Ling Chu would have to be reported to Scotland Yard, and that august institution would draw its own conclusions. In all probability they would be most unfavourable to Ling Chu, who would come immediately under suspicion.

Tarling, however, was satisfied – or perhaps it would be more accurate to say inclined to be satisfied – with his retainer's statement. Some of his story was susceptible to verification, and the detective lost no time in making his way to the Stores. The topographical situation was as Ling Chu had described it. Tarling went to the back of the big block of buildings, into the small, quiet street of which Ling Chu had spoken, and was able to distinguish the iron rain pipe (one of many) up which the Chinaman had clambered. Ling Chu would negotiate that task without any physical distress. He could climb like a cat, as Tarling knew, and that part of his story put no great tax upon the detective's credulity.

He walked back to the front of the shop, passed the huge plate-glass windows, fringed now with shoppers with whom Lyne's Store had acquired a new and morbid interest, and through the big swinging doors on to the crowded floor. Mr Milburgh was in his office, said a shopwalker, and led the way.

Mr Milburgh's office was much larger and less ornate than his late employer's. He greeted Tarling effusively, and pushed an armchair forward and produced a box of cigars.

"We're in rather a turmoil and upset now, Mr Tarling," he said in his ingratiating voice, with that set smile of his which never seemed to leave his face. "The auditors – or rather I should say the accountants – have taken away all the books, and of course that imposes a terrible strain on me, Mr Tarling. It means that we've got to organise a system of interim accounts, and you as a businessman will understand just what that means."

"You work pretty hard, Mr Milburgh?" said Tarling.

"Why, yes, sir," smiled Milburgh. "I've always worked hard."

"You were working pretty hard before Mr Lyne was killed, were you not?" asked Tarling.

"Yes – " hesitated Milburgh. "I can say honestly that I was."

"Very late at night?"

Milburgh still smiled, but there was a steely look in his eye as he answered:

"Frequently I worked late at night."

"Do you remember the night of the eleventh?" asked Tarling.

Milburgh looked at the ceiling for inspiration.

"Yes, I think I do. I was working very late that night."

"In your own office?"

"No," replied the other readily, "I did most of my work in Mr Lyne's office – at his request," he added. A bold statement to make to a man who knew that Lyne suspected him of robbing the firm. But Milburgh was nothing if not bold.

"Did he also give you the key of his desk?" asked the detective dryly.

"Yes, sir," beamed Mr Milburgh, "of course he did! You see, Mr Lyne trusted me absolutely."

He said this so naturally and with such assurance that Tarling was staggered. Before he had time to speak the other went on:

"Yes, I can truthfully say that I was in Mr Lyne's confidence. He told me a great deal more about himself than he has told anybody and – "

"One moment," said Tarling, and he spoke slowly. "Will you please tell me what you did with the revolver which you found on Mr Lyne's desk? It was a Colt automatic, and it was loaded."

Blank astonishment showed in Mr Milburgh's eyes. "A loaded pistol?" he asked, raising his eyebrows, "but, my dear good Mr Tarling, whatever are you talking about? I never found a loaded pistol on Mr Lyne's desk – poor fellow! Mr Lyne objected as much to these deadly weapons as myself."

Here was a facer for Tarling, but he betrayed no sign either of disappointment or surprise. Milburgh was frowning as though he were attempting to piece together some half-forgotten recollection.

120

"Is it possible," he said in a shocked voice, "that when you examined my house the other day it was with the object of discovering such a weapon as this!"

"It's quite possible," said Tarling coolly, "and even probable. Now, I'm going to be very straightforward with you, Mr Milburgh. I suspect you know a great deal more about this murder than you have told us, and that you had ever so much more reason for wishing Mr Lyne was dead than you are prepared to admit at this moment. Wait," he said, as the other opened his mouth to speak. "I am telling you candidly that the object of my first visit to these Stores was to investigate happenings which looked very black against you. It was hardly so much the work of a detective as an accountant," he said, "but Mr Lyne thought that I should be able to discover who was robbing the firm."

"And did you?" asked Milburgh coolly. There was the ghost of a smile still upon his face, but defiance shone in his pale eyes.

"I did not, because I went no further in the matter after you had expressed your agreement with Mr Lyne that the firm had been robbed by Odette Rider."

He saw the man change colour, and pushed home his advantage.

"I am not going to inquire too closely into your reasons for attempting to ruin an innocent girl," he said sternly. "That is a matter for your own conscience. But I tell you, Mr Milburgh, that if you are innocent – both of the robbery and of the murder – then I've never met a guilty person in my life."

"What do you mean?" asked the man loudly. "Do you dare to accuse me – ?"

"I accuse you of nothing more than this," said Tarling, " that I am perfectly satisfied that you have been robbing the firm for years. I am equally satisfied that, even if you did not kill Mr Lyne, you at least know who did."

"You're mad," sneered Milburgh, but his face was white. "Supposing it were true that I had robbed the firm, why should I want to kill Mr Thornton Lyne? The mere fact of his death would have brought an examination into the accounts."

This was a convincing argument – the more so as it was an argument which Tarling himself had employed.

"As to your absurd and melodramatic charges of robbing the firm," Milburgh went on, "the books are now in the hands of an eminent firm of chartered accountants, who can give the lie to any such statement as you have made."

He had recovered something of his old urbanity, and now stood, or rather straddled, with his legs apart, his thumbs in the armholes of his waistcoat, beaming benignly upon the detective.

"I await the investigation of that eminent firm, Messrs Dashwood and Solomon, with every confidence and without the least perturbation," he said. "Their findings will vindicate my honour beyond any question. I shall see this matter through!"

Tarling looked at him.

"I admire your nerve," he said, and left the office without another word.

COVERING THE TRAIL

Tarling had a brief interview with his assistant Whiteside, and the Inspector, to his surprise, accepted his view of Ling Chu's confession.

"I always thought Milburgh was a pretty cool customer," Whiteside said thoughtfully. "But he has more gall than I gave him credit for I would certainly prefer to believe your Chink than I would believe Milburgh. And, by the way, your young lady has slipped the shadow."

"What are you talking about?" asked Tarling in surprise.

"I am referring to your Miss Odette Rider – and why on earth a grown-up police officer with your experience should blush, I can't imagine."

"I'm not blushing," said Tarling. "What about her?"

"I've had two men watching her," explained Whiteside, "and whenever she has taken her walks abroad she has been followed, as you know. In accordance with your instructions I was taking off those shadows tomorrow, but today she went to Bond Street, and either Jackson was careless – it was Jackson who was on the job – or else the young lady was very sharp; at any rate, he waited for half an hour for her to come out of the shop, and when she didn't appear he walked in and found there was another entrance through which she had gone. Since then she has not been back to the hotel."

"I don't like that," said Tarling, a little troubled. "I wished her to be under observation as much for her own protection as anything else. I wish you would keep a man at the hotel and telephone me just as soon as she returns."

Whiteside nodded.

"I've anticipated your wishes in that respect," he said. "Well, what is the next move?"

"I'm going to Hertford to see Miss Rider's mother; and incidentally, I may pick up Miss Rider, who is very likely to have gone home."

Whiteside nodded.

"What do you expect to find out from the mother?" he asked.

"I expect to learn a great deal," said Tarling. "There is still a minor mystery to be discovered. For example, who is the mysterious man who comes and goes to Hertford, and just why is Mrs Rider living in luxury whilst her daughter is working for her living at Lyne's Store?"

"There's something in that," agreed Whiteside. "Would you like me to come along with you?"

"Thanks," smiled Tarling, "I can do that little job by myself."

"Reverting to Milburgh," began Whiteside.

"As we always revert to Milburgh," groaned Tarling. "Yes?"

"Well, I don't like his assurance," said Whiteside. "It looks as if all our hopes of getting a clue from the examination of Lyne's accounts are fated to be dashed."

"There's something in that," said Tarling. "I don't like it myself. The books are in the hands of one of the best chartered accountants in the country, and if there has been any monkey business, he is the fellow who is certain to find it; and not only that, but to trace whatever defalcations there are to the man responsible. Milburgh is not fool enough to imagine that he won't be found out once the accountants get busy, and his cheeriness in face of exposure is to say the least disconcerting."

Their little conference was being held in a prosaic public tea room opposite the House of Commons – a tea room the walls of which, bad they ears, could have told not a few of Scotland Yard's most precious secrets.

Tarling was on the point of changing the subject when he remembered the parcel of books which had arrived at the accountant's office that morning.

"Rather late," said Whiteside thoughtfully. "By Jove! I wonder!"

"You wonder what?"

"I wonder if they were the three books that Milburgh bought yesterday?"

"The three ledgers?"

Whiteside nodded.

"But why on earth should he want to put in three new ledgers – they were new, weren't they? That doesn't seem to me to be a very intelligent suggestion. And yet – "

He jumped up, almost upsetting the table in his excitement.

"Quick, Whiteside! Get a cab while I settle the bill," he said.

"Where are you going?"

"Hurry up and get the cab!" said Tarling, and when he had rejoined his companion outside, and the taxi was bowling along the Thames Embankment: "I'm going to St Mary Axe."

"So I gathered from your directions to the cabman," said Whiteside. "But why St Mary Axe at this time of the afternoon? The very respectable Dashwood and Solomon will not be glad to see you until tomorrow."

"I'm going to see these books," said Tarling, "the books which Milburgh sent to the accountants this morning."

"What do you expect to find?"

"I'll tell you later," was Tarling's reply. He looked at his watch. "They won't be closed yet, thank heaven!"

The taxi was held up at the juncture of the Embankment and Blackfriars Bridge, and was held up again for a different reason in Queen Victoria Street. Suddenly there was a clang-clang of gongs, and all traffic drew to one side to allow the passage of a flying motor fire-engine. Another and another followed in succession.

"A big fire," said Whiteside. "Or it may be a little one, because they get very panicky in the City, and they'll put in a divisional call for a smoking chimney!"

The cab moved on, and had crossed Cannon Street, when it was again held up by another roaring motor, this time bearing a fire escape.

"Let's get out of the cab; we'll walk," said Tarling.

They jumped out, and Whiteside paid the driver.

"This way," said Tarling. "We'll make a short cut."

Whiteside had stopped to speak to a policeman.

"Where's the fire, constable?" he asked.

"St Mary Axe, sir," was the policeman's reply. "A big firm of chartered accountants – Dashwood and Solomon. You know them, sir? I'm told the place is blazing from cellar to garret."

Tarling showed his teeth in an unamused grin as the words came to him.

"And all the proof of Milburgh's guilt gone up in smoke, eh?" he said. "I think I know what those books contained – a little clockwork detonator and a few pounds of thermite to burn up all the clues to the Daffodil Murder!"

THE HEAVY WALLET

All that remained of the once stately, if restricted, premises of Messrs Dashwood and Solomon was a gaunt-looking front wall, blackened by the fire. Tarling interviewed the Chief of the Fire Brigade.

"It'll be days before we can get inside," said that worthy, "and I very much doubt if there's anything left intact. The whole of the building has been burnt out – you can see for yourself the roof has gone in – and there's very little chance of recovering anything of an inflammable nature unless it happens to be in a safe."

Tarling caught sight of the brusque Sir Felix Solomon gazing, without any visible evidence of distress, upon the wreckage of his office.

"We are covered by insurance," said Sir Felix philosophically, "and there is nothing of any great importance, except, of course, those documents and books from Lyne's Store."

"They weren't in the fireproof vault?" asked Tarling, and Sir Felix shook his head.

"No," he said, "they were in a strongroom; and curiously enough, it was in that strongroom where the fire originated. The room itself was not fireproof, and it would have been precious little use if it had been, as the fire started inside. The first news we received was when a clerk, going down to the basement, saw flames leaping out between the steel bars which constitute the door of No. 4 vault."

Tarling nodded.

"I need not ask you whether the books which Mr Milburgh brought this morning had been placed in that safe, Sir Felix," he said, and the knight looked surprised.

"Of course not. They were placed there whilst you were in the office," he said, "Why do you ask?"

"Because in my judgment those books were not books at all in the usually understood sense. Unless I am at fault, the parcel contained three big ledgers glued together, the contents being hollowed out and that hollow filled with thermite, a clockwork detonator, or the necessary electric apparatus to start a spark at a given moment."

The accountant stared at him.

"You're joking," he said, but Tarling shook his head.

"I was never more serious in my life."

"But who would commit such an infernal act as that? Why, one of my clerks was nearly burnt to death!"

"The man who would commit such an infernal act as that," repeated Tarling slowly, "is the man who has every reason for wishing to avoid an examination of Lyne's accounts."

"You don't mean – "

"I'll mention no names for the moment, and if inadvertently I have conveyed the identity of the gentleman of whom I have been speaking, I hope you will be good enough to regard it as confidential," said Tarling, and went back to his crestfallen subordinate.

"No wonder Milburgh was satisfied with the forthcoming examination," he said bitterly. "The devil had planted that parcel, and had timed it probably to the minute. Well, there's nothing more to be done tonight – with Milburgh."

He looked at his watch.

"I'm going back to my flat, and afterwards to Hertford," he said.

He had made no definite plan as to what line he should pursue after he reached Hertford. He had a dim notion that his investigation hereabouts might, if properly directed, lead him nearer to the heart of the mystery. This pretty, faded woman who lived in such style, and whose husband was so seldom visible, might give him a key. Somewhere it was in existence, that key, by which he could decipher the jumbled code of the Daffodil Murder, and it might as well be at Hertford as nearer at hand.

It was dark when he came to the home of Mrs Rider, for this time he had dispensed with a cab, and had walked the long distance between the station and the house, desiring to avoid attention. The dwelling stood on the main road. It had a high wall frontage of about three hundred and fifty feet. The wall was continued down the side of a lane, and at the other end marked the boundary of a big paddock.

The entrance to the grounds was through a wrought-iron gate of strength, the design of which recalled something which he had seen before. On his previous visit the gate had been unfastened, and he had had no difficulty in reaching the house. Now, however, it was locked.

He put his flashlight over the gate and the supporting piers, and discovered a bell, evidently brand new, and recently fixed. He made no attempt to press the little white button, but continued his reconnaissance. About half a dozen yards inside the gateway was a small cottage, from which a light showed, and apparently the bell communicated with this dwelling. Whilst he was waiting, he heard a whistle and a quick footstep coming up the road, and drew into the shadow. Somebody came to the gate; he heard the faint tinkle of a bell and a door opened.

The newcomer was a newspaper boy, who pushed a bundle of evening papers through the iron bars and went off again. Tarling waited until he heard the door of the cottage or lodge close. Then he made a circuit of the house, hoping to find another entrance. There was evidently a servants' entrance at the back, leading from the lane, but this too was closed. Throwing his light up, he saw that there was no broken glass on top of the wall, as there had been in the front of the house, and, making a jump, he caught the stone coping and drew himself up and astride.

He dropped into the darkness on the other side without any discomfort to himself, and made his cautious way towards the house. Dogs were the danger, but apparently Mrs Rider did not keep dogs, and his progress was unchallenged.

He saw no light either in the upper or lower windows until he got to the back. Here was a pillared porch, above which had been built what appeared to be a conservatory. Beneath the porch was a door and a barred window, but it was from the conservatory above that a faint light emanated. He looked round for a ladder without success. But the portico presented no more difficulties than the wall had done. By stepping on to the windowsill and steadying himself against one of the pillars, he could reach an iron stanchion, which had evidently been placed to support the framework of the superstructure. From here to the parapet of the conservatory itself was but a swing. This glass-house had casement windows, one of which was open, and he leaned on his elbows and cautiously intruded his head.

The place was empty. The light came from an inner room opening into the glass sheltered balcony. Quickly he slipped through the windows and crouched under the shadow of a big oleander. The atmosphere of the conservatory was close and the smell was earthy. He judged from the hot-water pipes which his groping hands felt that it was a tiny winter garden erected by the owner of the house for her enjoyment in the dark, cold days. French windows admitted to the inner room, and, peering through the casement curtains which covered them, Tarling saw Mrs Rider. She was sitting at a desk, a pen in her hand, her chin on her fingertips. She was not writing, but staring blankly at the wall, as though she were at a loss for what to say.

The light came from a big alabaster bowl hanging a foot below the ceiling level, and it gave the detective an opportunity of making a swift examination. The room was furnished simply if in perfect taste, and had the appearance of a study. Beside her desk was a green safe, half let into the wall and half exposed. There were a few prints hanging on the walls, a chair or two, a couch half-hidden from the detective's view, and that was all. He had expected to see Odette Rider with her mother, and was disappointed. Not only was Mrs Rider alone, but she conveyed the impression that she was practically alone in the house.

Tarling knelt, watching her, for ten minutes, until he heard a sound outside. He crept softly back and looked over the edge of the portico in time to see a figure moving swiftly along the path. It was riding a bicycle which did not carry a light. Though he strained his eyes, he could not tell whether the rider was man or woman. It disappeared under the portico and he heard the grating of the machine as it was leant against one of the pillars, the click of a key in the lock and the sound of a door opening. Then he crept back to his observation post overlooking the study.

Mrs Rider had evidently not heard the sound of the door opening below, and sat without movement still staring at the wall before her. Presently she started and looked round towards the door. Tarling noted the door – noted, too the electric switch just in view. Then the door opened slowly. He saw Mrs Rider's face light up with pleasure, then somebody asked a question in a whisper, and she answered – he could just hear her words:

"No darling, nobody."

Tarling held his breath and waited. Then, of a sudden, the light in the room was extinguished. Whoever had entered had turned out the light. He heard a soft footfall coming towards the window looking into the conservatory and the rattle of the blinds as they were lowered. Then the light went up again, but he could see nothing or hear nothing.

Who was Mrs Rider's mysterious visitor? There was only one way to discover, but he waited a little longer – waited, in fact, until he heard the soft slam of a safe door closing – before he slipped again through the window and dropped to the ground.

The bicycle was, as he had expected, leaning against one of the pillars. He could see nothing, and did not dare flash his lamp, but his sensitive fingers ran over its lines, and he barely checked an exclamation of surprise. It was a lady's bicycle!

He waited a little while, then withdrew to a shrubbery opposite the door on the other side of the drive up which the cyclist had come. He had not long to wait before the door under the portico opened again and closed. Somebody jumped on to the bicycle as Tarling leaped from his place of concealment. He pressed the key of his electric lamp, but for some reason it did not act. He felt rather than heard a shiver of surprise from the person on the machine.

"I want you," said Tarling, and put out his hands.

He missed the rider by the fraction of an inch, but saw the machine swerve and heard the soft thud of something falling. A second later the machine and rider had disappeared in the pitch darkness.

He re-fixed his lamp. Pursuit, he knew, was useless without his lantern, and, cursing the maker thereof, he adjusted another battery, and put the light on the ground to see what it was that the fugitive had dropped. He thought he heard a smothered exclamation behind him and turned swiftly. But nobody came within the radius of his lamp. He must be getting nervy, he thought, and continued his inspection of the wallet.

It was a long, leather portfolio, about ten inches in length and five inches in depth, and it was strangely heavy. He picked it up, felt for the clasp, and found instead two tiny locks. He made another examination by the light of his lantern, an examination which was interrupted by a challenge from above.

"Who are you?"

It was Mrs Rider's voice, and just then it was inconvenient for him to reveal himself. Without a word in answer, he switched off his light and slipped into the bushes, and, more as the result of instinct than judgment, regained the wall, at almost the exact spot he had crossed it.

The road was empty, and there was no sign of the cyclist. There was only one thing to do and that was to get back to town as quickly as possible and examine the contents of the wallet at his leisure. It was extraordinarily heavy for its size, he was reminded of that fact by his sagging pocket.

The road back to Hertford seemed interminable and the clocks were chiming a quarter of eleven when he entered the station yard.

"Train to London, sir?" said the porter. "You've missed the last train to London by five minutes!"

THE NIGHT VISITOR

Tarling was less in a dilemma than in that condition of uncertainty which is produced by having no definite plans one way or the other. There was no immediate necessity for his return to town and his annoyance at finding the last train gone was due rather to a natural desire to sleep in his own bed, than to any other cause. He might have got a car from a local garage, and motored to London, if there had been any particular urgency, but, he told himself, he might as well spend the night in Hertford as in Bond Street.

If he had any leanings towards staying at Hertford it was because he was anxious to examine the contents of the wallet at his leisure. If he had any call to town it might be discovered in his anxiety as to what had happened to Odette Rider; whether she had returned to her hotel or was still marked "missing" by the police. He could, at any rate, get into communication with Scotland Yard and satisfy his mind on that point. He turned back from the station in search of lodgings. He was to find that it was not so easy to get rooms as he had imagined. The best hotel in the place was crowded out as a result of an agricultural convention which was being held in the town. He was sent on to another hotel, only to find that the same state of congestion existed, and finally after half an hour's search he found accommodation at a small commercial hotel which was surprisingly empty.

His first step was to get into communication with London and this was established without delay. Nothing had been heard of Odette Rider, and the only news of importance was that the ex-convict, Sam

Stay, had escaped from the county lunatic asylum to which he had been removed.

Tarling went up to the commodious sitting-room. He was mildly interested in the news about Stay, for the man had been a disappointment. This criminal, whose love for Thornton Lyne had, as Tarling suspected rightly, been responsible for his mental collapse, might have supplied a great deal of information as to the events which led up to the day of the murder, and his dramatic breakdown had removed a witness who might have offered material assistance to the police.

Tarling closed the door of his sitting-room behind him, pulled the wallet from his pocket and laid it on the table. He tried first with his own keys to unfasten the flap but the locks defied him. The heaviness of the wallet surprised and piqued him, but he was soon to find an explanation for its extraordinary weight. He opened his pocket-knife and began to cut away the leather about the locks, and uttered an exclamation.

So that was the reason for the heaviness of the pouch – it was only leather-covered! Beneath this cover was a lining of fine steel mail. The wallet was really a steel chain bag, the locks being welded to the chain and absolutely immovable. He threw the wallet back on the table with a laugh. He must restrain his curiosity until he got back to the Yard, where the experts would make short work of the best locks which were ever invented. Whilst he sat watching the thing upon the table and turning over in his mind the possibility of its contents, he heard footsteps pass his door and mount the stairway opposite which his sitting-room was situated. Visitors in the same plight as himself, he thought.

Somehow, being in a strange room amidst unfamiliar surroundings, gave the case a new aspect. It was an aspect of unreality. They were all so unreal, the characters in this strange drama.

Thornton Lyne seemed fantastic, and fantastic indeed was his end. Milburgh, with his perpetual smirk, his little stoop, his broad, fat face and half bald head; Mrs Rider, a pale ghost of a woman who flitted in and out of the story, or rather hovered about it, never seeming to intrude, yet never wholly separated from its tragic process; Ling Chu, imperturbable, bringing with him the atmosphere of that land of intrigue and mystery and motive, China. Odette Rider alone was real. She was life; warm, palpitating, wonderful.

Tarling frowned and rose stiffly from his chair. He despised himself a little for this weakness of his. Odette Rider! A woman still under suspicion of murder, a woman whom it was his duty, if she were guilty, to bring to the scaffold, and the thought of her turned him hot and cold!

He passed through to his bedroom which adjoined the sitting-room, put the wallet on a table by the side of his bed, locked the bedroom door, opened the windows and prepared himself, as best be could, for the night.

There was a train leaving Hertford at five in the morning and he had arranged to be called in time to catch it. He took off his boots, coat, vest, collar and tie, unbuckled his belt – he was one of those eccentrics to whom the braces of civilisation were anathema – and lay down on the outside of the bed, pulling the eiderdown over him. Sleep did not come to him readily. He turned from side to side, thinking, thinking, thinking.

Suppose there had been some mistake in the time of the accident at Ashford? Suppose the doctors were wrong and Thornton Lyne was murdered at an earlier hour? Suppose Odette Rider was in reality a cold-blooded – He growled away the thought.

He heard the church clock strike the hour of two and waited impatiently for the quarter to chime – he had heard every quarter since he had retired to bed. But he did not hear that quarter. He must have fallen into an uneasy sleep for he began to dream. He dreamt he was in China again and had fallen into the hands of that baneful society, the "Cheerful Hearts." He was in a temple, lying on a great black slab of stone, bound hand and foot, and above him he saw the leader of the gang, knife in hand, peering down into his face with a malicious grin – and it was the face of Odette Rider! He saw the knife raised and woke sweating.

The church clock was booming three and a deep silence lay on the world. But there was somebody in his room. He knew that and lay motionless, peering out of half-closed eyes from one corner to the other. There was nobody to be seen, nothing to be heard, but his sixth sense told him that somebody was present. He reached out his hand carefully and silently to the table and searched for the wallet. It was gone!

Then he heard the creak of a board and it came from the direction of the door leading to the sitting room. With one bound he was out of bed in time to see the door flung open and a figure slip through. He was after it in a second. The burglar might have escaped, but unexpectedly there was a crash and a cry. He had fallen over a chair and before he could rise Tarling was on him and had flung him back. He leapt to the door, it was open. He banged it close and turned the key.

"Now, let's have a look at you," said Tarling grimly and switched on the light.

He fell back against the door, his mouth open in amazement, for the intruder was Odette Rider, and in her hand she held the stolen wallet.

THE CONFESSION OF
ODETTE RIDER

He could only gaze in stupified silence.

"You!" he said wonderingly.

The girl was pale and her eyes never left his face.

She nodded.

"Yes, it is I," she said in a low voice.

"You!" he said again and walked towards her. He held out his hand and she gave him the wallet without a word.

"Sit down," he said kindly.

He thought she was going to faint.

"I hope I didn't hurt you? I hadn't the slightest idea – "

She shook her head.

"Oh, I'm not hurt," she said wearily, "not hurt in the way you mean."

She drew a chair to the table and dropped her face upon her hands and he stood by, embarrassed, almost terrified, by this unexpected development.

"So you were the visitor on the bicycle," he said at last, "I didn't suspect – "

It struck him at that moment that it was not an offence for Odette Rider to go up to her mother's house on a bicycle, or even to take away a wallet which was probably hers. If there was any crime at all, he had committed it in retaining something to which he had no right. She looked up at his words.

"I? On the bicycle?" she asked. "No, it was not I."

"Not you?"

She shook her head.

"I was in the grounds – I saw you using your lamp and I was quite close to you when you picked up the wallet," she said listlessly, "but I was not on the bicycle."

"Who was it?" he asked.

She shook her head.

"May I have that please?"

She held out her hand and he hesitated.

After all, he had no right or title to this curious purse. He compromised by putting it on the table and she did not attempt to take it.

"Odette," he said gently and walked round to her, laying his hand on her shoulder. "Why don't you tell me?"

"Tell you what?" she asked, without looking up.

"Tell me all there is to be told," he said. "I could help you. I want to help you."

She looked up at him.

"Why do you want to help me?" she asked simply.

He was tongue-tied for a second.

"Because I love you," he said, and his voice shook.

It did not seem to him that he was talking. The words came of their own volition. He had no more intention of telling her he loved her, indeed he had no more idea that he did love her, than Whiteside would have had. Yet he knew he spoke the truth and that a power greater than he had framed the words and put them on his lips.

The effect on the girl seemed extraordinary to him. She did not shrink back, she did not look surprised. She showed no astonishment whatever. She just brought her eyes back to the table and said: "Oh!"

That calm, almost uncannily calm acceptance of a fact which Tarling had not dared to breathe to himself, was the second shock of the evening.

It was as though she had known it all along. He was on his knees by her side and his arm was about her shoulders, even before his brain had willed the act.

"My girl, my girl," he said gently. "Won't you please tell me?"

Her head was still bent and her voice was so low as to he almost inaudible.

"Tell you what?" she asked.

"What you know of this business?" he said. "Don't you realise how every new development brings you more and more under suspicion?"

"What business do you mean?"

He hesitated.

"The murder of Thornton Lyne? I know nothing of that."

She made no response to that tender arm of his, but sat rigid. Something in her attitude chilled him and he dropped her hand and rose. When she looked up she saw that his face was white and set. He walked to the door and unlocked it.

"I'm not going to ask you any more," he said quietly. "You know best why you came to me tonight – I suppose you followed me and took a room. I heard somebody going upstairs soon after I arrived."

She nodded.

"Do yon want – this?" she asked and pointed to the wallet on the table.

"Take it away with you."

She got up to her feet unsteadily and swayed toward him. In a second he was by her side, his arms about her. She made no resistance, but rather he felt a yielding towards him which he had missed before. Her pale face was upturned to his and he stooped and kissed her.

"Odette! Odette!" he whispered. "Don't you realise that I love you and would give my life to save you from unhappiness? Won't you tell me everything, please?"

"No, no, no," she murmured with a little catch in her voice. "Please don't ask me! I am afraid. Oh, I am afraid!"

He crushed her in his arms, his cheek against hers, his lips tingling with the caress of her hair.

"But there is nothing to be afraid of, nothing," he said eagerly. "If you were as guilty as hell, I would save you! If you are shielding somebody I would shield them because I love you, Odette!"

139

"No, no!" she cried and pushed him back, both her little hands pressing against his chest. "Don't ask me, don't ask me – "

"Ask me!"

Tarling swung round. There was a man standing in the doorway, in the act of closing the door behind him.

"Milburgh!" he said between his teeth.

"Milburgh!" smiled the other mockingly. "I am sorry to interrupt this beautiful scene, but the occasion is a desperate one and I cannot afford to stand on ceremony, Mr Tarling."

Tarling put the girl from him and looked at the smirking manager. One comprehensive glance the detective gave him, noted the cycling clips and the splashes of mud on his trousers, and understood.

"So you were the cyclist, eh?" he said.

"That's right," said Milburgh, "it is an exercise to which I am very partial."

"What do you want?" asked Tarling, alert and watchful.

"I want you to carry out your promise, Mr Tarling," said Milburgh smoothly.

Tarling stared at him.

"My promise," he said, "what promise?"

"To protect, not only the evil-doer, but those who have compromised themselves in an effort to shield the evil-doer from his or her own wicked act."

Tarling started.

"Do you mean to say – " he said hoarsely. "Do you mean to accuse – ?"

"I accuse nobody," said Milburgh with a wide sweep of his hands. "I merely suggest that both Miss Rider and myself are in very serious trouble and that you have it in your power to get us safely out of this country to one where extradition laws cannot follow."

Tarling took one step towards him and Milburgh shrank back.

"Do you accuse Miss Rider of complicity in this murder?" he demanded.

Milburgh smiled, but it was an uneasy smile.

"I make no accusation," he said, "and as to the murder?" he shrugged his shoulders. "You will understand better when you read the contents of the wallet which I was endeavouring to remove to a place of safety."

Tarling picked up the wallet from the table and looked at it.

"I shall see the contents of this wallet tomorrow," he said. "Locks will present very little difficulty – "

"You can read the contents tonight," said Milburgh smoothly, and pulled from his pocket a chain, at the end of which dangled a bunch of keys. "Here is the key," he said. "Unlock and read tonight."

Tarling took the key in his hand, inserted it in first one tiny lock and then in the other. The catches snapped open and he threw back the flap. Then a hand snatched the portfolio from him and he turned to see the girl's quivering face and read the terror in her eyes.

"No, no!" she cried, almost beside herself, "no, for God's sake, no!"

Tarling stepped back. He saw the malicious little smile on Milburgh's face and could have struck him down.

Miss Rider does not wish me to see what is in this case," he said.

"And for an excellent reason," sneered Milburgh,

"Here!"

It was the girl's voice, surprisingly clear and steady. Her shaking hands held the paper she had taken from the wallet and she thrust it toward the detective.

"There is a reason," she said in a low voice But it is not the reason you suggest."

Milburgh had gone too far. Tarling saw his face lengthen and the look of apprehension in his cold blue eyes Then, without further hesitation, he opened the paper and read.

The first line took away his breath.

"THE CONFESSION OF ODETTE RIDER."

"Good God!" he muttered and read on. There were only half a dozen lines and they were in the firm calligraphy of the girl.

"I, Odette Rider, hereby confess that for three years I have been robbing the firm of Lyne's Stores, Limited, and during that period have taken the sum of £25,000."

Tarling dropped the paper and caught the girl as she fainted.

MILBURGH'S LAST BLUFF

Milburgh had gone too far. He had hoped to carry through this scene without the actual disclosure of the confession. In his shrewd, clever way he had realised before Tarling himself, that the detective from Shanghai, this heir to the Lyne millions, had fallen under the spell of the girl's beauty, and all his conjectures had been confirmed by the scene he had witnessed, no less than by the conversation he had overheard before the door was opened.

He was seeking immunity and safety. The man was in a panic, though this Tarling did not realise, and was making his last desperate throw for the life that he loved, that life of ease and comfort to secure which he had risked so much.

Milburgh had lived in terror that Odette Rider would betray him, and because of his panicky fear that she had told all to the detective that night he brought her back to London from Ashford, he had dared attempt to silence the man whom he believed was the recipient of the girl's confidence.

Those shots in the foggy night which had nearly ended the career of Jack Tarling had their explanation in Milburgh's terror of exposure. One person in the world, one living person, could place him in the felon's dock, and if she betrayed him –

Tarling had carried the girl to a couch and had laid her down. He went quickly into his bedroom, switching on the light, to get a glass of water. It was Milburgh's opportunity. A little fire was burning in the sitting-room. Swiftly he picked the confession from the floor and thrust it into his pocket.

On a little table stood a writing cabinet. From this he took a sheet of the hotel paper, crumpled it up and thrust it into the fire, it was blazing when Tarling returned.

"What are you doing?" he asked, halting by the side of the couch.

"I am burning the young lady's confession," said Milburgh calmly. "I do not think it is desirable in the interests – "

"Wait," said Tarling calmly.

He lowered the girl's head and sprinkled some of the water on her face, and she opened her eyes with a little shudder.

Tarling left her for a second and walked to the fire. The paper was burnt save a scrap of the edge that had not caught, and this he lifted gingerly, looked at it for a moment, then cast his eyes round the room. He saw that the stationery cabinet had been disturbed and laughed. It was neither a pleasant nor an amused laugh.

"That's the idea, eh?" he said, walked to the door, closed it and stood with his back to it.

"Now, Milburgh, you can give me that confession you've got in your pocket."

"I've burnt it, Mr Tarling."

"You're a liar," said Tarling calmly. "You knew very well I wouldn't let you go out of this room with that confession in your pocket and you tried to bluff me by burning a sheet of writing paper. I want that confession."

"I assure you – " began Milburgh.

"I want that confession," said Tarling, and with a sickly smile Milburgh put his hand in his pocket and drew out the crumpled sheet.

"Now, if you are anxious to see it burn," said Tarling, "you will have an opportunity."

He read the statement again and put it into the fire, watched it until it was reduced to ashes, then beat the ashes down with a poker.

"That's that," said Tarling cheerfully.

"I suppose you know what you've done," said Milburgh. "You've destroyed evidence which you, as an officer of the law – "

"Cut that out," replied Tarling shortly.

For the second time that night he unlocked the door and flung it wide open.

"Milburgh, you can go. I know where I can find you when I want you," he said.

"You'll be sorry for this," said Milburgh.

"Not half as sorry as you'll be by the time I'm through with you," retorted Tarling.

"I shall go straight to Scotland Yard," fumed the man, white with passion.

"Do, by all means," said the detective coolly, "and be good enough to ask them to detain you until I come."

With this shot he closed the door upon the retreating man.

The girl was sitting now on the edge of the sofa, her brave eyes surveying the man who loved her.

"What have you done?" she asked.

"I've destroyed that precious confession of yours," said Tarling cheerfully. "It occurred to me in the space of time it took to get from you to my washstand, that that confession may have been made under pressure. I am right, aren't I?"

She nodded.

"Now, you wait there a little while I make myself presentable and I'll take you home."

"Take me home?" said the startled girl. "Not to mother, no, no. She mustn't ever know."

"On the contrary, she must know. I don't know what it is she mustn't know," said Tarling with a little smile, "but there has been a great deal too much mystery already, and it is not going to continue."

She rose and walked to the fireplace, her elbows on the mantelpiece, and her head back.

"I'll tell you all I can. Perhaps you're right," she said. "There has been too much mystery. You asked me once who was Milburgh."

She turned and half-faced him.

"I won't ask you that question any more," he said quietly, "I know!"

"You know?"

"Yes, Milburgh is your mother's second husband."

Her eyes opened.

"How did you find out that?"

"I guessed that," he smiled, "and she keeps her name Rider at Milburgh's request. He asked her not to reveal the fact that she was married again. Isn't that so?"

She nodded.

"Mother met him about seven years ago. We were at Harrogate at the time. You see, mother had a little money, and I think Mr Milburgh thought it was much more than it actually was. He was a very agreeable man and told mother that he had a big business in the city. Mother believes that he is very well off."

Tarling whistled.

"I see," he said. "Milburgh has been robbing his employers and spending the money on your mother."

She shook her head.

"That is partly true and partly untrue," she said. "Mother has been an innocent participant. He bought this house at Hertford and furnished it lavishly, he kept two cars until a year ago, when I made him give them up and live more simply. You don't know what these years have meant, Mr Tarling, since I discovered how deeply mother would be dragged down by the exposure of his villainy."

"How did you find it out?"

"It was soon after the marriage," said the girl. "I went into Lyne's Store one day and one of the employees was rude to me. I shouldn't have taken much notice, but an officious shopwalker dismissed the girl on the spot, and when I pleaded for her reinstatement, he insisted that I should see the manager. I was ushered into a private office, and there I saw Mr Milburgh and realised the kind of double life he was living. He made me keep his secret, painted a dreadful picture of what would happen, and said he could put everything right if I would come into the business and help him. He told me he had large investments which were bringing in big sums and that he would apply this money to making good his defalcations. That was why I went into Lyne's Store, but he broke his word from the very beginning."

"Why did he put you there?" asked Tarling.

"Because, if there had been another person," said the girl, "he might have been detected. He knew that any inquiries into irregularities of accounts would come first to my department, and he wanted to have somebody there who would let him know. He did not betray this thought," said the girl, "but I guessed that that was the idea at the back of his mind..."

She went on to tell him something of the life she had lived, the humiliation she suffered in her knowledge of the despicable part she was playing.

"From the first I was an accessory," she said. "It is true that I did not steal, but my reason for accepting the post was in order to enable him, as I thought, to right a grievous wrong and to save my mother from the shame and misery which would follow the exposure of Milburgh's real character."

She looked at him with a sad little smile.

"I hardly realise that I am speaking to a detective," she said, "and all that I have suffered during these past years has been in vain; but the truth must come now, whatever be the consequences."

She paused.

"And now I am going to tell you what happened on the night of the murder."

IN MRS RIDER'S ROOM

There was a deep silence. Tarling could feel his heart thumping almost noisily.

"After I had left Lyne's Store," she said, "I had decided to go to mother to spend two or three days with her before I began looking for work. Mr Milbrugh only went to Hertford for the weekends, and I couldn't stay in the same house with him, knowing all that I knew.

"I left my flat at about half-past six that evening, but I am not quite sure of the exact time. It must have been somewhere near then, because I was going to catch the seven o'clock train to Hertford. I arrived at the station and had taken my ticket, and was stooping to pick up my bag, when I felt a hand on my arm, and turning, saw Mr Milburgh. He was in a state of great agitation and distress, and asked me to take a later train and accompany him to the Florentine Restaurant where he had taken a private room. He told me he had very bad news and that I must know.

"I put my bag in the cloakroom and went off with him, and over the dinner – I only had a cup of tea, as a matter of fact – he told me that he was on the verge of ruin. He said that Mr Lyne had sent for a detective (which was you), and had the intention of exposing him, only Mr Lyne's rage against me was so great, that for the moment he was diverted from his purpose.

" 'Only you can save me,' said Milburgh.

" 'I? I said in astonishment, 'how can I save you?'

" 'Take the responsibility for the theft upon yourself,' he said. 'Your mother is involved in this heavily.'

" 'Does she know?'

"He nodded. I found afterwards that he was lying to me and was preying upon my love for mother.

"I was dazed and horrified," said the girl, "at the thought that poor dear mother might be involved in this horrible scandal, and when he suggested that I should write a confession at his dictation and should leave by the first train for the Continent until the matter blew over, I fell in with his scheme without protest – and that is all."

"Why did you come to Hertford tonight" asked Tarling.

Again she smiled

"To get the confession," she said simply "I knew Milburgh would keep it in the safe. I saw him when I left the hotel – he had telephoned to me and made the appointment at the shop where I slipped the detectives, and it was there that he told me – " she stopped suddenly and went red.

"He told you I was fond of you," said Tarling quietly, and she nodded.

"He threatened to take advantage of that fact, and wanted to show you the confession."

"I see," said Tarling, and heaved a deep sigh of relief. "Thank God!" he said fervently.

"For what?" she asked, looking at him in astonishment.

"That everything is clear. Tomorrow I will arrest the murderer of Thornton Lyne!"

"No, no, not that," she said, and laid her hand on his shoulder, her distressed face looking into his, "surely not that. Mr Milburgh could not have done it, he could not be so great a scoundrel."

"Who sent the wire to your mother saying you were not coming down?"

"Milburgh," replied the girl.

"Did he send two wires, do you remember?" said Tarling.

She hesitated.

"Yes, he did," she said, "I don't know who the other was to."

"It was the same writing anyway," he said.

149

"But – "

"Dear," he said, "you must not worry any more about it. There is a trying time ahead of you, but you must he brave, both for your own sake and for your mother's, and for mine," he added.

Despite her unhappiness she smiled faintly.

"You take something for granted, don't you?" she asked.

"Am I doing that?" he said in surprise.

"You mean – " she went redder than ever – "that I care enough for you – that I would make an effort for your sake?"

"I suppose I do," said Tarling slowly, "it's vanity, I suppose?"

"Perhaps it is instinct," she said, and squeezed his arm.

"I must take you back to your mother's place," he said.

The walk from the house to the station had been a long and tedious one. The way back was surprisingly short, even though they walked at snail's pace. There never was a courting such as Tarling's, and it seemed unreal as a dream. The girl had a key of the outer gate and they passed through together.

"Does your mother know that you are in Hertford?" asked Tarling suddenly.

"Yes," replied the girl. "I saw her before I came after you."

"Does she know – "

He did not care to finish the sentence.

"No," said the girl, "she does not know, Poor woman, it will break her heart. She is – very fond of Milburgh. Sometimes he is most kind to mother. She loves him so much that she accepted his mysterious comings and goings and all the explanations which he offered, without suspicion."

They had reached the place where he had picked up the wallet, and above him gloomed the dark bulk of the portico with its glass-house atop. The house was in darkness, no lights shone anywhere.

"I will take you in through the door under the portico. It is the way Mr Milburgh always comes. Have you a light?"

He had his electric lamp in his pocket and he put a beam upon the keyhole. She inserted the key and uttered a note of exclamation, for the door yielded under her pressure and opened.

"It is unlocked," she said. "I am sure I fastened it."

Tarling put his lamp upon the lock and made a little grimace. The catch had been wedged back into the lock so that it could not spring out again.

"How long were you in the house?" he asked quickly.

"Only a few minutes," said the girl. "I went in just to tell mother, and I came out immediately."

"Did you close the door behind you when you went in?"

The girl thought a moment.

"Perhaps I didn't," she said. "No, of course not – I didn't come back this way; mother let me out by the front door."

Tarling put his light into the hall and saw the carpeted stairs half a dozen feet away. He guessed what had happened. Somebody had seen the door ajar, and guessing from the fact that she had left it open that she was returning immediately, had slipped a piece of wood, which looked to be and was in fact the stalk of a match, between the catch of the spring lock and its sheath.

"What has happened?" asked the girl in a troubled voice.

"Nothing," said Tarling airily. "It was probably your disreputable stepfather did this. He may have lost his key."

"He could have gone in the front door," said the girl uneasily.

"Well, I'll go first," said Tarling with a cheerfulness which he was far from feeling.

He went upstairs, his lamp in one hand, an automatic pistol in the other. The stairs ended in a balustraded landing from which two doors opened.

"That is mother's room," said the girl, pointing to the nearest.

A sense of impending trouble made her shiver. Tarling put his arms about her encouragingly. He walked to the door of the room, turned the handle and opened it. There was something behind the door which held it close, and exerting all his strength he pushed the door open sufficiently far to allow of his squeezing through.

On the desk a table lamp was burning, the light of which was hidden from the outside by the heavily curtained windows, but it was neither at the window nor at the desk that he was looking.

Mrs Rider lay behind the door, a little smile on her face, the haft of a dagger standing out with hideous distinctness beneath her heart.

THE LAUGH IN THE NIGHT

Tarling gave one glance before he turned to the girl, who was endeavouring to push past him, and catching her by the arm gently thrust her back into the passage.

"What is wrong? What is wrong?" she asked in a terrified whisper. "Oh, let me go to mother."

She struggled to escape from his grip, but he held her firmly.

"You must be brave, for your own sake – for everybody's sake," he entreated her.

Still holding her arm, he forced her to the door of the second inner room. His hand felt for the electric switch and found it.

He was in what appeared to be a spare bedroom, plainly furnished, and from this a door led, apparently into the main building.

"Where does that door lead?" he asked, but she did not appear to hear him.

"Mother, mother!" she was moaning, "what has happened to my mother?"

"Where does that door lead?" he asked again, and for answer she slipped her trembling hand into her pocket and produced a key.

He opened the door and found himself in a rectangular gallery overlooking the hall.

She slipped past him, but he caught her and pushed her back.

"I tell you, you must be calm, Odette," he said firmly, "you must not give way. Everything depends upon your courage. Where are the servants?"

Then, unexpectedly, she broke away from him and raced back through the door into the wing they had left. He followed in swift pursuit.

"For God's sake, Odette, don't, don't," he cried, as she flung herself against the door and burst into her mother's room.

One glance she gave, then she fell on the floor by the side of her dead mother, and flinging her arms about the form kissed the cold lips.

Tarling pulled her gently away, and half-carried, half-supported her back to the gallery. A dishevelled man in shirt and trousers whom Tarling thought might be the butler was hurrying along the corridor.

"Arouse any women who are in the house," said Tarling in a low voice. "Mrs Rider has been murdered."

"Murdered, sir!" said the startled man. "You don't mean that?"

"Quick," said Tarling sharply, "Miss Rider has fainted again."

They carried her into the drawing-room and laid her on the couch, and Tarling did not leave her until he had seen her in the hands of two women servants.

He went back with the butler to the room where the body lay. He turned on all the lights and made a careful scrutiny of the room. The window leading on to the glass-covered balcony where he had been concealed a few hours before, was latched, locked and bolted.

The curtains, which had been drawn, presumably by Milburgh when he came for the wallet, were undisturbed. From the position in which the dead woman lay and the calm on her face he thought death must have come instantly and unexpectedly. Probably the murderer stole behind her whilst she was standing at the foot of the sofa which he had partly seen through the window. It was likely that, to beguile the time of waiting for her daughter's return, she had taken a book from a little cabinet immediately behind the door, and support for this theory came in the shape of a book which had evidently fallen out of her hand between the position in which she was found and the book-case.

Together the two men lifted the body on to the sofa.

"You had better go down into the town and inform the police," said Tarling. "Is there a telephone here?"

"Yes, sir," replied the butler.

"Good, that will save you a journey," said the detective.

He notified the local police officials and then got on to Scotland Yard and sent a messenger to arouse Whiteside. The faint pallor of dawn was in the sky when he looked out of the window, but the pale light merely served to emphasise the pitch darkness of the world.

He examined the knife, which had the appearance of being a very ordinary butcher's knife. There were some faint initials burnt upon the hilt, but these had been so worn by constant handling that there was only the faintest trace of what they had originally been. He could see an "M" and two other letters that looked like "C" and "A."

"M C A?"

He puzzled his brain to interpret the initials. Presently the butler came back.

"The young lady is in a terrible state, sir, and I have sent for Dr Thomas."

Tarling nodded.

"You have done very wisely," he said. "Poor girl, she has had a terrible shock."

Again he went to the telephone, and this time he got into connection with a nursing home in London and arranged for an ambulance to pick up the girl without further delay. When he had telephoned to Scotland Yard he had asked as an afterthought that a messenger should be sent to Ling Chu, instructing him to come without delay. He had the greatest faith in the Chinaman, particularly in a case like this where the trail was fresh, for Ling Chu was possessed of superhuman gifts which only the bloodhound could rival.

"Nobody must go upstairs," he instructed the butler. "When the doctor and the coroner's officer come, they must be admitted by the principal entrance, and if I am not here, you must understand that under no circumstances are those stairs leading to the portico to be used."

He himself went out of the main entrance to make a tour of the grounds. He had little hope that that search would lead to anything. Clues there might be in plenty when the daylight revealed them, but the likelihood of the murderer remaining in the vicinity of the scene of his crime was a remote one.

The grounds were extensive and well-wooded. Numerous winding paths met, and forked aimlessly, radiating out from the broad gravel paths about the house to the high walls which encircled the little estate.

In one corner of the grounds was a fairly large patch, innocent of bush and offering no cover at all. He made a casual survey of this, sweeping his light across the ordered rows of growing vegetables, and was going away when he saw a black bulk which had the appearance, even in the darkness, of a gardener's house. He swept this possible cover with his lamp.

Was his imagination playing him a trick, or had he caught the briefest glimpse of a white face peering round the corner? He put on his light again. There was nothing visible. He walked to the building and round it. There was nobody in sight. He thought he saw a dark form under the shadow of the building moving towards the belt of pines which surrounded the house on the three sides. He put on his lamp again, but the light was not powerful enough to carry the distance required, and he went forward at a jog trot in the direction he had seen the figure disappear. He reached the pines and went softly. Every now and again he stopped, and once he could have sworn he heard the cracking of a twig ahead of him.

He started off at a run in pursuit, and now there was no mistaking the fact that somebody was still in the wood. He heard the quick steps of his quarry and then there was silence. He ran on, but must have overshot the mark, for presently he heard a stealthy noise behind him. In a flash he turned back.

"Who are you?" he said. "Stand out or I'll fire!"

There was no answer and he waited. He heard the scraping of a boot against the brickwork and he knew that the intruder was climbing the wall. He turned in the direction of the sound, but again found nothing.

Then from somewhere above him came such a trill of demoniacal laughter as chilled his blood. The top of the wall was concealed by the overhanging branch of a tree and his light was valueless.

"Come down," he shouted, "I've got you covered!"

Again came that terrible laugh, half-fear, half-derision, and a voice shrill and harsh came down to him.

"Murderer! Murderer! You killed Thornton Lyne, damn you! I've kept this for you – take it!"

Something came crashing through the trees, something small and round, a splashing drop, as of water, fell on the back of Tarling's hand and he shook it off with a cry, for it burnt like fire. He heard the mysterious stranger drop from the coping of the wall and the sound of his swift feet. He stooped and picked up the article which had been thrown at him. It was a small bottle bearing a stained chemist's label and the word "Vitriol."

THE THUMBPRINT

It was ten o'clock in the morning, and Whiteside and Tarling were sitting on a sofa in their shirtsleeves, sipping their coffee. Tarling was haggard and weary, in contrast to the dapper inspector of police. Though the latter had been aroused from his bed in the early hours of the morning, he at least had enjoyed a good night's sleep.

They sat in the room in which Mrs Rider had been murdered, and the rusty brown stains on the floor where Tarling had found her were eloquent of the tragedy.

They sat sipping their coffee, neither man talking, and they maintained this silence for several minutes, each man following his own train of thought. Tarling for reasons of his own had not revealed his own adventure and he had told the other nothing of the mysterious individual (who he was, he pretty well guessed) whom he had chased through the grounds.

Presently Whiteside lit a cigarette and threw the match in the grate, and Tarling roused himself from his reverie with a jerk.

"What do you make of it?" he asked.

Whiteside shook his head.

"If there had been property taken, it would have had a simple explanation. But nothing has gone. Poor girl!"

Tarling nodded.

"Terrible!" he said. "The doctor had to drug her before he could get her to go."

"Where is she?" asked Whiteside.

"I sent her on an ambulance to a nursing home in London," said Tarling shortly. "This is awful, Whiteside."

"It's pretty bad," said the detective-inspector, scratching his chin. "The young lady could supply no information?"

"Nothing, absolutely nothing. She had gone up to see her mother and had left the door ajar, intending to return by the same way after she had interviewed Mrs Rider. As a matter of fact, she was let out by the front door. Somebody was watching and apparently thought that she was coming out by the way she went in, waited for a time, and then as she did not reappear, followed her into the building."

"And that somebody was Milburgh?" said Whiteside.

Tarling made no reply. He had his own views and for the moment was not prepared to argue.

"It was obviously Milburgh," said Whiteside. "He comes to you in the night – we know that he is in Hertford. We know, too, that he tried to assassinate you because he thought the girl had betrayed him and you had unearthed his secret. He must have killed his wife, who probably knows much more about the murder than the daughter."

Tarling looked at his watch.

"Ling Chu should be here by now," he said.

"Oh, you sent for Ling Chu, did you?" said Whiteside in surprise. "I thought that you'd given up that idea."

"I 'phoned again a couple of hours ago," said Tarling.

"H'm!" said Whiteside. "Do you think that he knows anything about this?"

Tarling shook his head.

"I believe the story he told me. Of course, when I made the report to Scotland Yard I did not expect that you people would be as credulous as I am, but I know the man. He has never lied to me."

"Murder is a pretty serious business," said Whiteside. "If a man didn't lie to save his neck, he wouldn't lie at all."

There was the sound of a motor below, and Tarling walked to the window.

"Here is Ling Chu," he said, and a few minutes later the Chinaman came noiselessly into the room. Tarling greeted him with a curt nod, and without any preliminary told the story of the crime. He spoke in English – he had not employed Chinese since he discovered that Ling

Chu understood English quite as well as he understood Cantonese, and Whiteside was able from time to time to interject a word, or correct some little slip on Tarling's part. The Chinaman listened without comment and when Tarling had finished he made one of his queer jerky bows and went out of the room.

"Here are the letters," said Whiteside, after the man had gone.

Two neat piles of letters were arranged on Mrs Rider's desk, and Tarling drew up a chair.

"This is the lot?" he said.

"Yes," said Whiteside. "I've been searching the house since eight o'clock and I can find no others. Those on the right are all from Milburgh. You'll find they're simply signed with an initial – a characteristic of his – but they bear his town address."

"You've looked through them?" asked Tarling.

"Read 'em all," replied the other. "There's nothing at all incriminating in any of them. They're what I would call bread-and-butter letters, dealing with little investments which Milburgh has made in his wife's name – or rather, in the name of Mrs Rider. It's easy to see from these how deeply the poor woman was involved without her knowing that she was mixing herself up in a great conspiracy."

Tarling assented. One by one he took the letters from their envelopes, read them and replaced them. He was halfway through the pile when he stopped and carried a letter to the window.

"Listen to this," he said:

"Forgive the smudge, but I am in an awful hurry, and I have got my fingers inky through the overturning of an ink bottle."

"Nothing startling in that," said Whiteside with a smile.

"Nothing at all," admitted Tarling. "But it happens that our friend has left a very good and useful thumbprint. At least, it looks too big for a fingerprint."

"Let me see it," said Whiteside, springing up. He went to the other's side and looked over his shoulder at the letter in his hand, and whistled. He turned a glowing face upon Tarling and gripped his chief by the shoulder.

"We've got him!" he said exultantly. "We've got him as surely as if we had him in the pen!"

"What do you mean?" asked Tarling.

"I'll swear to that thumbprint," replied Whiteside. "It's identical with the blood mark which was left on Miss Rider's bureau on the night of the murder!"

"Are you sure?"

"Absolutely," said Whiteside, speaking quickly. "Do you see that whorl? Look at those lineations! They're the same. I have the original photograph in my pocket somewhere." He searched his pocketbook and brought out a photograph of a thumbprint considerably enlarged.

"Compare them!" cried Whiteside in triumph. Line for line, ridge for ridge, and furrow for furrow, it is Milburgh's thumbprint and Milburgh is my man!"

He took up his coat and slipped it on.

"Where are you going?"

"Back to London," said Whiteside grimly, "to secure a warrant for the arrest of George Milburgh, the man who killed Thornton Lyne, the man who murdered his wife – the blackest villain at large in the world today!"

THE THEORY OF LING CHU

Upon this scene came Ling Chu, imperturbable, expressionless, bringing with him his own atmosphere of mystery.

"Well," said Tarling, "what have you discovered?" and even Whiteside checked his enthusiasm to listen.

"Two people came up the stairs last night," said Ling Chu, "also the master." He looked at Tarling, and the latter nodded. "Your feet are clear," he said; "also the feet of the small-piece woman; also the naked feet."

"The naked feet?" said Tarling, and Ling Chu assented.

"What was the naked foot – man or woman?" asked Whiteside.

"It may have been man or woman," replied the Chinaman, "but the feet were cut and were bleeding. There is mark of blood on the gravel outside."

"Nonsense!" said Whiteside sharply.

"Let him go on," warned Tarling.

"A woman came in and went out – " continued Ling Chu.

"That was Miss Rider," said Tarling.

"Then a woman and a man came; then the barefooted one came, because the blood is over the first women's footmarks."

"How do you know which was the first woman and which was the second?" asked Whiteside, interested in spite of himself.

"The first woman's foot was wet," said Ling Chu.

"But there had been no rain," said the detective in triumph.

"She was standing on the grass," said Ling Chu, and Tarling nodded his head, remembering that the girl had stood on the grass in the shadow of the bushes, watching his adventure with Milburgh.

"But there is one thing I do not understand master," said Ling Chu. "There is the mark of another woman's foot which I cannot find on the stair in the hall. This woman walked all round the house; I think she walked round twice; and then she walked into the garden and through the trees."

Tarling stared at him.

"Miss Rider came straight from the house on to the road," he said, "and into Hertford after me."

"There is the mark of a woman who has walked round the house," insisted Ling Chu, "and, therefore, I think it was a woman whose feet were bare."

"Are there any marks of a man beside us three?"

"I was coming to that," said Ling Chu. "There is a very faint trace of a man who came early, because the wet footsteps are over his; also he left, but there is no sign of him on the gravel, only the mark of a wheel-track."

"That was Milburgh," said Tarling.

"If a foot has not touched the ground," explained Ling Chu, "it would leave little trace. That is why the woman's foot about the house is so hard for me, for I cannot find it on the stair. Yet I know it came from the house because I can see it leading from the door. Come, master, I will show you."

He led the way down the stairs into the garden, and then for the first time Whiteside noticed that the Chinaman was barefooted.

"You haven't mixed your own footmarks up with somebody else's?" he asked jocularly.

Ling Chu shook his head.

"I left my shoes outside the door because it is easier for me to work so," he said calmly. slipping his feet into his small shoes.

He led the way to the side of the house, and there pointed out the footprints. They were unmistakably feminine. Where the heel was, was a deep crescent-shaped hole, which recurred at intervals all round the house. Curiously enough, they were to be found in front of almost every window, as though the mysterious visitor had walked over the garden border as if seeking to find an entrance.

"They look more like slippers than shoes to me. They're undoubtedly a woman's," said Whiteside, examining one of the impressions. "What do you think, Tarling?"

Tarling nodded and led the way back to the room.

"What is your theory, Ling Chu?" he asked.

"Somebody came into the house," said the Chinaman, "squeezed through the door below and up the stairs. First that somebody killed and then went to search the house, but could not get through the door."

"That's right," said Whiteside. "You mean the door that shuts off this little wing from the rest of the house. That was locked, was it not, Tarling, when you made the discovery?"

"Yes," said Tarling, "it was locked."

"When they found they could not get into the house," Ling Chu went on, "they tried to get through one of the windows."

"They, they?" said Tarling impatiently. "Who are they? Do you mean the woman?"

The new theory was disturbing. He had pierced the second actor in the tragedy – a brown vitriol burn on the back of his hand reminded him of his existence – but who was the third?"

"I mean the woman," replied Ling Chu quietly.

"But who in God's name wanted to get into the house after murdering Mrs Rider?" asked Whiteside irritably. "Your theory is against all reason, Ling Chu. When a person has committed a murder they want to put as much distance between themselves and the scene of the crime as they can in the shortest possible space of time."

Ling Chu did not reply.

"How many people are concerned in this murder?" said Tarling. "A bare-footed man or woman came in and killed Mrs Rider; a second person made the round of the house, trying to get in through one of the windows – "

"Whether it was one person or two I cannot tell," replied Ling Chu.

Tarling made a further inspection of the little wing. It was, as Ling Chu had said and as he had explained to the Chinaman, cut off from the rest of the house, and had evidently been arranged to give Mr Milburgh the necessary privacy upon his visits to Hertford. The wing consisted of three rooms; a bedroom, leading from the sitting room, evidently used by Mrs Rider, for her clothes were hanging in the wardrobe; the sitting-room in which the murder was committed, and the spare room through which he had passed with Odette to the gallery over the hall.

It was through the door in this room that admission was secured to the house.

"There's nothing to be done but to leave the local police in charge and get back to London," said Tarling when the inspection was concluded.

"And arrest Milburgh," suggested Whiteside. "Do you accept Ling Chu's theory?"

Tarling shook his head.

"I am loath to reject it," he said, "because he is the most amazingly clever tracker. He can trace footmarks which are absolutely invisible to the eye, and he has a bushman's instinct which in the old days in China led to some extraordinary results."

They returned to town by car, Ling Chu riding beside the chauffeur, smoking an interminable chain of cigarettes. Tarling spoke very little during the journey, his mind being fully occupied with the latest development of a mystery, the solution of which still evaded him.

The route through London to Scotland Yard carried him through Cavendish Place, where the nursing home was situated in which Odette Rider lay. He stopped the car to make inquiries, and found that the girl had recovered from the frenzy of grief into which the terrible discovery of the morning had thrown her, and had fallen into a quiet sleep.

"That's good news, anyway," he said, rejoining his companion. "I was half beside myself with anxiety."

"You take a tremendous interest in Miss Rider, don't you?" asked Whiteside dryly.

Tarling brindled, then laughed.

165

"Oh, yes, I take an interest," he admitted, "but it is very natural."

"Why natural?" asked Whiteside.

"Because," replied Tarling deliberately, "Miss Rider is going to be my wife."

"Oh!" said Whiteside in blank amazement, and had nothing more to say.

The warrant for Milburgh's arrest was waiting for them, and placed in the hands of Whiteside for execution.

"We'll give him no time," said the officer. "I'm afraid he's had a little too much grace, and we shall be very lucky if we find him at home."

As he had suspected, the house in Camden Town was empty, and the woman who came daily to do the cleaning of the house was waiting patiently by the iron gate. Mr Milburgh, she told them, usually admitted her at half-past eight. Even if he was "in the country" he was back at the house before her arrival.

Whiteside fitted a skeleton key into the lock of the gate, opened it (the charwoman protesting in the interests of her employer) and went up the flagged path. The door of the cottage was a more difficult proposition, being fitted with a patent lock. Tarling did not stand on ceremony, but smashed one of the windows, and grinned as he did so.

"Listen to that?"

The shrill tinkle of a bell came to their ears.

"Burglar alarm," said Tarling laconically, and pushed back the catch, threw up the window, and stepped into the little room where he had interviewed Mr Milburgh.

The house was empty. They went from room to room, searching the bureaux and cupboards. In one of these Tarling made a discovery. It was no more than a few glittering specks which he swept from a shelf into the palm of his hand.

"If that isn't thermite, I'm a Dutchman," he said. "At any rate, we'll be able to convict Mr Milburgh of arson if we can't get him for murder. We'll send this to the Government analyst right away, Whiteside. If Milburgh did not kill Thornton Lyne, he certainly burnt down the premises of Dashwood and Solomon to destroy the evidence of his theft."

It was Whiteside who made the second discovery. Mr Milburgh slept on a large wooden four-poster.

"He's a luxurious devil," said Whiteside. "Look at the thickness of those box springs." He tapped the side of that piece of furniture and looked round with a startled expression.

"A bit solid for a box spring, isn't it?" he asked, and continued his investigation, tearing down the bed valance.

Presently he was rewarded by finding a small eyelet hole in the side of the mattress. He took out his knife, opened the pipe cleaner, and pressed the narrow blade into the aperture. There was a click and two doors, ludicrously like the doors which deaden the volume of gramophone music, flew open.

Whiteside put in his hand and pulled something out.

"Books," he said disappointedly. Then, brightening up. "They are diaries; I wonder if the beggar kept a diary?"

He piled the little volumes on the bed and Tarling took one and turned the leaves.

"Thornton Lyne's diary," he said. "This may be useful."

One of the volumes was locked. It was the newest of the books, and evidently an attempt had been made to force the lock, for the hasp was badly wrenched. Mr Milburgh had, in fact, made such an attempt, but as he was engaged in a systematic study of the diaries from the beginning he had eventually put aside the last volume after an unsuccessful effort to break the fastening.

"Is there nothing else?" asked Tarling.

"Nothing," said the disappointed inspector, looking into the interior. "There may be other little cupboards of this kind," he added. But a long search revealed no further hiding place.

"Nothing more is to be done here," said Tarling. "Keep one of your men in the house in case Milburgh turns up. Personally I doubt very much whether he will put in an appearance."

"Do you think the girl has frightened him?"

"I think it is extremely likely," said Tarling. "I will make an inquiry at the Stores, but I don't suppose he will be there either."

This surmise proved to be correct. Nobody at Lyne's Store had seen the manager or received word as to his whereabouts. Milburgh had disappeared as though the ground had opened and swallowed him.

No time was lost by Scotland Yard in communicating particulars of the wanted man to every police station in England. Within twenty-four hours his description and photograph were in the hands of every chief constable; and if he had not succeeded in leaving the country – which was unlikely – during the time between the issue of the warrant and his leaving Tarling's room in Hertford, his arrest was inevitable.

At five o'clock that afternoon came a new clue. A pair of ladies' shoes, mud-stained and worn, had been discovered in a ditch on the Hertford road, four miles from the house where the latest murder had been committed. This news came by telephone from the Chief of the Hertford Constabulary, with the further information that the shoes had been despatched to Scotland Yard by special messenger.

It was half-past seven when the little parcel was deposited on Tarling's table. He stripped the package of its paper, opened the lid of the cardboard box, and took out a distorted-looking slipper which had seen better days.

"A woman's, undoubtedly," he said. "Do you note the crescent-shaped heel."

"Look!" said Whiteside, pointing to some stains on the whitey-brown inner sock. "That supports Ling Chu's theory. The feet of the person who wore these were bleeding."

Tarling examined the slippers and nodded. He turned up the tongue in search of the maker's name, and the shoe dropped from his hand.

"What's on earth the matter?" asked Whiteside, and picked it up.

He looked and laughed helplessly; for on the inside of the tongue was a tiny label bearing the name of a London shoemaker, and beneath, written in ink, "Miss O Rider."

WHO KILLED MRS RIDER?

The matron of the nursing home received Tarling. Odette, she said, had regained her normal calm, but would require a few days' rest. She suggested she should be sent to the country.

"I hope you're not going to ask her a lot of questions, Mr Tarling," said the matron, "because she really isn't fit to stand any further strain."

"There's only one question I'm going to ask," said Tarling grimly.

He found the girl in a prettily-furnished room, and she held out her hand to him in greeting. He stooped and kissed her, and without further ado produced the shoe from his pocket.

"Odette dear," he said gently, "is this yours?"

She looked at it and nodded.

"Why yes, where did you find it?"

"Are you sure it is yours?"

"I'm perfectly certain it's mine," she smiled. "It's an old slipper I used to wear. Why do you ask?"

"Where did you see it last?"

The girl closed her eyes and shivered.

"In mother's room," she said. "Oh, mother, mother!"

She turned her head to the cushion of the chair and wept, and Tarling soothed her.

It was some time before she was calm, but then she could give no further information.

"It was a shoe that mother liked because it fitted her. We both took the same size…"

Her voice broke again and Tarling hastened to change the conversation.

More and more he was becoming converted to Ling Chu's theory. He could not apply to that theory the facts which had come into his possession. On his way back from the nursing home to police headquarters, he reviewed the Hertford crime.

Somebody had come into the house bare-footed, with bleeding feet, and, having committed the murder, had looked about for shoes. The old slippers had been the only kind which the murderer could wear, and he or she had put them on and had gone out, again, after making the circuit of the house. Why had this mysterious person tried to get into the house again, and for whom or what were they searching?

If Ling Chu was correct, obviously the murderer could not be Milburgh. If he could believe the evidence of his senses, the man with the small feet had been he who had shrieked defiance in the darkness and had hurled the vitriol at his feet. He put his views before his subordinate and found Whiteside willing to agree with him.

"But it does not follow," said Whiteside, "that the bare-footed person who was apparently in Mrs Rider's house committed the murder. Milburgh did that right enough, don't worry! There is less doubt that he committed the Daffodil Murder."

Tarling swung round in his chair; he was sitting on the opposite side of the big table that the two men used in common.

"I think I know who committed the Daffodil Murder," he said steadily. "I have been working things out, and I have a theory which you would probably describe as fantastic."

"What is it?" asked Whiteside, but the other shook his head.

He was not for the moment prepared to reveal his theory.

Whiteside leaned back in his chair and for a moment cogitated.

"The case from the very beginning is full of contradictions," he said. "Thornton Lyne was a rich man – by the way, you're a rich man, now, Tarling, and I must treat you with respect."

Tarling smiled.

"Go on," he said.

"He had queer tastes – a bad poet, as is evidenced by his one slim volume of verse. He was a poseur, proof of which is to be found in his patronage of Sam Stay – who, by the way, has escaped from the lunatic asylum; I suppose you know that?"

"I know that," said Tarling. "Go on."

"Lyne falls in love with a pretty girl in his employ," continued Whiteside. "Used to having his way when he lifted his finger, all women that in earth do dwell must bow their necks to the yoke. He is repulsed by the girl and in his humiliation immediately conceives for her a hatred beyond the understanding of any sane mortal."

"So far your account doesn't challenge contradiction," said Tarling with a little twinkle in his eye.

"That is item number one," continued Whiteside, ticking the item off on his fingers. "Item number two is Mr Milburgh, an oleaginous gentleman who has been robbing the firm for years and has been living in style in the country on his ill-earned gains. From what he hears, or knows, he gathers that the jig is up. He is in despair when he realises that Thornton Lyne is desperately in love with his step-daughter. What is more likely than that he should use his step-daughter in order to influence Thornton Lyne to take the favourable view of his delinquencies?"

"Or what is more likely," interrupted Tarling, than that he would put the blame for the robberies upon the girl and trust to her paying a price to Thornton Lyne to escape punishment?"

"Right again. I'll accept that possibility," said Whiteside. "Milburgh's plan is to get a private interview, under exceptionally favourable circumstances, with Thornton Lyne. He wires to that gentleman to meet him at Miss Rider's flat, relying upon the magic of the name."

"And Thornton Lyne comes in list slippers," said Tarling sarcastically. "That doesn't wash, Whiteside."

"No, it doesn't," admitted the other. "But I'm getting at the broad aspects of the case. Lyne comes. He is met by Milburgh, who plays his trump card of confession and endeavours to switch the young man on to the solution which Milburgh had prepared. Lyne refuses, there is a row, and in desperation Milburgh shoots Thornton Lyne."

Tarling shook his head. He mused a while, then:

"It's queer," he said.

The door opened and a police officer came in.

"Here are the particulars you want," he said and handed Whiteside a typewritten sheet of paper.

"What is this?" said Whiteside when the man had gone. "Oh, here is our old friend, Sam Stay. A police description." He read on: "Height five foot four, sallow complexion…wearing a grey suit and underclothing bearing the markings of the County Asylum… Hullo!"

"What is it?" said Tarling.

"This is remarkable," said Whiteside, and read:

"When the patient escaped, he had bare feet. He takes a very small size in shoes, probably four or five. A kitchen knife is missing and the patient may be armed. Boot-makers should be warned…"

"Bare feet!" Tarling rose from the table with a frown on his face. "Sam Stay hated Odette Rider."

The two men exchanged glances.

"Now, do you see who killed Mrs Rider?" asked Tarling. "She was killed by one who saw Odette Rider go into the house, and did not see her come out; who went in after her to avenge, as he thought, his dead patron. He killed this unhappy woman – the initials on the knife, MCA, stand for Middlesex County Asylum, and he brought the knife with him – and discovered his mistake; then, having searched for a pair of shoes to cover his bleeding feet, and having failed to get into the house by any other way, made a circuit of the building, looking for Odette Rider and seeking an entrance at every window."

Whiteside looked at him in astonishment.

"It's a pity you've got money," he said admiringly. "When you retire from this business there'll be a great detective lost."

SAM STAY TURNS UP

"I have seen you somewhere before, ain't I?" The stout clergyman in the immaculate white collar beamed benevolently at the questioner and shook his head with a gentle smile.

"No, my dear friend, I do not think I have ever seen you before."

It was a little man, shabbily dressed, and looking ill. His face was drawn and lined; he had not shaved for days, and the thin, black stubble of hair gave him a sinister look. The clergyman bad just walked out of Temple Gardens and was at the end of Villiers Street leading up to the Strand, when he was accosted. He was a happy-looking clergyman, and something of a student, too, if the stout and serious volume under his arm had any significance.

"I've seen you before," said the little man, "I've dreamt about you."

"If you'll excuse me," said the clergyman, "I am afraid I cannot stay. I have an important engagement."

"Hold hard," said the little man, in so fierce a tone that the other stopped. "I tell you I've dreamt about you. I've seen you dancing with four black devils with no clothes on, and you were all fat and ugly."

He lowered his voice and was speaking in a fierce earnest monotone, as though he was reciting some lesson he had been taught.

The clergyman took a pace back in alarm.

"Now, my good man," he said severely, "you ought not to stop gentlemen in the street and talk that kind of nonsense. I have never met you before in my life. My name is the Reverend Josiah Jennings."

"Your name is Milburgh," said the other. "Yes, that's it, Milburgh. *He* used to talk about you! That lovely man – here!" He clutched the clergyman's sleeve and Milburgh's face went a shade paler. There was a concentrated fury in the grip on his arm and a strange wildness in the man's speech. "Do you know where he is? In a beautivault built like an 'ouse in Highgate Cemetery. There's two little doors that open like the door of a church, and you go down some steps to it."

"Who are you?" asked Milburgh, his teeth chattering.

"Don't you know me?" The little man peered at him. "You've heard him talk about me. Sam Stay – why, I worked for two days in your Stores, I did. And you – you've only got what he's given you. Every penny you earned he gave you, did Mr Lyne. He was a friend to everybody – to the poor, even to a hook like me."

His eyes filled with tears and Mr Milburgh looked round to see if he was being observed.

"Now, don't talk nonsense!" he said under his breath, "and listen, my man; if anybody asks you whether you have seen Mr Milburgh, you haven't, you understand?"

"Oh, I understand," said the man. "But I knew you! There's nobody connected with him that I don't remember. He lifted me up out of the gutter, he did. He's my idea of God!"

They had reached a quiet corner of the Gardens and Milburgh motioned the man to sit beside him on a garden seat.

For the first time that day he experienced a sense of confidence in the wisdom of his choice of disguise. The sight of a clergyman speaking with a seedy-looking man might excite comment, but not suspicion. After all, it was the business of clergymen to talk to seedy-looking men, and they might be seen engaged in the most earnest and confidential conversation and he would suffer no loss of caste.

Sam Stay looked at the black coat and the white collar in doubt.

"How long have you been a clergyman, Mr Milburgh?" he asked.

"Oh – er – for a little while," said Mr Milburgh glibly, trying to remember what he had heard about Sam Stay. But the little man saved him the labour of remembering.

"They took me away to a place in the country," he said, "but you know I wasn't mad, Mr Milburgh. *He* wouldn't have had a fellow hanging round him who was mad, would he? You're a clergyman, eh?" He nodded his head wisely, then asked, with a sudden eagerness: "Did he make you a clergyman? He could do wonderful things, could Mr Lyne, couldn't he? Did you preach over him when they buried him in that little vault in 'Ighgate? I've seen it – I go there every day, Mr Milburgh," said Sam. "I only found it by accident. 'Also Thornton Lyne, his son.' There's two little doors that open like church doors."

Mr Milburgh drew a long sigh. Of course, he remembered now. Sam Stay had been removed to a lunatic asylum, and he was dimly conscious of the fact that the man had escaped. It was not a pleasant experience, talking with an escaped lunatic. It might, however, be a profitable one. Mr Milburgh was a man who let very few opportunities slip. What could he make out of this, he wondered? Again Sam Stay supplied the clue.

"I'm going to settle with that girl – " He stopped and dosed his lips tightly, and looked with a cunning little smile at Milburgh. "I didn't say anything, did I?" he asked with a queer little chuckle. "I didn't say anything that would give me away, did I?"

"No, my friend," said Mr Milburgh, still in the character of the benevolent pastor. "To what girl do you refer?"

The face of Sam Stay twisted into a malignant smile.

"There's only one girl," he said between his teeth, "and I'll get her. I'll settle with her! I've got something here – " he felt in his pocket in a vague, aimless way. "I thought I had it, I've carried it about so long; but I've got it somewhere, I know I have!"

"So you hate Miss Rider, do you?" asked Milburgh.

"Hate her!"

The little fellow almost shouted the words, his face purple, his eyes starting from his head, his two hands twisted convulsively.

"I thought I'd finished her last night," he began, and stopped.

The words had no significance for Mr Milburgh, since he had seen no newspapers that day.

"Listen," Sam went on. "Have you ever loved anybody?"

Mr Milburgh was silent. To him Odette Rider was nothing, but about the woman Odette Rider had called mother and the woman he called wife, circled the one precious sentiment in his life.

"Yes, I think I have," he said after a pause. "Why?"

"Well, you know how I feel, don't you?" said Sam Stay huskily. "You know how I want to get the better of this party who brought him down. She lured him on – lured him on – oh, my God!" He buried his face in his hands and swayed from side to side.

Mr Milburgh looked round in some apprehension. No one was in sight.

Odette would be the principal witness against him and this man hated her. He had small cause for loving her. She was the one witness that the Crown could produce, now that he had destroyed the documentary evidence of his crime. What case would they have against him if they stood him in the dock at the Old Bailey, if Odette Rider were not forthcoming to testify against him?

He thought the matter over cold-bloodedly, as a merchant might consider some commercial proposition which is put before him. He had learnt that Odette Rider was in London in a nursing home, as the result of a set of curious circumstances.

He had called up Lyne's Store that morning on the telephone to discover whether there had been any inquiries for him and had heard from his chief assistant that a number of articles of clothing had been ordered to be sent to this address for Miss Rider's use. He had wondered what had caused her collapse, and concluded that it was the result of the strain to which the girl had been subjected in that remarkable interview which she and he had had with Tarling at Hertford on the night before.

"Suppose you met Miss Rider?" he said. "What could you do?"

Sam Stay showed his teeth in a grin.

"Well, anyway, you're not likely to meet her for some time. She is in a nursing home," said Milburgh, "and the nursing home," he went on deliberately, "is at 304, Cavendish Place."

"304, Cavendish Place," repeated Sam. "That's near Regent Street, isn't it?"

"I don't know where it is," said Mr Milburgh. "She is at 304, Cavendish Place, so that it is very unlikely that you will meet her for some time."

He rose to his feet, and he saw the man was shaking from head to foot like a man in the grip of ague.

"304, Cavendish Place," he repeated, and without another word turned his back on Mr Milburgh and slunk away.

That worthy gentleman looked after him and shook his head, and then rising, turned and walked in the other direction. It was just as easy to take a ticket for the Continent at Waterloo station as it was at Charing Cross. In many ways it was safer.

THE DIARY OF THORNTON LYNE

Tarling should have been sleeping. Every bone and sinew in him ached for rest. His head was sunk over a table in his flat. Lyne's diaries stood in two piles on the table, the bigger pile that which he had read, the lesser being those which Tarling had yet to examine.

The diaries had been blank books containing no printed date lines. In some cases one book would cover a period of two or three years, in other cases three or four books would be taken up by the record of a few months. The pile on the left grew, and the pile on the right became smaller, until there was only one book – a diary newer than the others which had been fastened by two brass locks, but had been opened by the Scotland Yard experts.

Tarling took up this volume and turned the leaves. As he had expected, it was the current diary – that on which Thornton Lyne had been engaged at the time of his murder. Tarling opened the book in a spirit of disappointment. The earlier books had yielded nothing save a revelation of the writer's egotism. He had read Lyne's account of the happenings in Shanghai, but after all that was nothing fresh, and added little to the sum of the detective's knowledge.

He did not anticipate that the last volume would yield any more promising return for his study. Nevertheless, he read it carefully, and presently drawing a writing pad toward him, he began to note down excerpts from the diary. There was the story, told in temperate language and with surprising mildness, of Odette Rider's rejection of Thornton Lyne's advances. It was a curiously uninteresting record, until he came to a date following the release of Sam Stay from gaol, and here Thornton Lyne enlarged upon the subject of his "humiliation."

"Stay is out of prison," the entry ran. "It is pathetic to see how this man adores me. I almost wish sometimes that I could keep him out of gaol; but if I did so, and converted him into a dull, respectable person, I should miss these delicious experiences which his worship affords. It is good to bask in the bright sunlight of his adoration! I talked to him of Odette. A strange matter to discuss with a lout, but he was so wonderful a listener! I exaggerated, the temptation was great. How he loathed her by the time I was through…he actually put forward a plan to 'spoil her looks,' as he put it. He had been working in the same prison gang as a man who was undergoing a term of penal servitude for 'doing in' his girl that way…vitriol was used, and Sam suggested that he should do the work… I was horrified, but it gave me an idea. He says he can give me a key that will open any door. Suppose I went…in the dark? And I could leave a clue behind. What clue? Here is a thought. Suppose I left something unmistakably Chinese? Tarling had evidently been friendly with the girl…something Chinese might place him under suspicion…"

The diary ended with the word "suspicion," an appropriate ending. Tarling read the passages again and again until he almost had them by heart. Then he closed the book and locked it away in his drawer.

He sat with his chin on his hand for half an hour. He was piecing together the puzzle which Thornton Lyne had made so much more simple. The mystery was clearing up. Thornton Lyne had gone to that flat not in response to the telegram, but with the object of compromising and possibly ruining the girl. He had gone with the little slip of paper inscribed with Chinese characters, intending to leave the Hong in a conspicuous place, that somebody else might be blamed for his infamy.

Milburgh had been in the flat for another purpose. The two men had met; there had been a quarrel; and Milburgh had fired the fatal shot. That part of the story solved the mystery of Thornton Lyne's list slippers and his Chinese characters; his very presence there was cleared up. He thought of Sam Stay's offer.

It came in a flash to Tarling that the man who had thrown the bottle of vitriol at him, who had said he had kept it for years – was Sam Stay. Stay, with his scheme for blasting the woman who, he believed, had humiliated his beloved patron.

And now for Milburgh, the last link in the chain.

Tarling had arranged for the superintendent in charge of the Cannon Row Police Station to notify him if any news came through. The inspector's message did not arrive, and Tarling went down through Whitehall to hear the latest intelligence at first hand. That was to be precious little. As he was talking there arrived on the scene an agitated driver, the proprietor of a taxicab which had been lost. An ordinary case such as come the way of the London police almost every day. The cabman had taken a man and a woman to one of the West End theatres, and had been engaged to wait during the evening and pick them up when the performance was through. After setting down his fares, he had gone to a small eating-house for a bit of supper. When he came out the cab had disappeared.

"I know who done it," he said vehemently, "and if I had him here, I'd…"

"How do you know?"

"He looked in at the coffee-shop while I was eating my bit of food."

"What did he look like?" asked the station inspector.

"He was a man with a white face." said the victim, "I could pick him out of a thousand. And what's more, he had a brand new pair of boots on."

Tarling had strolled away from the officer's desk whilst this conversation was in progress, but now he returned.

"Did he speak at all?" he asked.

"Yes, sir," said the cabman. "I happened to ask him if he was looking for anybody, and he said no, and then went on to talk a lot of rubbish about a man who had been the best friend any poor chap could have had. My seat happened to be nearest the door, that's how I got into conversation with him. I thought he was off his nut."

"Yes, yes, go on," said Tarling impatiently. "What happened then?"

"Well, he went out," said the cabman, "and presently I heard a cab being cranked up. I thought it was one of the other drivers – there were several cabs outside. The eating-house is a place which cabmen use, and I didn't take very much notice until I came out and found my cab gone and the old devil I'd left in charge in a public house drinking beer with the money this fellow had given him."

"Sounds like your man, sir," said the inspector, looking at Tarling.

"That's Sam Stay all right," he said, "but it's news to me that he could drive a taxi."

The inspector nodded.

"Oh, I know Sam Stay all right, sir. We've had him in here two or three times. He used to be a taxi-driver – didn't you know that?"

Tarling did not know that. He had intended looking up Sam's record that day, but something had occurred to put the matter out of his mind.

"Well, he can't go far," he said. "You'll circulate the description of the cab, I suppose? He may be easier to find. He can't hide the cab as well as he can hide himself, and if he imagines that the possession of a car is going to help him to escape he's making a mistake."

Tarling was going back to Hertford that night, and had informed Ling Chu of his intention. He left Cannon Row Police Station, walked across the road to Scotland Yard, to confer with Whiteside, who had promised to meet him. He was pursuing independent inquiries and collecting details of evidence regarding the Hertford crime.

Whiteside was not in when Tarling called, and the sergeant on duty in the little office by the main door hurried forward.

"This came for you two hours ago, sir," he said "We thought you were in Hertford."

"This" was a letter addressed in pencil, and Mr Milburgh had made no attempt to disguise his handwriting. Tarling tore open the envelope and read the contents:

> "Dear Mr Tarling," it began. "I have just read in the *Evening Press*, with the deepest sorrow and despair, the news that my dearly beloved wife, Catherine Rider, has been foully murdered. How terrible to think that a few hours ago I was conversing with her assassin, as I believe Sam Stay to be, and had inadvertently given him information as to where Miss Rider was to be found! I beg of you that you will lose no time in saving her from the hands of this cruel madman, who seems to have only one idea, and that to avenge the death of the late Mr Thornton Lyne. When this reaches you I shall be beyond the power of human vengeance, for I have determined to end a life which has held so much sorrow and disappointment – M."

He was satisfied that Mr Milburgh would not commit suicide, and the information was superfluous that Sam Stay had murdered Mrs Rider. It was the knowledge that this vengeful lunatic knew where Odette Rider was staying which made Tarling sweat.

"Where is Mr Whiteside?" he asked.

"He has gone to Cambours Restaurant to meet somebody, sir," said the sergeant.

The somebody was one of Milburgh's satellites at Lyne's Store. Tarling must see him without delay. The inspector had control of all the official arrangements connected with the case, and it would be necessary to consult him before he could place detectives to watch the nursing home in Cavendish Place.

He found a cab and drove to Cambours, which was in Soho, and was fortunate enough to discover Whiteside in the act of leaving.

"I didn't get much from that fellow," Whiteside began, when Tarling handed him the letter.

The Scotland Yard man read it through without comment and handed it back.

"Of course he hasn't committed suicide. It's the last thing in the world that men of the Milburgh type ever think about seriously. He is a cold-blooded villain. Imagine him sitting down to write calmly about his wife's murderer!"

"What do you think of the other matter – the threat against Odette?"

Whiteside nodded.

"There may be something in it," he said. "Certainly we cannot take risks. Has anything been heard of Stay?"

Tarling told the story of the stolen taxicab.

"We'll have him," said Whiteside confidently. "He'll have no pals, and without pals in the motor business it is practically impossible to get a car away."

He got into Tarling's cab, and a few minutes later they were at the nursing home.

The matron came to them, a sedate, motherly lady.

"I'm sorry to disturb you at this hour of the night," said Tarling, sensing her disapproval. "But information has come to me this evening which renders it necessary that Miss Rider should be guarded."

"Guarded?" said the matron in surprise. "I don't quite understand you, Mr Tarling. I had come down to give you rather a blowing up about Miss Rider. You know she is absolutely unfit to go out. I thought I made that clear to you when you were here this morning?"

"Go out?" said the puzzled Tarling. "What do you mean? She is not going out."

It was the matron's turn to be surprised.

"But you sent for her half an hour ago," she said. "I sent for her?" said Tarling, turning pale.

"Tell me, please, what has happened?"

"About half an hour ago, or it may be a little longer," said the matron, "a cabman came to the door and told me that he had been sent by the authorities to fetch Miss Rider at once – she was wanted in connection with her mother's murder."

Something in Tarling's face betrayed his emotion.

"Did you not send for her?" she asked in alarm.

Tarling shook his head.

"What was the man like who called?" he asked.

"A very ordinary-looking man, rather under-sized and ill-looking – it was the taxi-driver."

"You have no idea which way they went?"

"No," replied the matron. "I very much objected to Miss Rider going at all, but when I gave her the message, which apparently had come from you, she insisted upon going."

Tarling groaned. Odette Rider was in the power of a maniac who hated her, who had killed her mother and had cherished a plan for disfiguring the beauty of the girl whom he believed had betrayed his beloved master.

Without any further words he turned and left the waiting-room, followed by Whiteside.

"It's hopeless," he said, when they were outside, "hopeless, hopeless! My God! How terrible! I dare not think of it. If Milburgh is alive he shall suffer."

He gave directions to the cab-driver and followed Whiteside into the cab.

"I'm going back to my flat to pick up Ling Chu," he said. "I can't afford to lose any help he may be able to give us."

Whiteside was pardonably piqued.

"I don't know if your Ling Chu will be able to do very much in the way of trailing a taxicab through London." And then, recognising something of the other's distress, he said more gently, "Though I agree with you that every help we can get we shall need."

On their arrival at the Bond Street flat, Tarling opened the door and went upstairs, followed by the other. The flat was in darkness – an extraordinary circumstance, for it was an understood thing that Ling Chu should not leave the house whilst his master was out. And Ling Chu had undoubtedly left. The dining-room was empty. The first thing Tarling saw, when he turned on the light, was a strip of rice paper on which the ink was scarcely dry. Just half a dozen Chinese characters and no more.

"If you return before I, learn that I go to find the little-little woman," read Tarling in astonishment.

"Then he knows she's gone! Thank God for that!" he said. "I wonder – "

He stopped. He thought he had heard a low moan, and catching the eye of Whiteside, he saw that the Scotland Yard man had detected the same sound.

"Sounds like somebody groaning," he said. "Listen!"

He bent his head and waited, and presently it came again.

In two strides Tarling was at the door of Ling Chu's sleeping place, but it was locked. He stooped to the keyhole and listened, and again heard the moan. With a thrust of his shoulder he had broken the door open and dashed in.

The sight that met his eyes was a remarkable one. There was a man lying on the bed, stripped to the waist. His hands and his legs were bound and a white cloth covered his face. But what Tarling saw before all else was that across the centre of the broad chest were four little red lines, which Tarling recognised. They were "persuaders," by which native Chinese policemen secretly extract confessions from unwilling criminals – light cuts with a sharp knife on the surface of the skin, and after –

He looked around for the "torture bottle," but it was not in sight.

"Who is this?" he asked, and lifted the cloth from the man's face.

It was Milburgh.

LING CHU – TORTURER

Much had happened to Mr Milburgh between the time of his discovery lying bound and helpless and showing evidence that he had been in the hands of a Chinese torturer and the moment he left Sam Stay. He had read of the murder, and had been shocked, and, in his way, grieved.

It was not to save Odette Rider that he sent his note to Scotland Yard, but rather to avenge himself upon the man who had killed the only woman in the world who had touched his warped nature. Nor had he any intention of committing suicide. He had the passports which he had secured a year before in readiness for such a step (he had kept that clerical uniform of his by him all that time) and was ready at a moment's notice to leave the country.

His tickets were in his pocket, and when he despatched the district messenger to Scotland Yard he was on his way to Waterloo station to catch the Havre boat train. The police, he knew, would be watching the station, but he had no fear that they would discover beneath the benign exterior of a country clergyman, the wanted manager of Lyne's Store, even supposing that there was a warrant out for his arrest.

He was standing at a bookstall, purchasing literature to while away the hours of the journey, when he felt a hand laid on his arm and experienced a curious sinking sensation. He turned to look into a brown mask of a face he had seen before.

"Well, my man," he asked with a smile, "what can I do for you?"

He had asked the question in identical terms of Sam Stay – his brain told him that much, mechanically.

"You will come with me, Mr Milburgh," said Ling Chu. "It will be better for you if you do not make any trouble."

"You are making a mistake."

"If I am making a mistake," said Ling Chu calmly, "you have only to tell that policeman that I have mistaken you for Milburgh, who is wanted by the police on a charge of murder, and I shall get into very serious trouble."

Milburgh's lips were quivering with fear and his face was a pasty grey.

"I will come," he said.

Ling Chu walked by his side, and they passed out of Waterloo station. The journey to Bond Street remained in Milburgh's memory like a horrible dream. He was not used to travelling on omnibuses, being something of a sybarite who spared nothing to ensure his own comfort. Ling Chu on the contrary had a penchant for buses and seemed to enjoy them.

No word was spoken until they reached the sitting-room of Tarling's flat. Milburgh expected to see the detective. He had already arrived at the conclusion that Ling Chu was but a messenger who had been sent by the man from Shanghai to bring him to his presence. But there was no sign of Tarling.

"Now, my friend, what do you want?" he asked. "It is true I am Mr Milburgh, but when you say that I have committed murder you are telling a wicked lie."

He had gained some courage, because he had expected in the first place to be taken immediately to Scotland Yard and placed in custody. The fact that Tarling's flat lay at the end of the journey seemed to suggest that the situation was not as desperate as he had imagined.

Ling Chu, turning suddenly upon Milburgh, gripped him by the wrist, half-turning as he did so. Before Milburgh knew what was happening, he was lying on the floor, face downwards, with Ling Chu's knee in the small of his back. He felt something like a wire loop slipped about his wrists, and suffered an excruciating pain as the Chinaman tightened the connecting link of the native handcuff.

"Get up," said Ling Chu sternly, and, exerting a surprising strength, lifted the man to his feet.

"What are you going to do?" said Milburgh, his teeth chattering with fear.

There was no answer. Ling Chu gripped the man by one hand and opening the door with the other, pushed him into a room which was barely furnished. Against the wall there was an iron bed, and on to this the man was pushed, collapsing in a heap.

The Chinese thief-catcher went about his work in a scientific fashion. First he fastened and threaded a length of silk rope through one of the rails of the bed and into the slack of this he lifted Milburgh's head, so that he could not struggle except at the risk of being strangled.

Ling Chu turned him over, unfastened the handcuffs, and methodically bound first one wrist and then the other to the side of the bed.

"What are you going to do?" repeated Milburgh, but the Chinaman made no reply.

He produced from a belt beneath his blouse a wicked-looking knife, and the manager opened his mouth to shout. He was beside himself with terror, but any cause for fear had yet to come. The Chinaman stopped the cry by dropping a pillow on the man's face, and began deliberately to cut the clothing on the upper part of his body.

"If you cry out," he said calmly, "the people will think it is I who am singing! Chinamen have no music in their voices, and sometimes when I have sung my native songs, people have come up to discover who was suffering."

"You are acting illegally," breathed Milburgh, in a last attempt to save the situation. "For your crime you will suffer imprisonment."

"I shall be fortunate," said Ling Chu; "for prison is life. But you will hang at the end of a long rope."

He had lifted the pillow from Milburgh's face, and now that pallid man was following every movement of the Chinaman with a fearful eye. Presently Milburgh was stripped to the waist, and Ling Chu regarded his handiwork complacently.

He went to a cupboard in the wall, and took out a small brown bottle, which he placed on a table by the side of the bed. Then he himself sat upon the edge of the bed and spoke. His English was almost perfect, though now and again he hesitated in the choice of a word, and there were moments when he was a little stilted in his speech, and more than a little pedantic. He spoke slowly and with great deliberation.

"You do not know the Chinese people? You have not been or lived in China? When I say lived I do not mean staying for a week at a good hotel in one of the coast towns. Your Mr Lyne lived in China in that way. It was not a successful residence."

"I know nothing about Mr Lyne," interrupted Milburgh, sensing that Ling Chu in some way associated him with Thornton Lyne's misadventures.

"Good!" said Ling Chu, tapping the flat blade of his knife upon his palm. "If you had lived in China – in the real China – you might have a dim idea of our people and their characteristics. It is said that the Chinaman does not fear death or pain, which is a slight exaggeration, because I have known criminals who feared both."

His thin lips curved for a second in the ghost of a smile, as though at some amusing recollection. Then he grew serious again.

"From the Western standpoint we are a primitive people. From our own point of view we are rigidly honourable. Also – and this I would emphasise." He did, in fact, emphasise his words to the terror of Mr Milburgh, with the point of his knife upon the other's broad chest, though so lightly was the knife held that Milburgh felt nothing but the slightest tingle.

"We do not set the same value upon the rights of the individual as do you people in the West. For example," he explained carefully, "we are not tender with our prisoners, if we think that by applying a little pressure to them we can assist the process of justice."

"What do you mean?" asked Milburgh, a grisly thought dawning upon his mind.

EDGAR WALLACE

"In Britain – and in America too, I understand – though the Americans are much more enlightened on this subject – when you arrest a member of a gang you are content with cross-examining him and giving him full scope for the exercise of his inventive power. You ask him questions and go on asking and asking, and you do not know whether he is lying or telling the truth."

Mr Milburgh began to breathe heavily.

"Has that idea sunk into your mind?" asked Ling Chu.

"I don't know what you mean," said Mr Milburgh in a quavering voice. "All I know is that you are committing a most – "

Ling Chu stopped him with a gesture.

"I am perfectly well aware of what I am doing," he said. "Now listen to me. A week or so ago, Mr Thornton Lyne, your employer, was found dead in Hyde Park. He was dressed in his shirt and trousers, and about his body, in an endeavour to stanch the wound, somebody had wrapped a silk nightdress. He was killed in the flat of a small lady, whose name I cannot pronounce, but you will know her."

Milburgh's eyes never left the Chinaman's, and he nodded.

"He was killed by you," said Ling Chu slowly "because he had discovered that you had been robbing him, and you were in fear that he would hand you over to the police."

"That's a lie," roared Milburgh. "It's a lie – I tell you it's a lie!"

"I shall discover whether it is a lie in a few moments," said Ling Chu.

He put his hand inside his blouse and Milburgh watched him fascinated, but he produced nothing more deadly than a silver cigarette case, which he opened. He selected a cigarette and lit it, and for a few minutes puffed in silence, his thoughtful eyes fixed upon Milburgh. Then he rose and went to the cupboard and took out a larger bottle and placed it beside the other.

Ling Chu pulled again at his cigarette and then threw it into the grate.

"It is in the interests of all parties." he said in his slow, halting way, "that the truth should be known, both for the sake of my honourable master, Lieh Jen, the Hunter, and his honourable Little Lady."

190

He took up his knife and bent over the terror-stricken man.

"For God's sake don't, don't," half screamed, half sobbed Milburgh.

"This will not hurt you," said Ling Chu, and drew four straight lines across the other's breast. The keen razor edge seemed scarcely to touch the flesh, yet where the knife had passed was a thin red mark like a scratch.

Milburgh scarcely felt a twinge of pain, only a mild irritating smarting and no more. The Chinaman laid down the knife and took up the smaller bottle.

"In this," he said, "is a vegetable extract. It is what you would call capsicum, but it is not quite like your pepper because it is distilled from a native root. In this bottle," he picked up the larger, "is a Chinese oil which immediately relieves the pain which capsicum causes."

"What are you going to do?" asked Milburgh, struggling. "You dog! You fiend!"

"With a little brush I will paint capsicum on these places." He touched Milburgh's chest with his long white fingers. "Little by little, millimetre by millimetre my brush will move, and you will experience such pain as you have never experienced before. It is pain which will rack you from head to foot, and will remain with you all your life in memory. Sometimes," he said philosophically, "it drives me mad, but I do not think it will drive you mad."

He took out the cork and dipped a little camel hair brush in the mixture, withdrawing it moist with fluid. He was watching Milburgh all the time, and when the stout man opened his mouth to yell he thrust a silk handkerchief, which he drew with lightning speed from his pocket, into the open mouth.

"Wait, wait!" gasped the muffled voice of Milburgh. "I have something to tell you – something that your master should know."

"That is very good," said Ling Chu coolly, and pulled out the handkerchief. "You shall tell me the truth."

"What truth can I tell you?" asked the man, sweating with fear. Great beads of sweat were lying on his face.

"You shall confess the truth that you killed Thornton Lyne," said Ling Chu. "That is the only truth I want to hear."

"I swear I did not kill him! I swear it, I swear it!" raved the prisoner. "Wait, wait!" he whimpered as the other picked up the handkerchief. "Do you know what has happened to Miss Rider?"

The Chinaman checked his movement.

"To Miss Rider?" he said quickly. (He pronounced the word "Lider.")

Brokenly, gaspingly, breathlessly, Milburgh told the story of his meeting with Sam Stay. In his distress and mental anguish he reproduced faithfully not only every word, but every intonation, and the Chinaman listened with half-closed eyes. Then, when Milburgh had finished, he put down his bottle and thrust in the cork.

"My master would wish that the little woman should escape danger," he said. "Tonight he does not return, so I must go myself to the hospital – you can wait."

"Let me go," said Milburgh. "I will help you."

Ling Chu shook his head.

"You can wait," he said with a sinister smile.

"I will go first to the hospital and afterwards, if all is well, I will return for you."

He took a clean white towel from the dressing table and laid it over his victim's face. Upon the towel he sprinkled the contents of a third bottle which he took from the cupboard, and Milburgh remembered no more until he looked up into the puzzled face of Tarling an hour later.

THE ARREST

Tarling stooped down and released the cords which bound Milburgh to the couch. The stout man was white and shaking, and had to be lifted into a sitting position. He sat there on the edge of the bed, his face in his hands, for five minutes, and the two men watched him curiously. Tarling had made a careful examination of the cuts on his chest, and was relieved to discover that Ling Chu – he did not doubt that the Chinaman was responsible for Milburgh's plight – had not yet employed that terrible torture which had so often brought Chinese criminals to the verge of madness.

Whiteside picked up the clothes which Ling Chu had so systematically stripped from the man's body, and placed them on the bed by Milburgh's side. Then Tarling beckoned the other into the outer room.

"What does it all mean? "asked Whiteside.

"It means," said Tarling grimly, "that my friend, Ling Chu, has been trying to discover the murderer of Thornton Lyne by methods peculiarly Chinese. Happily he was interrupted, probably as a result of Milburgh telling him that Miss Odette Rider had been spirited away."

He looked back to the drooping figure by the side of the bed.

"He's a little bigger than I," he said, "but I think some of my clothes will fit him."

He made a hasty search of his wardrobe and came back with an armful of clothes.

"Come, Milburgh," he said, "rouse yourself and dress."

The man looked up, his lower lip trembling pathetically.

"I rather think these clothes, though they may be a bad fit, will suit you a little better than your clerical garb," said Tarling sardonically.

Without a word, Milburgh took the clothes in his arms, and they left him to dress. They heard his heavy footfall, and presently the door opened and he came weakly into the sitting-room and dropped into a chair.

"Do you feel well enough to go out now?" asked Whiteside.

"Go out?" said Milburgh, looking up in alarm. "Where am I to go?"

"To Cannon Row Police Station," said the practical Whiteside. "I have a warrant for your arrest, Milburgh, on a charge of wilful murder, arson, forgery, and embezzlement."

"Wilful murder!" Milburgh's voice was high and squeaky and his shaking hands went to his mouth. "You cannot charge me with wilful murder. No, no, no! I swear to you I am innocent!"

"Where did you see Thornton Lyne last?" asked Tarling, and the man made a great effort to compose himself.

"I saw him last alive in his office," he began.

"When did you see Thornton Lyne last?" asked Tarling again. "Alive or dead."

Milburgh did not reply. Presently Whiteside dropped his hand on the man's shoulder and looked across at Tarling.

"Come along," he said briskly. "It is my duty as a police officer to warn you that anything you now say will be taken down and used as evidence against you at your trial."

"Wait, wait!" said Milburgh. His voice was husky and thick. He looked round. "Can I have a glass of water?" he begged, licking his dry lips.

Tarling brought the refreshment, which the man drank eagerly. The water seemed to revive something of his old arrogant spirit, for he got up from his chair, jerked at the collar of his ill-fitting coat – it was an old shooting-coat of Tarling's – and smiled for the first time.

"I think, gentlemen," he said with something of his old airiness, "you will have a difficulty in proving that I am concerned in the

194

murder of Thornton Lyne. You will have as great a difficulty in proving that I had anything to do with the burning down of Solomon's office – I presume that constitutes the arson charge? And most difficult of all will be your attempt to prove that I was concerned in robbing the firm of Thornton Lyne. The lady who robbed that firm has already made a confession, as you, Mr Tarling, are well aware." He smiled at the other, but Tarling met his eye.

"I know of no confession," he said steadily.

Mr Milburgh inclined his head with a smirk. Though he still bore the physical evidence of the bad time through which he had been, he had recovered something of his old confidence.

"The confession was burnt," he said, "and burnt by you, Mr Tarling. And now I think your bluff has gone on long enough."

"My bluff!" said Tarling, in his turn astonished. "What do you mean by bluff?"

"I am referring to the warrant which you suggest has been issued for my arrest," said Milburgh.

"That's no bluff." It was Whiteside who spoke, and he produced from his pocket a folded sheet of paper, which he opened and displayed under the eyes of the man. "And in case of accidents," said Whiteside, and deftly slipped a pair of handcuffs upon the man's wrists.

It may have been Milburgh's overweening faith in his own genius. It may have been, and probably was, a consciousness that he had covered his trail too well to be detected. One or other of these causes had kept him up, but now he collapsed. To Tarling it was amazing that the man had maintained this show of bravado to the last, though in his heart he knew that the Crown had a very poor case against Milburgh if the charge of embezzlement and arson were proceeded with. It was on the murder alone that a conviction could be secured; and this Milburgh evidently realised, for he made no attempt in the remarkable statement which followed to do more than hint that he had been guilty of robbing the firm. He sat huddled up in his chair, his manacled hands clasped on the table before him, and then with a jerk sat upright.

"If you'll take off these things, gentlemen," he said, jangling the connecting chain of the handcuffs, "I will tell you something which may set your mind at rest on the question of Thornton Lyne's death."

Whiteside looked at his superior questioningly, and Tarling nodded. A few seconds later the handcuffs had been removed, and Mr Milburgh was soothing his chafed wrists.

The psychologist who attempted to analyse the condition of mind in which Tarling found himself would be faced with a difficult task. He had come to the flat beside himself with anxiety at the disappearance of Odette Rider. He had intended dashing into his rooms and out again, though what he intended doing thereafter he had no idea. The knowledge that Ling Chu was on the track of the kidnapper had served as an opiate to his jagged nerves; otherwise he could not have stayed and listened to the statement Milburgh was preparing to make.

Now and again it came back to him, like a twinge of pain, that Odette Rider was in danger; and he wanted to have done with this business, to bundle Milburgh into a prison cell, and devote the whole of his energies to tracing her. Such a twinge came to him now as he watched the stout figure at the table.

"Before you start," he said, "tell me this: What information did you give to Ling Chu which led him to leave you?"

"I told him about Miss Rider," said Milburgh, "and I advanced a theory – it was only a theory – as to what had happened to her."

"I see," said Tarling. "Now tell your story and tell it quickly, my friend, and try to keep to the truth. Who murdered Thornton Lyne?"

Milburgh twisted his head slowly towards him and smiled.

"If you could explain how the body was taken from Odette Rider's flat," he said slowly, "and left in Hyde Park, I could answer you immediately. For to this minute, I believe that Thornton Lyne was killed by Odette Rider."

Tarling drew a long breath.

"That is a lie," he said.

Mr Milburgh was in no way put out.

"Very well," he said. "Now, perhaps you will be kind enough to listen to my story."

MILBURGH'S STORY

"I do not intend," said Mr Milburgh in his best oracular manner, "describing all the events which preceded the death of the late Thornton Lyne. Nor will I go to any length to deal with his well-known and even notorious character. He was not a good employer; he was suspicious, unjust, and in many ways mean. Mr Lyne was, I admit, suspicious of me. He was under the impression that I had robbed the firm of very considerable sums of money – a suspicion which I in turn had long suspected, and had confirmed by a little conversation which I overheard on the first day I had the pleasure of seeing you, Mr Tarling"

Tarling remembered that fatal day when Milburgh had come into the office at the moment that Lyne was expressing his views very freely about his subordinate.

"Of course, gentlemen," said Milburgh, "I do not for one moment admit that I robbed the firm, or that I was guilty of any criminal acts. I admit there were certain irregularities, certain carelessnesses, for which I was morally responsible; and beyond that I admit nothing. If you are making a note" – he turned to Whiteside, who was taking down the statement in shorthand, "I beg of you to make a special point of my denial. Irregularities and carelessnesses, " he repeated carefully. "Beyond that I am not prepared to go."

"In other words, you are not confessing anything?"

"I am not confessing anything," agreed Mr Milburgh with heavy gravity. "It is sufficient that Mr Lyne suspected me, and that lie was prepared to employ a detective in order to trace my defalcations, as he termed them. It is true that I lived expensively, that I own two houses, one in Camden Town and one at Hertford; but then I had speculated on the Stock Exchange and speculated very wisely.

"But I am a sensitive man, gentlemen; and the knowledge that I was responsible for certain irregularities preyed upon my mind. Let us say, for example, that I knew somebody had been robbing the firm, but that I was unable to detect that somebody. Would not the fact that I was morally responsible for the finances of Lyne's Stores cause me particular unhappiness?"

"You speak like a book," said Whiteside, "and I for one don't believe a word you say. I think you were a thief, Milburgh; but go on your own sweet way."

"I thank you," said Mr Milburgh sarcastically. "Well, gentlemen, matters had come to a crisis I felt my responsibility. I knew somebody had been robbing the house and I had an idea that possibly I would be suspected, and that those who were dear to me" – his voice shook for a moment, broke, and grew husky – "those who were dear to me," he repeated, "would be visited with my sins of omission.

"Miss Odette Rider had been dismissed from the firm of Lyne's Stores in consequence of her having rejected the undesirable advances of the late Mr Lyne. Mr Lyne turned the whole weight of his rage against this girl, and that gave me an idea.

"The night after the interview – or it may have been the same night – I refer to the interview which Mr Tarling had with the late Thornton Lyne – I was working late at the office. I was, in fact, clearing up Mr Lyne's desk. I had occasion to leave the office, and on my return found the place in darkness. I reconnected the light, and then discovered on the desk a particularly murderous-looking revolver.

"In the statement I made for you, sir," he turned to Tarling, "I said that that pistol had not been found by me; and indeed, I professed the profoundest ignorance of its existence. I regret to confess to you that I was telling an untruth. I did find the pistol; I put it in my pocket and I took it home. It is possible that with that pistol Mr Lyne was fatally shot."

Tarling nodded.

"I haven't the slightest doubt about that, Milburgh. You also had another automatic pistol, purchased subsequent to the murder from John Wadham's of Holborn Circus."

Mr Milburgh bowed his head.

"That is perfectly true, sir," he said. "I have such a weapon. I live a very lonely kind of life, and – "

"You need not explain. I merely tell you," said Tarling, "that I know where you got the pistol with which you shot at me on the night I brought Odette Rider back from Ashford."

Mr Milburgh closed his eyes and there was resignation written largely on his face – the resignation of an ill-used and falsely-accused man.

"I think it would be better not to discuss controversial subjects," he said. "If you will allow me, I will keep to the facts."

Tarling could have laughed at the sublime impertinence of the man, but that he was growing irritable with the double strain which was being imposed upon him. It was probable that, had not this man accused Odette Rider of the murder, he would have left him to make his confession to Whiteside, and have gone alone in his hopeless search for the taxicab driven by Sam Stay.

"To resume," continued Mr Milburgh, "I took the revolver home. You will understand that I was in a condition of mind bordering upon a nervous breakdown, I felt my responsibilities very keenly, and I felt that if Mr Lyne would not accept my protestations of innocence, there was nothing left for me but to quit this world."

"In other words, you contemplated suicide?" said Whiteside.

"You have accurately diagnosed the situation," said Milburgh ponderously. "Miss Rider had been dismissed, and I was on the point of ruin. Her mother would be involved in the crash – those were the thoughts which ran through my mind as I sat in my humble dining-room in Camden Town. Then the idea flashed upon me. I wondered whether Odette Rider loved her mother sufficiently well to make the great sacrifice, to take full responsibility for the irregularities which had occurred in the accounts' department of Lyne's Stores, and clear away to the Continent until the matter blew over. I intended seeing her the next day, but I was still doubtful as to whether she would fall in with my views. Young people nowadays," he said sententiously, "are terribly selfish."

"As it happened, I just caught her as she was leaving for Hertford, and I put the situation before her. The poor girl was naturally shocked, but she readily fell in with my suggestion and signed the confession which you, Mr Tarling, so thoughtfully burnt."

Whiteside looked at Tarling.

"I knew nothing of this," he said a little reproachfully.

"Go on," said Tarling. "I will explain that afterwards."

"I had previously wired the girl's mother that she would not be home that night. I also wired to Mr Lyne, asking him to meet me at Miss Rider's flat. I took the liberty of fixing Miss Rider's name to the invitation, thinking that that would induce him to come."

"It also covered you," said Tarling, "and kept your name out of the business altogether."

"Yes," said Mr Milburgh, as though the idea had not struck him before, "yes, it did that. I had sent Miss Rider off in a hurry. I begged that she would not go near the flat, and I promised that I myself would go there, pack the necessary articles for the journey and take them down in a taxi to Charing Cross."

"I see," said Tarling, "so it was you who packed the bag?"

"Half-packed it," corrected Mr Milburgh. "You see, I'd made a mistake in the time the train left. It was only when I was packing the bag that I realised it was impossible for me to get down to the station in time. I had made arrangements with Miss Rider that if I did not turn up I would telephone to her a quarter of an hour before the train left. She was to await me in the lounge of a near-by hotel. I had hoped to get to her at least an hour before the train left, because I did not wish to attract attention to myself, or," he added, "to Miss Rider. When I looked at my watch, and realised that it was impossible to get down, I left the bag as it was, half-packed and went outside to the tube station and telephoned."

"How did you get in and out?" asked Tarling. "The porter on duty at the door said he saw nobody."

"I went out the back way," explained Mr Milburgh. "It is really the simplest thing in the world to get into Miss Rider's basement flat by way of the mews behind. All the tenants have keys to the back door so that they can bring their cycles in and out, or get in their coals."

"I know that," said Tarling. "Go on."

"I am a little in advance of the actual story," said Milburgh. "The business of packing the bag takes my narrative along a little farther than I intended it to go. Having said good-bye to Miss Rider, I passed the rest of the evening perfecting my plans. It would serve no useful purpose," said Milburgh with an airy wave of his hand, "if I were to tell you the arguments I intended putting before him."

"If they did not include the betrayal of Miss Rider, I'm a Dutchman," said Tarling. "I pretty well know the arguments you intended using."

"Then, Mr Tarling, allow me to congratulate you upon being a thought-reader," said Milburgh, "because I have not revealed my secret thoughts to any human being. However, that is beside the point. I intended to plead with Mr Lyne. I intended to offer him the record of years of loyal service to his sainted father; and if the confession was not accepted, and if he still persisted in his revengeful plan, then, Mr Tarling, I intended shooting myself before his eyes."

He said this with rare dramatic effect; but Tarling was unimpressed, and Whiteside looked up from his notes with a twinkle in his eye.

"Your hobby seems to be preparing for suicide and changing your mind," he said.

"I am sorry to hear you speak so flippantly on a solemn subject," said Milburgh. "As I say, I waited a little too long; but I was anxious for complete darkness to fall before I made my way into the flat. This I did easily because Odette had lent me her key. I found her bag with no difficulty – it was in the dining-room on a shelf, and placing the case upon her bed, I proceeded, as best I could, for I am not very familiar with the articles of feminine toilette, to put together such things as I knew she would require on the journey.

"I was thus engaged when, as I say, it occurred to me that I had mistaken the time of the train, and, looking at my watch, I saw to my consternation that I should not he able to get down to the station in time. Happily I had arranged to call her up, as I have already told you."

"One moment," said Tarling. "How were you dressed?"

"How was I dressed? Let me think. I wore a heavy overcoat, I know," said Mr Milburgh, "for the night was chilly and a little foggy, if you remember."

"Where was the revolver?"

"In the overcoat pocket," replied Milburgh immediately.

"Had you your overcoat on?"

Milburgh thought for a moment.

"No, I had not. I had hung it up on a hook at the foot of the bed, near the alcove which I believe Miss Rider used as a wardrobe."

"And when you went out to telephone, had you your overcoat?"

"No, that I am perfectly certain about," said Milburgh readily. "I remember thinking later how foolish it was to bring an overcoat out and not use it."

"Go on," said Tarling.

"Well, I reached the station, called up the hotel, and to my surprise and annoyance Miss Rider did not answer. I asked the porter who answered my 'phone call whether he had seen a young lady dressed in so-and-so waiting in the lounge, and he replied 'no.' Therefore," said Mr Milburgh emphatically, "you will agree that it is possible that Miss Rider was not either at the station or at the hotel, and there was a distinct possibility that she had doubled back."

"We want the facts," interrupted Whiteside. "We have enough theories. Tell us what happened. Then we will draw our own conclusions."

"Very good, sir," replied Milburgh courteously. "By the time I had telephoned it was half-past nine o'clock. You will remember that I had wired to Mr Lyne to meet me at the flat at eleven. Obviously there was no reason why I should go back to the flat until a few minutes before Mr Lyne was due, to let him in. You asked me just now, sir," he turned to Tarling, "whether I had my overcoat on, and I can state most emphatically that I had not. I was going back to the flat with the intention of collecting my overcoat, when I saw a number of people walking about the mews behind the block. I had no desire to attract attention, as I have told you before, so I stood waiting until these people, who were employees of a motor car company which had a garage behind the flat, had dispersed.

"Now, waiting at the corner of a mews on a cold spring night is a cold business, and seeing that it would be some time before the mews would be clear, I went back to the main street and strolled along until I came to a picture palace. I am partial to cinematograph displays," explained Mr Milburgh, "and, although I was not in the mood for entertainment, yet I thought the pictures would afford a pleasant attraction. I forget the name of the film – "

"It is not necessary that you should tell us for the moment," said Tarling. "Will you please make your story as short as possible?"

Milburgh was silent for a moment.

"I am coming now to the most extraordinary fact," he said, "and I would ask you to bear in mind every detail I give you. It is to my interest that the perpetrator of this terrible crime should be brought to justice – "

Tarling's impatient gesture arrested his platitudes, but Mr Milburgh was in no way abashed.

"When I got back to the mews I found it deserted. Standing outside the door leading to the storeroom and cellars was a two-seater car. There was nobody inside or in attendance and I looked at it curiously, not realising at the moment that it was Mr Thornton Lyne's. What did interest me was the fact that the back gate, which I had left locked, was open. So, too, was the door leading to what I would call the underground room – it was little better – through which one had to pass to reach Odette's flat by the back way.

"I opened the door of the flat," said Mr Milburgh impressively, "and walked in. I had extinguished the light when I went, but to my surprise I saw through the transom of Odette's bedroom that a light was burning within. I turned the handle, and even before I saw into the room, my nose was assailed by a smell of burning powder.

"The first sight which met my gaze was a man lying on the floor. He was on his face, but I turned him over, and to my horror it was Mr Thornton Lyne. He was unconscious and bleeding from a wound in the chest," said Mr Milburgh, "and at the moment I thought he was dead. To say that I was shocked would be mildly to describe my terrible agitation.

"My first thought – and first thoughts are sometimes right – was that he had been shot down by Odette Rider, who for some reason had returned. The room, however, was empty, and a curious circumstance, about which I will tell you, was that the window leading out to the area of the flat was wide open."

"It was protected with heavy bars," said Tarling, "so nobody could have escaped that way."

"I examined the wound," Milburgh went on, nodding his agreement with Tarling's description, "and knew that it was fatal. I do not think, however, that Mr Thornton Lyne was dead at this time. My next thought was to stanch the wound, and I pulled open the drawer and took out the first thing which came to my hand, which was a nightdress. I had to find a pad and employed two of Odette's handkerchiefs for the purpose. First of all I stripped him of his coat and his vest, a task of some difficulty, then I fixed him up as best I could. I knew his case was hopeless, and indeed I believe," said Mr Milburgh soberly, "I believe he was dead even before the bandaging was completed.

"Whilst I was doing something I found it was possible to forget the terrible position in which I would find myself if somebody came into the room. The moment I saw the case was hopeless, and had a second think, I was seized with a blind panic. I snatched my overcoat from the peg and ran out of the room; through the back way into the mews, and reached Camden Town that night, a mental and physical wreck."

"Did you leave the lights burning?" asked Tarling.

Mr Milburgh thought for a moment.

"Yes," he said, "I left the lights burning."

"And you left the body in the flat?"

"That I swear," replied Milburgh.

"And the revolver – when you got home was it in your pocket?"

Mr Milburgh shook his head.

"Why did you not notify the police?"

"Because I was afraid," admitted Mr Milburgh. "I was scared to death. It is a terrible confession to make, but I am a physical coward."

"There was nobody in the room?" persisted Tarling.

"Nobody so far as I could see. I tell you the window was open. You say it is barred – that is true, but a very thin person could slip between those bars. A woman – "

"Impossible," said Tarling shortly. "The bars have been very carefully measured, and nothing bigger than a rabbit could get through. And you have no idea who carried the body away?"

"None whatever," replied Milburgh firmly.

Tarling had opened his mouth to say something, when a telephone bell shrilled, and he picked up the instrument from the table on which it stood.

It was a strange voice that greeted him, a voice husky and loud, as though it were unused to telephoning.

"Tarling the name?" shouted the voice quickly.

"That is my name," said Tarling.

"She's a friend of yours, ain't she?" asked the voice.

There was a chuckle. A cold shiver ran down Tarling's spine; for, though he had never met the man, instinct told him that he was speaking to Sam Stay.

"You'll find her tomorrow," screamed the voice, "what's left of her. The woman who lured him on…what's left of her…"

There was a click, and the receiver was hung up. Tarling was working the telephone hook like a madman.

"What exchange was that?" he asked, and the operator after a moment supplied the information that it was Hampstead.

AT HIGHGATE CEMETERY

Odette Rider sat back in a corner of the smooth-running taxicab. Her eyes were closed, for the inevitable reaction had come. Excitement and anxiety had combined to give her the strength to walk to the cab with a firm step which had surprised the matron; but now, in the darkness and solitude, she was conscious of a depression, both physical and mental, which left her without the will or power for further effort.

The car sped through interminably long streets – in what direction she neither knew nor cared. Remember that she did not even know where the nursing home was situated. It might have been on the edge of London for all she was aware. Once, that was as the car was crossing Bond Street from Cavendish Square, she saw people turn and look at the cab and a policeman pointed and shouted something. She was too preoccupied to worry her head as to the cause.

She appreciated in a dim, vague way the skill of the taxi-driver, who seemed to be able to grope his way through and around any obstruction of traffic; and it was not until she found the cab traversing a country road that she had any suspicion that all was not well. Even then her doubts were allayed by her recognition of certain landmarks which told her she was on the Hertford Road.

"Of course," she thought. "I should be wanted at Hertford rather than in London," and she settled herself down again.

Suddenly the cab stopped, backed down a side lane, and turned in the direction from whence they had come. When he had got his car's head right, Sam Stay shut off his engine, descended from his seat, and opened the door.

"Come on out of that!" he said sharply.

"Why – what – " began the bewildered girl, but before she could go much farther the man dived in, gripped her by the wrist, and pulled her out with such violence that she fell.

"You don't know me, eh?" The words were his as he thrust his face into hers, gripping her shoulders so savagely that she could have cried out in pain.

She was on her knees, struggling to get to her feet, and she looked up at the little man wonderingly.

"I know you," she gasped. "You are the man who tried to get into my flat!"

He grinned.

"And I know you!" he laughed harshly. "You're the devil that lured him on! The best man in the world…he's in the little vault in Highgate Cemetery. The door is just like a church. And that's where you'll be tonight, damn you! Down there I'm going to take you. Down, down, down, and leave you with him, because he wanted you!"

He was gripping her by both wrists, glaring down into her face, and there was something so wolfish, so inhuman, in the madman's staring eyes that her mouth went dry, and when she tried to scream no sound came. Then she lurched forward towards him, and he caught her under the arms and dragged her to her feet.

"Fainted, eh? You'll faint, me lady," he chuckled. "Don't you wish you might never come round, eh? I'll bet you would if you knew…if you knew!"

He dropped her on the grass by the side of the road, took a luggage strap from the front of the cab, and bound her hands. Then he picked up the scarf she had been wearing and tied it around her mouth.

With an extraordinary display of strength he lifted her without effort and put her back into the corner of the seat. Then he slammed the door, mounted again to his place, and sent the car at top speed in the direction of London. They were on the outskirts of Hampstead when he saw a sign over a tobacconist's shop, and stopped the car a little way beyond, at the darkest part of the road. He gave a glance into the interior. The girl had slid from the seat to the floor and lay motionless.

He hurried back to the tobacconist's where the telephone sign had been. At the back of his fuddled brain lingered an idea that there was somebody who would be hurt. That cruel-looking devil who was cross-examining him when he fell into a fit – Tarling. Yes, that was the name, Tarling.

It happened to be a new telephone directory, and by chance Tarling's name, although a new subscriber, had been included. In a few seconds he was talking to the detective.

He hung up the receiver and came out of the little booth, and the shopman, who had heard his harsh, loud voice, looked at him suspiciously; but Sam Stay was indifferent to the suspicions of men. He half ran, half walked back to where his cab was standing, leaped into the seat, and again drove the machine forward.

To Highgate Cemetery! That was the idea. The gates would be closed, but he could do something. Perhaps he would kill her first and then get her over the wall afterwards. It would be a grand revenge if he could get her into the cemetery alive and thrust her, the living, down amongst the dead, through those little doors which opened like church doors to the cold, dank vault below.

He screamed and sang with joy at the thought, and those pedestrians who saw the cab flash past, rocking from side to side, turned at the sound of the wild snatch of song, for Sam Stay was happy as he had not been happy in his life before.

But Highgate Cemetery was closed. The gloomy iron gates barred all entrance, and the walls were high. It was a baffling place, because houses almost entirely surrounded it; and he was half an hour seeking a suitable spot before he finally pulled up before a place where the wall did not seem so difficult. There was nobody about and little fear of interruption on the part of the girl. He had looked into the cab and had seen nothing save a huddled figure on the floor. So she was still unconscious, he thought.

He ran the car on to the sidewalk, then slipped down into the narrow space between car and wall and jerked open the door.

"Come on!" he cried exultantly. He reached out his fingers – and then something shot from the car, something lithe and supple, something that gripped the little man by the throat and hurled him back against the wall.

Stay struggled with the strength of lunacy, but Ling Chu held him in a grip of steel.

LING CHU RETURNS

Tarling dropped the telephone receiver on its hook and had sunk into a chair with a groan. His face was white – whiter than the prisoner's who sat opposite him, and he seemed to have gone old all of a sudden.

"What is it?" asked Whiteside quietly. "Who was the man?"

"Stay," said Tarling. "Stay. He has Odette! It's awful, awful!"

Whiteside, thoughtful, preoccupied; Milburgh, his face twitching with fear, watched the scene curiously.

"I'm beaten," said Tarling – and at that moment the telephone bell rang again.

He lifted the receiver and bent over the table, and Whiteside saw his eyes open in wide amazement. It was Odette's voice that greeted him.

"It is I, Odette!"

"Odette! Are you safe? Thank God for that!" he almost shouted. "Thank God for that! Where are you?"

"I am at a tobacconist's shop in – " there was a pause while she was evidently asking somebody the name of the street, and presently she came back with the information.

"But, this is wonderful!" said Tarling. "I'll be with you immediately. Whiteside, get a cab, will you? How did you get away?"

"It's rather a long story," she said. "Your Chinese friend saved me. That dreadful man stopped the cab near a tobacconist's shop to telephone. Ling Chu appeared by magic. I think he must have been lying on top of the cab, because I heard him come down by the side.

211

He helped me out and stood me in a dark doorway, taking my place. Please don't ask me any more. I am so tired."

Half an hour later Tarling was with the girl and heard the story of the outrage. Odette Rider had recovered something of her calm, and before the detective had returned her to the nursing home she had told him the story of her adventure.

"I must have fainted," she said. "When I woke up I was lying at the bottom of the cab, which was moving at a tremendous rate. I thought of getting back to the seat, but it occurred to me that if I pretended to be faint I might have a chance of escape. When I heard the cab stop I tried to rise, but I hadn't sufficient strength. But help was near. I heard the scraping of shoes on the leather top of the car, and presently the door opened and I saw a figure which I knew was not the cabman's. He lifted me out, and fortunately the cab had stopped opposite a private house with a big porch and to this he led me.

" 'Wait,' he said. 'There is a place where you may telephone a little way along. Wait till we have gone.'

"Then he went back to the cab, closed the door noiselessly, and immediately afterwards I saw Stay running along the path. In a few seconds the cab had disappeared and I dragged myself to the shop – and that's all."

No news had been received of Ling Chu when Tarling returned to his flat. Whiteside was waiting and told him that he had put Milburgh into the cells and that he would be charged the following day.

"I can't understand what has happened to Ling Chu. He should be back by now," said Tarling.

It was half-past one in the morning, and a telephone inquiry to Scotland Yard had produced no information.

"It is possible, of course," Tarling went on, "that Stay took the cab on to Hertford. The man has developed into a dangerous lunatic."

"All criminals are more or less mad," said the philosophical Whiteside. "I wonder what turned this fellow's brain."

"Love!" said Tarling.

The other looked at him in surprise.

"Love?" he repeated incredulously, and Tarling nodded.

"Undoubtedly Sam Stay adored Lyne. It was the shock of his death which drove him mad."

Whiteside drummed his fingers on the table thoughtfully.

"What do you think of Milburgh's story?" he asked, and Tarling shrugged his shoulders.

"It is most difficult to form a judgment," he said. "The man spoke as though he were telling the truth, and something within me convinces me that he was not lying. And yet the whole thing is incredible."

Of course, Milburgh has had time to make up a pretty good story," warned Whiteside. "He is a fairly shrewd man, this Milburgh, and it was hardly likely that he would tell us a yarn which was beyond the range of belief."

"That is true," agreed the other, "nevertheless, I am satisfied he told almost the whole of the truth."

"Then, who killed Thornton Lyne?"

Tarling rose with a gesture of despair.

"You are apparently as far from the solution of that mystery as I am, and yet I have formed a theory which may sound fantastic – "

There was a light step upon the stair and Tarling crossed the room and opened the door.

Ling Chu came in, his calm, inscrutable self, and but for the fact that his forehead and his right hand were heavily bandaged, carrying no evidence of his tragic experience.

"Hello, Ling Chu," said Tarling in English, "you're hurt?"

"Not badly," said Ling Chu. "Will the master be good enough to give me a cigarette? I lost all mine in the struggle."

"Where is Sam Stay?"

Ling Chu lit the cigarette before he answered, blew out the match and placed it carefully in the ash tray on the centre of the table.

"The man is sleeping on the Terrace of Night," said Ling Chu simply.

"Dead?" said the startled Tarling.

The Chinaman nodded.

"Did you kill him?"

213

Again Ling Chu paused and puffed a cloud of cigarette smoke into the air.

"He was dying for many days, so the doctor at the big hospital told me. I hit his head once or twice, but not very hard. He cut me a little with a knife, but it was nothing."

"Sam Stay is dead, eh?" said Tarling thoughtfully. "Well, that removes a source of danger to Miss Rider, Ling Chu."

The Chinaman smiled.

"It removes many things, master, because before this man died, his head became good."

"You mean he was sane?"

"He was sane, master," said Ling Chu, "and he wished to speak to paper. So the big doctor at the hospital sent for a judge, or one who sits in judgment."

"A magistrate?"

"Yes, a magistrate," said Ling Chu, nodding, "a little old man who lives very near the hospital, and he came, complaining because it was so late an hour. Also there came a man who wrote very rapidly in a book, and when the man had died, he wrote more rapidly on a machine and gave me these papers to bring to you, detaining others for himself and for the judge who spoke to the man."

He fumbled in his blouse and brought out a roll of paper covered with typewriting.

Tarling took the documents and saw that it consisted of several pages. Then he looked up at Ling Chu.

"First tell me, Ling Chu," he said, "what happened? You may sit."

Ling Chu with a jerky little bow pulled a chair from the wall and sat at a respectful distance from the table, and Tarling, noting the rapid consumption of his cigarette, passed him the box.

"You must know, master, that against your wish and knowledge, I took the large-faced man and put him to the question. These things are not done in this country, but I thought it best that the truth should be told. Therefore, I prepared to give him the torture when he told me that the small-small girl was in danger. So I left him, not thinking that your excellency would return until the morning, and I went to the big house where the small-small girl was kept, and as I came to the corner of the street I saw her get into a quick-quick car.

"It was moving off long before I came to it, and I had to run; it was very fast. But I held on behind, and presently when it stopped at this street to cross, I scrambled up the back and lay flat upon the top of the cab. I think people saw me do this and shouted to the driver, but he did not hear. Thus I lay for a long time and the car drove out into the country and after a while came back, but before it came back it stopped and I saw the man talking to the small-small woman in angry tones. I thought he was going to hurt her and I waited ready to jump upon him, but the lady went into the realms of sleep and he lifted her back into the car.

"Then he came back to the town and again he stopped to go into a shop. I think it was to telephone, for there was one of those blue signs which you can see outside a shop where the telephone may be used by the common people. Whilst he had gone in I got down and lifted the small-small woman out, taking the straps from her hands and placing her in a doorway. Then I took her place. We drove for a long time till he stopped by a high wall, and then, master, there was a fight," said Ling Chu simply.

"It took me a long time to overcome him and then I had to carry him. We came to a policeman who took us in another car to a hospital where my wounds were dressed. Then they came to me and told me the man was dying and wished to see somebody because he had that in his heart for which he desired ease.

"So he talked, master, and the man wrote for an hour, and then he passed to his fathers, that little white-faced man."

He finished abruptly as was his custom. Tarling took the papers up and opened them, glanced through page after page, Whiteside sitting patiently by without interrupting.

When Tarling had finished the documents, he looked across the table.

"Thornton Lyne was killed by Sam Stay," he said, and Whiteside stared at him.

"But – " he began.

"I have suspected it for some time, but there were one or two links in the evidence which were missing and which I was unable to supply. Let me read you the statement of Sam Stay."

THE STATEMENT OF SAM STAY

"My name is Sam Stay. I was born at Maidstone in the County of Kent. My age is twenty-nine years. I left school at the age of eleven and got mixed up with a bad set, and at the age of thirteen I was convicted for stealing from a shop, and was sent to Borstal Institute for four years.

"On my release from Borstal I went to London, and a year later was convicted of housebreaking, receiving a sentence of twelve months' imprisonment with hard labour. On my release from prison I was taken up by a society who taught me motor driving, and I secured a licence in another name as a taxicab driver and for twelve months drove a cab on the streets. At the end of that period I was convicted for stealing passengers' baggage and was sent to prison for eighteen months.

"It was after my release from this term of imprisonment that I first met Mr Thornton Lyne. I met him in the following manner. I had been given a letter from the Prisoners' Aid Society and went to Mr Thornton Lyne to get a job. He took a great interest in me and from the very first was the best friend I had ever had. His kindness was wonderful and I think there never was a man in the world with such a beautiful nature as his.

"He assisted me many times, and although I went back to prison, he never deserted me, but helped me as a friend and was never disgusted when I got into trouble.

"I was released from gaol in the spring of this year and was met at the prison gates by Mr Thornton Lyne in a beautiful motor car. He

217

treated me as though I were a prince and took me home to his grand house and gave me food and beautiful wine.

"He told me that he had been very much upset by a young lady whom he had looked after. This young lady worked for him and he had given her work when she was starving. He said that she had been spreading lies about him and that she was a bad girl. I had never seen this person, whose name was Odette Rider, but I felt full of hatred towards her, and the more he spoke about the girl the more determined I was to have revenge on her.

"When he told me that she was very beautiful, I remembered in the same gang as me at Wandsworth Gaol there had been a man named Selser. That is the name as far as I can remember. He was serving a lagging [a term of penal servitude] for throwing vitriol in the face of his girl. She had let him down and had married another man while he was serving a term of imprisonment. I believe she was very beautiful. When Selser got out he laid wait for her and threw vitriol in her face, and he has often told me that he didn't regret it.

"So that when Mr Lyne told me that the girl was beautiful, this idea struck me that I would have revenge upon her. I was living in Lambeth at the house of an old lag, who practically took nobody but crooks as lodgers. It cost more than ordinary lodging but it was worth it, because if the police made any inquiries the landlord or his wife would always give wrong information. I went to this place because I intended committing a burglary at Muswell Hill with a man who was released from gaol two or three days before me, who knew the crib and asked me, when we were at work one day, if I would go in with him on the job. I thought there might be a chance of getting away with the stuff, if I could get somebody to swear that I hadn't left the house that night.

"I told the landlord I had a job on the 14th and gave him £1. I saw Mr Lyne on the 14th at his house and put the idea up to him. I showed him the vitriol which I had bought in the Waterloo Road and he said he would not hear of my doing it. I thought he only said that because he did not want to be mixed up in the case. He asked me to leave the girl to him and he would settle with her.

"I left his house about nine o'clock at night, telling him I was going back to my lodgings. But really I went to the block of flats in the Edgware Road where this girl Rider lived. I knew the flat because I had been there the night before at Mr Lyne's suggestion to plant some jewellery which had been taken from the store. His idea was that he would pinch her for theft. I had not been able to get into the house, owing to the presence there of a detective named Tarling, but I had had a very good look round and I knew the way in, without coming through the front door, where a porter was always on duty.

"I had no difficulty either in getting into the building or into the flat. I thought it best to go in early because the girl might be out at the theatre and I should have a chance of concealing myself before her return. When I got into the flat I found it was in darkness. This suited my purpose very well. I went from one room to another. At last I came to the bedroom. I made an inspection of the room, looking about for a likely place where I could hide.

"At the foot of the bed was an alcove covered by a curtain where several dresses and a dressing-gown were hanging, and I found that I could easily get in there behind the clothes and nobody would be the wiser. There were two clothes-hooks projecting outside the curtain just inside the alcove. I mention these because of something which happened later.

"Whilst I was prying around I heard a key turn in the lock and switched off the lights. I had just time to get into the alcove when the door opened and a man named Milburgh appeared. He turned on the lights as he came into the room and shut the door after him. He looked around as though he was thinking about something and then, taking off his coat, he hung it on one of the hooks near the alcove. I held my breath fearing that he would look inside, but he did not.

"He walked about the room as though he was looking for something, and again I was afraid that I should be discovered after all, but by and by he went out and came back with a small suitcase. It was after he had gone that I saw poking out of the pocket of the overcoat which had been hung on the hook, the butt of a pistol. I didn't quite know what to make of it, but thinking that it was better in my pocket than in his if I were discovered, I lifted it out of the pocket and slipped it into my own.

"After a while he came back as I say and started packing the bag on the bed. Presently he looked at his watch and said something to himself, turned out the lights and hurried out. I waited and waited for him to come back but nothing happened, and knowing that I would have plenty of time if he came back again, I had a look at the pistol I had. It was an automatic and it was loaded. I had never worked with a gun in my life, but I thought I might as well take this as I intended committing a crime which might land me in jug for the term of my natural life. I thought I might as well be hung as go to penal servitude.

"Then I put out the lights and sat down by the window, waiting for Miss Rider's return. I lit a cigarette, and opened the window to let out the smell of the smoke. I took out the bottle of vitriol, removed the cork and placed it on a stool nearby.

"I don't know how long I waited in the dark, but about eleven o'clock, as far as I can judge, I heard the outer door click very gently and a soft foot in the hall. I knew it wasn't Milburgh because he was a heavy man. This person moved like a cat. In fact, I did not hear the door of the bedroom open. I waited with the vitriol on the stool by my side, for the light to be switched on, but nothing happened. I don't know what made me do it but I walked towards the person who had come into the room.

"Then, before I knew what had happened, somebody had gripped me. I was half-strangled by an arm which had been thrown round my neck and I thought it was Milburgh who had detected me the first time and had come back to pinch me. I tried to push him away, but he struck me on the jaw.

"I was getting frightened for I thought the noise would rouse the people and the police would come, and I must have lost my head. Before I knew what had happened I had pulled the gun out of my pocket and fired point-blank. I heard a sound like a thud of the body falling. The pistol was still in my hand, and my first act was to get rid of it. I felt a basket by my legs in the darkness. It was full of cotton and wool and stuff and I pushed the pistol down to the bottom and then groped across the room and switched on the lights.

"As I did so, I heard the key turn in the lock again. I gave one glance at the body which had fallen on its face and then I dived for the alcove.

"The man who came in was Milburgh. His back was to me. As he turned the body over I could not see its face. I saw him take something out of the drawer and bind it round the chest and I saw him strip off the coat and vest, but not until he had gone out and I came from the recess, did I realise that the man I had killed was dear Mr Lyne.

"I think I must have gone raving mad with grief. I don't know what I did. All I thought of was that there must be some chance and he wasn't dead at all and he must be got away to a hospital. We had discussed the plan of going into the flat and he had told me how he would bring his car to the back. I rushed out of the flat, going through the back way. Sure enough there was the car waiting and nobody was about.

"I came back to the bedroom and lifted him in my arms and carried him back to the car, propping him up in the seat. Then I went back and got his coat and vest and threw them on to the seat by him. I found his boots were also in the car and then for the first time I noticed that he had slippers on his feet.

"I have been a taxi-driver so I know how to handle a car and in a few minutes I was going along the Edgware Road, on my way to St George's Hospital. I turned in through the park because I didn't want people to see me, and it was when I had got into a part where nobody was about that I stopped the car to have another look at him. I realised that he was quite dead.

"I sat in that car with him for the best part of two hours, crying as I never have cried, then after a while I roused myself and carried him out and laid him on the sidewalk, some distance from the car. I had enough sense to know that if he were found dead in my company it would go very badly with me, but I hated leaving him and after I had folded his arms I sat by him for another hour or two.

"He seemed so cold and lonely that it made my heart bleed to leave him at all. In the early light of morning I saw a bed of daffodils growing close by and I plucked a few and laid them on his breast because I loved him."

Tarling finished reading and looked at his assistant.

"That is the end of the Daffodil Mystery," he said. "A fairly simple explanation, Whiteside. Incidentally, it acquits our friend Milburgh, who looks like escaping conviction altogether."

A week later two people were walking slowly along the downs overlooking the sea. They had walked for a mile in complete silence, then suddenly Odette Rider said:

"I get very easily tired. Let us sit down."

Tarling obediently sank down by her side.

"I read in the newspapers this morning, Mr Tarling," she said, "that you have sold Lyne's Store."

"That's true," said Tarling. "There are very many reasons why I do not want to go into the business, or stay in London."

She did not look at him, but played with the blades of grass she had plucked.

"Are you going abroad?" she asked.

"We are," said Tarling.

"We?" she looked at him in surprise. "Who are we?"

"I am referring to myself and a girl to whom I made violent love at Hertford," said Tarling, and she dropped her eyes.

"I think you were sorry for me," she said, "and you were rather led into your wild declaration of – "

"Love?" suggested Tarling.

"That's the word," she replied with a little smile. "You were led to say what you did because of my hopeless plight."

"I was led to say what I did," said Tarling, "because I loved you."

"Where are you – we – going?" she asked awkwardly.

"To South America," said Tarling, "for a few months. Then afterwards to my well-beloved China for the cool season."

"Why to South America?" asked the girl.

"Because," said Tarling, "I was reading an article on horticulture in this morning's papers and I learnt that daffodils do not grow in the Argentine."

EDGAR WALLACE

BIG FOOT

Footprints and a dead woman bring together Superintendent Minton and the amateur sleuth Mr Cardew. Who is the man in the shrubbery? Who is the singer of the haunting Moorish tune? Why is Hannah Shaw so determined to go to Pawsy, 'a dog lonely place' she had previously detested? Death lurks in the dark and someone must solve the mystery before BIG FOOT strikes again, in a yet more fiendish manner.

BONES IN LONDON

The new Managing Director of Schemes Ltd has an elegant London office and a theatrically dressed assistant – however, Bones, as he is better known, is bored. Luckily there is a slump in the shipping market and it is not long before Joe and Fred Pole pay Bones a visit. They are totally unprepared for Bones' unnerving style of doing business, unprepared for his unique style of innocent and endearing mischief.

EDGAR WALLACE

BONES OF THE RIVER

'Taking the little paper from the pigeon's leg, Hamilton saw it was from Sanders and marked URGENT. *Send Bones instantly to Lujamalababa... Arrest and bring to headquarters the witch doctor.*'

It is a time when the world's most powerful nations are vying for colonial honour, a time of trading steamers and tribal chiefs. In the mysterious African territories administered by Commissioner Sanders, Bones persistently manages to create his own unique style of innocent and endearing mischief.

THE JOKER
(USA: THE COLOSSUS)

While the millionaire Stratford Harlow is in Princetown, not only does he meet with his lawyer Mr Ellenbury but he gets his first glimpse of the beautiful Aileen Rivers, niece of the actor and convicted felon Arthur Ingle. When Aileen is involved in a car accident on the Thames Embankment, the driver is James Carlton of Scotland Yard. Later that evening Carlton gets a call. It is Aileen. She needs help.

Edgar Wallace

The Square Emerald
(USA: The Girl From Scotland Yard)

'Suicide on the left,' says Chief Inspector Coldwell pleasantly, as he and Leslie Maughan stride along the Thames Embankment during a brutally cold night. A gaunt figure is sprawled across the parapet. But Coldwell soon discovers that Peter Dawlish, fresh out of prison for forgery, is not considering suicide but murder. Coldwell suspects Druze as the intended victim. Maughan disagrees. If Druze dies, she says, 'It will be because he does not love children!'

The Three Oak Mystery

While brothers Lexington and Socrates Smith, authority on fingerprints and blood stains, are guests of Peter Mandle and his stepdaughter, they observe a light flashing from the direction of Mr Jethroe's house. COME THREE OAKS, it spells in Morse. A ghostly figure is seen hurrying across the moonlit lawn. Early next morning the brothers take a stroll, and there, tied to an oak branch, is a body – a purple mark where the bullet struck.